WICKED INTENTIONS

STEELE SECURITY SERIES

A. D. JUSTICE

STEELE SECURITY SERIES

WICKED INTENTIONS

Steele Security Series
Book 4

A.D. JUSTICE

PROLOGUE

June 22, 2001

Heather,

I've watched you sleep for the past few hours, and I've racked my brain trying to remember what my life was like without you in it. We've known each other as long as I can remember, and I can't recall a time when I didn't love you. There hasn't been a single day gone by I didn't know exactly how much you meant to me. You've never kept secrets from me. Your heart has always been an open book, reserved only for me to devour every word, thought, and feeling.

When we first met as kids, I was only looking for someone to play with after school. The day I knocked on your front door changed me forever. You became my partner in crime, my best friend, and the love of my life. Remember how we were inseparable? Every day, we rushed to do our chores or homework, so we'd have more time to spend together. You were, and still are, the coolest girl in the world. You could hang with me on the bicycle. You'd hold frogs and touch snakes. Every other girl would run away screaming, but never you. Nothing could make you leave my side.

As we got older, those things weren't as important to me anymore, and I saw you in a whole new light. You still had just as much spunk about you.

Remember the time at the middle school dance when you punched that girl for flirting with me? I still laugh about that to this day. As if she was ever any threat to you. You said I belonged to you, even if I didn't realize it yet. You said you wouldn't put up with another girl disrespecting what we had. There are no words to describe how turned on I was when you said that. I knew I loved you then, but an awkward thirteen-year-old me didn't know how to tell you.

Then came the high school years. Yes, you remember those well, don't you? Our class schedules separated us, so I didn't see you as much during the day. The first semester of our freshman year, I thought I'd die from being apart from you for so long. Every day after school, I waited for you outside so we could go home together. Absence really did make the heart grow fonder, and I knew without a doubt it was time to tell you exactly how I felt. That day, I waited in the rain for you to come out of the school. I had my speech memorized down to the last syllable.

Then you walked out, and I watched in horror as David Richards put his arm around you and announced to the school that you were his girlfriend. You know me...there was no way I could let that stand. So I decked him. Punched his lights right out. The look on your face was priceless—you were shocked, awed, and dumbfounded all at once. You were shocked that I had finally admitted my feelings for you. Awed that I did it in such a public display. And dumbfounded that it took me so fucking long to realize what you'd always known. When I kissed you that day, you changed me again. You ruined me for any other woman. Your kiss, your taste, and your sweet scent—no one else on earth could compare to you.

So began our dating experience. We defied the odds, didn't we, babe? We showed everyone in this one-horse town that our love was real and lasting. Neither of us has ever even been on a date with anyone else. Never kissed another person in the intimate ways we kiss. Never made love to another and shared the special bond that we have together. Even after more than four years of officially dating, I can honestly say that I don't regret one minute of the time I've spent exclusively with you. Four years of football games, school dances, junior and senior proms. Weekend dates, weeknights sneaking out my bedroom window just to make out with you. Making plans and dreaming big—together.

Sometimes I look back and miss the "us" we used to be, even just a short year ago. The things we've been through have taken a hard toll on you, and I blame myself for that. You can blame me, too. I can take it, and I deserve it. More than anything, I wanted to be the one to always protect you, love you, and provide for you. Our life together was supposed to be perfect. Wonderful. Magical. Beautiful.

I failed you. I failed us. I'm sorry, baby. I'm sorry I couldn't be the man I should've been, the man you needed me to be. Because of my failures, you're all but estranged from your family, especially your dad. The stress of everything has just been too much on you, and my presence here is only adding to it.

We fight every day now over things we'd normally laugh about. We're slowly tearing each other apart, bit by bit, and I'm afraid there will be nothing left of the Heather I fell in love with before much longer. When he died, I think he took the best part of us with him. I can't keep putting you through this hell every day, baby. It's killing me to watch you slowly die right before my eyes. When you look at me, I know you blame me for not being able to protect him like I should have.

Saying all this to you in a letter is a really shitty thing to do, I know. I openly admit that I'm a coward when it comes to losing you. On one hand, I'm afraid that if I tell you I'm leaving, you'd cry and ask me to stay. And I would. For you, there's nothing I wouldn't do. On the other hand, I'm petrified that you'd tell me to go, because then I'd know that your love for me has truly died. Love that has been alive and growing since the day we met. That means I'm taking the coward's way out, so I can keep your love with me.

I'm apparently also selfish, because I can't stand to think of doing this any other way. But I'm not so selfish that I don't want you to be happy. I want you to find someone who makes you the Heather I once knew, before I brought so much pain and suffering to your life. Find someone who puts that spark in your eye, the spring in your step, and the smile on your face. Give him all of you, everything you possess, and hold nothing back so that you can be whole again. Put me in the past, where I belong, and don't look back.

Know that you have my love—all of my love, all of my heart, and all of me. Forever.

Until death do us part,

Braxton Reed

BRAXTON PLACED the folded letter on the empty pillow beside his wife's head and stared at her intently one last time. Over the years, he'd memorized every line, curve, and tiny freckle on her face. He knew her better than anyone else did. Better than her family members who'd done everything in their power to drive them apart. Better than her friends who'd tried to convince her to date other people before settling for him. Better than their teachers who thought they knew everything but had no idea how deeply Braxton and Heather's love ran.

Part of him wished they'd listened to at least one of the naysayers before they'd reached such a low point. Maybe if they'd broken up, dated other people, or just took a break from their all-consuming relationship, the sorrows they'd experienced wouldn't have ever happened. Maybe if they'd actually waited until they were adults, instead of pretending to be grown-ups, everything would've turned out differently.

But that wasn't the way of things. Being young and foolish, they'd made mistakes and tried to fix them. In doing so, Braxton realized they'd only made their follies worse. In his mind, the only way either of them would make it out alive was if they did something they'd never tried before. They had to split up and never look back.

In the weeks leading up to that day, Braxton had talked secretly to a recruiter about his choices and completed all the steps to enlist in the Army. By the time Heather awoke that morning, he planned to be long gone, far away from her so he couldn't hurt her again.

He paused at the door, and his hand gripped the knob as his heart shattered into a million pieces. "Eighteen, married, and divorced." He shook his head in disbelief. "How did we come to this?"

When Braxton walked out the door of the tiny, one-bedroom apartment they had briefly shared as husband and wife, he reflected on how it was the second hardest thing he'd ever done. He closed the door behind him quietly, ensured it was locked, and walked away from the woman who held his heart in her hands, who had been his best friend for as long as he could remember, and whom he'd failed in the worst way. He tried to block the visions of Heather waking and finding the letter on his pillow rather than seeing him lying there. He didn't want to think about her reaction when she read his words, regardless of what it was. The thought of her crying, brokenhearted, and feeling abandoned hurt him as much as the thought of her being relieved that he was gone.

As the bus pulled away from the station, he leaned his head on the seat back and closed his eyes. "I love you, baby. Until death do us part."

1

CHAPTER ONE

February, Present Day

Heather Reed stepped out of the hospital and inhaled a deep, cleansing breath before starting her trek to her car in the parking garage alone. The long, twelve-hour shift had morphed into fourteen hours, thanks to a shortage of nurses and an abundance of patients, and she was more than ready to go home. Her feet ached after the constant rushing from one room to another all day. Her lower back was stiff from all the time she spent standing in one place to complete her charting. She was more mentally drained than usual because of her heavy patient load, but taking care of others when they needed her the most was her passion. Nursing wasn't just a job she left behind when she left the floor.

When she'd found her calling in life many years ago, she'd known immediately she wouldn't be happy doing anything else. Her propensity to nurture and her desire to help others made her a natural in nursing school. Quickly rising to the top of her class, Heather insisted on taking the harder cases the other students shied away from. During her first clinical rotation in the oncology unit, she knew she'd found her niche. The work was hard and exhausting, but she knew her patients needed her more than the average.

Her mind drifted back to the first time she accompanied the oncologist to deliver the dreaded news that the treatments weren't helping and it was time to stop them. Her elderly patient was lying in the bed, watching TV like every other day. She remembered thinking how normal everything seemed, but within a matter of seconds, everything changed. The doctor sat on the edge of the bed and talked to the woman like an old friend rather than with the standard clinical distance.

By the time the doctor finished imparting the unfortunate news, the patient was at peace with the decision they'd agreed upon, while Heather was the emotional wreck. She stood at the foot of the bed and listened to the conversation, admired how well the patient accepted the bad news, and felt her heart break because she knew it wouldn't be long before the cancer ravaged the sweet lady's body. Heather's cries turned into muffled sobs, despite her desperate attempts to remain professional. When she and the doctor left the room, he stopped her in the hall and asked if she needed the sedative he'd prepared for the patient, trying to infuse humor into the situation.

No matter how many times she'd delivered the news since that day, it was always the same. She left the hospital carrying the weight of her patient's burden on her shoulders. Empathy was part of what made her such a good nurse, but it was also part of what brought all the memories flooding back. Along with the debilitating loneliness. The current patient who prompted the memories to resurface hadn't received bad news yet, but Heather couldn't shake the feeling it was coming.

She also couldn't shake the feeling she was being watched. The hairs on the back of her neck stood up at full attention. Anxiety filled her mind and a strong sense of dread filled her chest, squeezing her from the inside like a vise. Despite being tired, she quickened her steps and hurried to the safety of her car. Once she was securely locked inside, her eyes scanned the parking garage for anyone out of the ordinary. She knew just because she didn't see someone didn't mean he wasn't out there.

When she exited from the garage, she purposely turned in the opposite direction from the route she normally took home. She trusted the gut feeling that warned her she was in danger. On one hand, just the thought of it all threatened to shut off her rational mind and fill her with fear. On the other hand, her stubborn, determined side refused to be intimidated by anyone cowardly enough to watch from the shadows. Her drive took an extra hour longer than normal before she reached her house. Fortunately, the numerous stops at various stores, unexpected turns onto side streets, and a couple of double-backs revealed the car that had followed her continuously.

Armed with that knowledge, she was able to evade the person following her and reach the security of her enclosed garage. Once inside, she intentionally left the lights off and watched for approaching headlights through the bow window at the front of her house. When the car lights illuminated the street, she stepped to the side of the window, completely out of sight, and kept her eyes glued to the car as it made its way around the cul-de-sac.

The silhouette of a single occupant was visible from her viewpoint, and it had masculine characteristics. "What do you want, creeper?" she whispered to the darkness around her. "What the hell are you up to?"

The car crawled at a snail's pace back in the direction it had come from originally, before turning to continue the search on the next street over from hers. She was confident her exact location hadn't been discovered; however, she wasn't about to give up the advantage she had over him. Moving through her darkened rooms, she gathered the items she needed and showered in the hall bathroom, where the light wasn't visible from anywhere else.

She thought about driving her second vehicle instead, since he obviously knew her primary car by sight, but decided against it. If he waited in the parking garage again, he could easily spot her walking to it. "I'll park somewhere else instead," she reasoned to herself.

"Leave through a different door out of the hospital, move like a ninja, undetected, right to my car. Piece of cake."

With her plan for the next day in place, she crawled into the bed and welcomed the rest that would soon follow. As tired as she was after her long day, the events of the evening had her nerves keyed up and her mind racing. She picked up her cell from the nightstand and called the first number stored in her favorites. When the call rolled to voice mail, Heather listened to the familiar voice with longing before she disconnected.

"I miss you so much," she whispered.

The next morning, Heather left for work earlier than normal, hoping to avoid giving away her exact location by beating her stalker to the punch. In her dark blue Land Rover with blackout windows, she navigated the streets with ease, taking more turns than required while constantly keeping her eyes on the traffic behind her. Rather than parking in the regular parking garage, she pulled into the lot behind the doctors' offices across the street from the hospital.

One of the benefits of working there for the past ten years was she knew every access point to gain entry. Once inside, she worked her way to the oncology floor undetected, using the secure hallways that required employee access codes to enter. But when she actually reached her unit, she knew she'd be vulnerable and completely exposed for her entire twelve-hour shift. With the substantial number of patients under her care, she didn't have time to validate every visitor who appeared on the hall.

"Becca, I need a favor." Heather approached her charge nurse and best friend in the nurses' lounge.

"Sure, hon. You're here awful early this morning. What do you need?"

"I need you to watch for anyone suspicious on the hall today. Anyone hanging around without ever actually visiting someone's room."

"You got it. But what happened? Why are you so spooked?"

"Someone followed me home from here last night. I lost him

before I reached my house, but I watched him drive around my neighborhood looking for me."

"I'm alerting security right now. We need someone stationed up here until we figure out what's going on." Becca quickly moved to the desk and called security. She turned back to Heather when she hung up the phone. "Their shift changes when ours does, so they'll send someone up when the new crew gets in. We still have about forty-five minutes before shift change, though."

"Thanks, Becca. I'm going to go ahead and meet with Renee for briefing on what happened with my patients last night. The sooner I can finish the first round of pulling medications, the faster I can get out of the open hall and into my patients' rooms. With the door closed. So no one can see in."

"Don't worry, I know where to find you if I need you," Becca chuckled. "You can only hide from me for so long. If some strange guy shows up looking for you, I'll take care of him. We have plenty of shit around here that'll knock him on his ass."

"I love having you as my best friend. You are the best...and you're a little frightening when you're mad."

AFTER HE'D LOST her the previous night, he drove for hours along every street in the enormous subdivision, determined to find her. He had to give her credit for being one of the few people he'd ever underestimated. The morning's mission was to get her work schedule so he could better track her movements. Tracing her comings and goings was becoming more cumbersome and time-consuming for him. He'd walked the halls of the hospital on more than one occasion, just to confirm she was still in the building. She'd left at different times every day she'd worked, and some days she didn't show up at all.

He was angry with himself because the night before had been the best opportunity he'd had to follow the gorgeous nurse with the short black hair back to her house. His brother, Turan, had been the computer genius, able to find anything with just a few clicks, but computers weren't his forte. Rashad had taken a more conventional preference to learning what their uncle had to teach them. He had perfected his intimidation tactics and all but eradicated any kind of feeling, but it was his proficiency with high-yield explosives that set him apart from the others. He hated to admit the moment of nostalgia that hit him when the memory of his brother snuck up on him. That moment of weakness was dangerous.

Rashad chose a spot in the parking garage and waited for Heather to show up. Cars and trucks rushed by in a mad dash to make it to work on time. When the influx of traffic slowed to a trickle and she still hadn't shown up, he muttered a curse under his breath and jerked his car door open. He moved quickly through the garage to the covered breezeway that connected to the hospital, determined not to be bested by that woman, or any woman, ever again.

Once inside, Rashad walked casually through the hospital as if he didn't have a care in the world. When others smiled or spoke to him, he replied with a feigned warmth to avoid raising any alarms or giving anyone reason to remember him. When he stepped off the elevator on her floor, he moved more carefully so his target didn't see him. Not that he was hiding from her, but when they officially met for the first time, he didn't want a flicker of recognition to light in her eyes.

With the recent shift change, the nurses were extra busy preparing for their first round to check on their patients, giving him ample opportunity to fade into the background. Patients were just waking up, call lights were going off all up and down the hall, and the breakfast trays had just arrived. While everyone scurried from one room to another, Rashad slipped into the nurses' break room to look for any information he could find on her.

One wall had a row of gray metal lockers for the nurses to store their belongings, but they all had combination locks securely fastened. There was no way he could find hers, break in to it, and leave undetected. A computer sat on a desk against the opposite wall with an uncomfortable, plastic chair. He quickly sat and tapped on a couple of keys, and the screen lit up, requesting a secure login ID.

"Damn computers," he muttered under his breath as he rose from the chair. As he walked around the table in the center of the room, the corner of a paper sticking out from under a legal pad caught his eye. He slid the paper out and smiled to himself. "Thank you for leaving me a printed copy of the floor's six-week schedule."

As he folded the paper into quarters, the break room door opened and a nurse stopped dead in her tracks when she saw him. "Can I help you, sir?"

While slipping the paper into his back pocket, he flashed his most charming smile before he replied. "I'm trying to find the break room for the family to use. You know, the one with snack machines, coffee dispenser, and bottled drinks. I'm afraid I may be lost."

"I can show you the way," she offered. "This room is only for the nurses to use."

"Ah, well, that would explain a few things," he replied, pouring on the false charm. "Lead the way."

The nurse turned and led him back to the main corridor. "Take the next hall on the right, and the vending area will be about halfway down on the left. There's a sign hanging from the ceiling just over the doorway."

"Thank you so much for your help," he replied.

"No problem," she answered. "Have a good day."

Rashad made the trek to the break room, taking the opportunity to look around nonchalantly for Heather as he walked. Not seeing her on his initial pass, he waited in the break room and bought a few snack items for appearance's sake before making the return trip. When he turned the corner back into the main hall, the first person he noticed was the security guard at the nurses' station. His first thought was he'd been made, but he released his held breath when the guard leaned over the counter and kissed the nurse.

"I'm headed home now, babe. Have a good day," the guard said. "Love you."

"Drive carefully, honey. I love you. See you tonight," the nurse cooed back.

The guard left without a backward glance, making Rashad feel more secure in his quest. As he strode down the hall, he cut his eyes to each open door, blatantly disregarding the person's privacy as he looked for Heather. When the last door came into view, his pace slowed while he considered his next move.

"I see you found the vending machines," Becca called from behind him.

"Yes, I'm afraid I found a few too many treats," he replied with his charming smile intact.

"Who are you visiting?"

He hesitated for a heartbeat, knowing he couldn't lie about a patient name. "A family friend. I'm just giving them some privacy for a few minutes."

"What's the name? I'll check to see how long it'll be before you can go in."

As luck would have it, a nurse exited from a room a few doors down just as she asked for the name. "Looks like I'm good to go in now," he inclined his head toward the open door. "Thank you for the offer, though."

She smiled and nodded her head, but he recognized the suspicion in her eyes. She wasn't moving on to continue doing her job. She was waiting him out, testing him, and calling his bluff. He had no choice but to walk into the room and at least try to stay long enough to make her believe he was actually visiting a patient. He only hoped in doing so, Heather would finally make an appearance.

Rashad walked into the room apprehensively and watched the lady lying in the bed. She appeared to be in her later sixties and was obviously once very beautiful. But the pallor of her skin expressed the severity of her condition. He took a seat in the chair beside her bed and watched her sleep for several minutes, keeping up his ruse. When she stirred and opened her eyes, she started at seeing him in her room.

"Who the hell are you?"

"I'm Greg. Would you care for a snack today?" He lied, trying to use her confusion to his advantage.

"No, I don't want anything. I'm too sick to eat."

"Okay, I'll let you get some rest and check back with you later today." He rose, snacks in hand, and left the hospital by taking the same route he'd followed in. The suspicious nurse was back at the nurses' station as he passed, but she was too busy to notice him walking out.

2

CHAPTER TWO

June 2001

Braxton tried to sleep with the rhythmic rocking of the bus as it continued eastward, but it was no use even to try. He could've taken the option to fly to the South Carolina base for his basic training, but he wasn't required to be there for several more days. He decided to take his time on the trip and hopefully clear his head before the intensive two-month training program began.

He would be several hours into the fifteen-hour trip before Heather woke and found his letter. She would have no way to contact him and no indication of where he was headed. He'd planned it that way intentionally so she would be forced to move on with her life. Even at eighteen, he knew when she looked at him, all she saw was a constant reminder of the worst day of their lives. After all their years spent side by side, it killed him when he saw the regret in her eyes that left no doubt in his mind she wished she'd never fallen in love with him.

He had to face the fact he had become no more than an expensive growing pain, a lesson that life had to teach them, but they were both stubborn and had to learn the hard way. For the sake of her sanity and her happiness, he had to be the one to leave. That took all the strength, drive, and courage he could muster. She'd have to be the one to file for a divorce, though. That's where he drew the line. Regardless of what the future held for him, another marriage was nowhere in the cards.

She would be his one and only love until he died.

"Where are you headed?" the older man across the aisle asked aloud.

Braxton cut his eyes toward the man to see to whom he was speaking. Most everyone on the bus was asleep since it was still dark outside. When their eyes met, the man smiled at him and waited for a reply.

"Army basic training in South Carolina. You?"

"Visiting my daughter and her family in Georgia. My son-in-law is in the Army and stationed there," the man replied. "Name's Larry, by the way."

"Braxton," he replied and accepted the offer to shake hands. "Good to meet you."

"Good to meet you, son. You're awful young to join the Army, aren't you?"

"I'm eighteen. Legal to sign my name on the dotted line and give away the next four years of my life to them."

"So you're not making it a career?"

"I haven't thought that far ahead yet," Braxton admitted. A career in the Army may not be such a bad idea. Travel the world. Associate with the best men and women, serve his country, and leave Texas behind him for as long as possible.

"What does your wife think about that?" Larry asked.

The corners of Braxton's eyes squeezed together, and his head slightly tilted in question. "What?"

Larry pointed at Braxton's left hand where his wedding ring was still prominently displayed. "You're married, right?"

"For now," he shrugged. "It didn't work out. She made a mistake marrying me."

"Marriage is hard, there's no doubt about that. My wife and I married young, too. Everyone told us not to, said we should wait until we were older. But we were headstrong, and we knew better than they did," Larry laughed in reply. His gaze drifted to another time and place as his mind's eye relived the events of the past. "After the first month of living together, we were both ready to call it quits.

"But we stuck it out. You see, we had too many people to prove wrong. More than that, we meant it when we said those vows. For better or for worse is what we've lived by all these years. Don't give up on her just yet, son. There may still be hope."

Braxton's only reply was a lopsided smile that didn't reach his eyes. There was no point in telling the man that all hope was lost and had been dead for months. Three months, to be exact. Three months since he failed Heather in a way she could never forgive him, and he could never forgive himself. In a way he knew he didn't deserve forgiveness.

"It's none of my business, and I'm just a nosy old man, I know," Larry said warmly. "But I know the look of a tormented young man. I saw it too many times in my own mirror when I wasn't much older than you are now. You'll come out of basic training a different man, Braxton. You'll be harder, more focused, and more disciplined. Use that discipline to help your marriage, son. Not hurt it."

"I will," Braxton promised. Though he didn't elaborate on how. The only way he could help his marriage was to be disciplined enough to give Heather a real chance at happiness, far away from him. "There's nothing I wouldn't do for her."

"Then you're a good man, Braxton," Larry replied. "Never forget that."

Larry settled into his seat and was asleep within minutes. His words played over and over in Braxton's mind. More times than he could count, he considered telling the bus driver to stop and let him off. He'd find a way back home on his own. He'd find a way to work things out, regardless of what had happened. But every time he started to rise from his seat, the weight of his failure held him down.

With a heavy heart, Braxton closed his eyes and let sleep overtake him.

The bus shuddered to a halt, waking Braxton from the most sleep he'd had at one time in the last several months. "We'll take a thirty-minute break here, folks. Grab a bite to eat, stretch your legs, and be back on the bus at half past the hour."

Braxton's eyes surveyed the area after he exited the bus, trying to determine where they were and how much longer they had to go. The roadside diner had obviously been built first from the age of it. The truck stop next door was newer, bigger, and had a full range of facilities to cater to truck drivers. He felt someone move up beside him and knew who it was without looking.

"Want to grab a chicken sandwich and fries at four in the morning?" Larry asked with a chuckle.

"Sounds like the ultimate breakfast to me," he joked in return. "Maybe we can have apple pie for dessert. Breakfast dessert."

"That's the spirit."

The two men walked together into the diner and sat in a booth along the front windows. After the waitress took their orders, an uncomfortable silence crept into the booth, and Larry fidgeted nervously. Braxton sensed the older man wanted to resume their earlier conversation but wasn't sure how to broach it.

"It's a long, sad story." Braxton decided to save Larry the hassle. "We started out as best friends when we were kids. We finally became an official couple when we started high school. A lot of things went wrong. I'm not getting into all of the nitty-gritty details right now, though.

"In a nutshell, every day of my life that I can actually remember, I've loved her in one way or another. We were neighbors for a long time, but then her dad got one promotion after another at work. With his newfound wealth, he bought a bigger, nicer house in a ritzier neighborhood. Suddenly, I wasn't good enough for his daughter anymore.

"That didn't stop her, though. She loved me, so we stayed together despite his protests and threats and bellowing." Braxton paused and stared at a droplet of water as it slid down his glass. "As soon as we were old enough and didn't need anyone's permission, we got married. We had a go at it for a little while, tried to make it work. This is where I leave out the private details, but it all boils down to the fact that she's estranged from her entire family because of me. Especially her dad. He won't have anything to do with her as long as I'm still around.

"The stress of everything is killing her. She's torn between being with me and being with her family. I just can't stand by and watch the beautiful woman I love wither away to nothing. So, I left and made it easier for her to move on with her life."

"Did you ask her if that's what she wanted?"

The waitress returned with their orders, momentarily saving Braxton from answering what should've been an easy question. When the waitress left, Larry took a bite of his sandwich and waited for Braxton to answer.

In between bites of his food, Braxton continued recounting his story. "She's not the kind of person who would say she wanted me to leave. She can't stand hurting anyone else, so she'd take all the pain just to avoid inflicting any on someone else. Her dad or her mom called every day, pressuring her to come home, keeping her on the phone for hours at a time. She became more and more withdrawn from me. Selfishly, I hung around longer than I should have, but I just couldn't let her suffer anymore."

"Did you file for a divorce before you left?"

Braxton shook his head from side to side. "No. I won't be the one to do that."

"You really do love her, don't you?"

"It's always been her. It'll always be her."

"You know, other guys your age don't think like that."

"Those guys haven't met Heather."

Larry leaned back and studied Braxton, taking in his words and his overall demeanor. Braxton felt the appraising gaze, knew he was being sized up and measured, but he didn't care. The talk with Larry brought all the memories flooding back, tormenting him with mental pictures of the best and worst times of his life. His guts churned, the chicken sandwich and fries turned to lead in his stomach, and he had to work to swallow past the ball of emotions stuck in his throat.

"For the record, I think you're making a big mistake by leaving like this. She sounds like a great girl."

"She's the best."

"Girls like her aren't that common. Love like you just described comes once in a lifetime, if you're lucky. You won't find another one like her, Braxton."

He looked up and met Larry's gaze directly. "I know I won't. And I won't be looking for another one either. Especially not after all I've been through."

The waitress appeared with their checks. Larry picked up both at the same time and insisted on paying. "It's the least I can do for a young man who'll be serving our country. My trip ends at our next stop, so this is the last chance I'll have to do it."

"It's not necessary, but I appreciate it. Thank you."

"Take care of yourself, Braxton. I hope everything works out for you."

At the next stop, Braxton felt a deep loneliness when he said goodbye to Larry. The older man had been the first friend he'd really talked to about his predicament. He'd talked to his father often, but familial bias tainted their discussions. His friends were his age and didn't understand any of what he'd already experienced. Larry was the first person who wasn't related, wasn't too young, and didn't have any preconceived notions about their relationship. He listened, he grasped the depth of their love, and he offered advice without being condescending.

The ride from Georgia to South Carolina was both the longest and shortest of his life. He'd watched the sun rise and visualized Heather still asleep in their bed. He longed to be there with her, to hold her while she slept, to kiss her when she woke. As the bus pulled up to the station, he wondered how much longer it would be before she found his letter. Would she move out of their apartment right away, back in with her parents? Or would she wait a while to see if he came back?

"The truth is it doesn't matter what happens. Our courses are set now. In two days, I have to report to the base for basic training," he muttered to himself. He hailed a cab to take him to a hotel close to the base. After checking in and stowing his stuff, he set out on foot to take in the sights and spend the rest of his free time alone until the very last second. The two days passed by much too quickly, and it was time to check out of the hotel.

Before leaving his room, he called his mom to talk to her one last time before basic training started and all communication was cut off.

"Hello?"

"Hey, Mom." His tone was deflated, like his heart. "I'm about to leave the hotel. Just wanted to say I love you. I'll let you know when graduation is in case you and Dad can make it."

"Of course we'll be there, Brax. I love you, too, son. And I'm so worried about you."

"I'll be okay, Mom. Don't worry."

She paused for a heartbeat before replying. "Heather called this morning. She's worried to death about you, Braxton."

"Did you tell her where I am?"

"No, I didn't. You asked me not to, but you know I don't agree with how you're handling this."

"It's for the best, Mom. I have to go. Tell Dad I love him. I love you. I'll call you as soon as I can."

"Your father and I are so proud of you, Braxton. I want you to know that. We love you more than life itself."

～

August 2001

"WHERE DID MY LITTLE BOY GO?" Braxton's mother, Jackie, asked as she grasped her son's face in her palms.

"He left as a boy, and two months later, the Army gives us a man," his father, Bryan, beamed. "He even had a birthday while he was in basic training."

"You look so handsome in that uniform," Jackie commented through her tears. The pride and admiration she had for her son shone in her eyes and resonated in her voice.

Braxton scanned the crowd milling around the soldiers who had just graduated from basic training, searching for another familiar face he'd hoped to see. Without asking, Bryan knew exactly who his son was looking for.

"She's not here, son." Bryan placed his hand on Braxton's shoulder and squeezed to show his support. "She said..." He paused to consider his next words before he continued.

"You talked to her? What did she say?"

"She said you left her, so you know where to find her if you want to see her," Bryan replied, his face contorted with sympathy.

"She hasn't filed for a divorce?" Braxton couldn't keep the surprise from his tone. He was certain she would've filed within the first week of his absence.

"Not that we know of, Brax. She hasn't told us if she has."

"How is she?" There were a million and one questions he wanted to grill his parents with to find out every single detail about Heather. What had she been doing? Who was she talking to? Had she moved back in with her parents? Did she ask about him? Did she miss him? Did she still love him? Asking about how she was doing left the question open for interpretation, so they could share any information they thought was important.

"She's had a really rough time, son. She seemed to be doing a little better before we left to come here," Bryan replied.

"Maybe you should go talk to her, Brax. Sit down and do it face-to-face," Jackie suggested. "I think you both need that time together."

"I'm not sure I can," Braxton sighed. "I only have a couple of days to get to Arizona for AIT."

"AIT?" Jackie asked.

"Advanced Individual Training. It's training for my assigned job with the Army."

"How long will you be there?" Jackie's face fell with his reply.

"I'll be away for about six months total for AIT and jump school."

"Jump school? What is jump school?" Jackie demanded.

"Airborne School, Mom. I'm going to learn how to jump out of airplanes, control my parachute to land on specific targets, and use these skills in combat."

"I don't even want to think about that. Don't tell me anything else." Jackie shook her head from side to side, making Braxton chuckle at her discomfort.

"I'm tougher than you think, Mom."

With the graduation ceremony events completed, Braxton was able to spend what little free time he had with his parents before his more extensive training program began. While they talked, ate, and toured the grounds, his mother's words urging him to see Heather in person rang in his ears. His date to report to the training base in Arizona was nonnegotiable with the Army. But with a little extra effort, he'd already managed to get a connecting flight with an extra-long layover through the Houston airport.

The urge to see her, talk to her, be with her had been too strong for too long. He knew what he had to do the instant he was instructed to make his travel arrangements. There was no way he was flying across the country without stopping in Texas to see her again. Leaving her had been pure torture. He didn't know if seeing her again would make him feel better or worse. He only knew it had to be done.

At the end of their day together, he hugged his parents as they said goodbye, told them he loved them, and made his final preparations for leaving the base that had been his home for the previous nine weeks. The new base would be his home for the next eighteen weeks before he'd make the trek back across the country to attend the three-week jump school. He hadn't had the heart to tell his mother he'd decided to make a career of his time in the Army, and that the training he had in mind for the future would keep him away from home more and more.

Finally, the time had come to face the anguish he'd been running from for far too long. He walked out of the Houston airport with his duffle bag slung over his shoulder and hailed a taxi. They drove in complete silence to the apartment he shared with Heather. It amazed him how everything could look the same and simultaneously be completely different. The tiny little space that was barely big enough for them to turn around without bumping into each other held so many wonderful memories—and far too much pain.

He climbed the stairs, delaying the inevitable by only a couple of minutes, and stopped in front of their door. Part of him hoped she'd changed the locks, that his key wouldn't work, and he could at least say he tried as he walked away.

But he had no such luck.

His key slid into the lock without a hitch. He turned it, and the doorknob twisted with ease. He pushed the door open but stayed planted in the threshold. He felt like an intruder breaking into someone else's house, not a husband returning home to his wife after an extended leave.

His feet moved on their own into the place he'd called home just a short eight weeks before. His legs carried him into the apartment where the sights, scents, and belongings only served to intensify the pain in his chest. He dropped his duffel bag on the floor and robotically moved through the rooms, noting what had and hadn't changed. Her clothes still hung in the tiny closet. Her makeup and toiletries still cluttered the minuscule bathroom counter.

The pictures of the two of them throughout their lives were still everywhere. According to the story the pictures told, they were more than happy together. Images of them smiling, laughing, and kissing said they couldn't get enough of each other. Their wedding picture said they belonged to each other for all time.

He walked into the kitchen and began searching for paper and a pen to write her a letter. In the event she didn't come home before he had to get back to the airport, he planned to leave her a note asking her to contact him. Telling her how monumentally he'd fucked up. Laying his feelings out on the table, without holding anything back, without regard to his vulnerability.

He wanted her back, and he could no longer deny it.

Rifling through the stack of mail and papers on the counter as he searched for a blank sheet, his eyes landed on a set of documents that made everything else fade to black around him. The black hole they created drew all of the air out of the room, leaving his chest burning as his lungs demanded oxygen. All sound instantly disappeared, replaced by the sound of his pulse beating on drums in his ears. His capacity to rationalize and reason like any other sane person dissolved, leaving only instability in its place.

Name of person filing for divorce (Petitioner): Heather Reed
Your spouse's name (Respondent): Braxton Reed

Petition For Divorce

3

CHAPTER THREE

February, Present Day

In a deep sleep, Sara rolled over and snuggled against her husband, her front to his back. The contact instantly startled her awake and filled her with so much fear that she sat up and called his name out in the dark.

"Steve! Honey, what's wrong?"

She reached over to turn on the lamp beside the bed and gasped when she saw him in the light. His skin was so pale it was almost translucent, his arms were drawn up close to his chest, and his entire body appeared to be in convulsions. Had she not felt the heat radiating from his every pore, she would've thought he was having a seizure from the severity of his shivers. She placed her hand on his forehead and immediately knew she needed to call for an ambulance.

As she flew out of the bed, she grabbed the cordless phone on the nightstand and dialed 911. When the line connected to the dispatcher, she immediately began rambling information and demands.

"We're in room 1345 at Sterling Luxury Resort on Broad Street. My husband has colon cancer and is undergoing experimental chemotherapy. His fever has spiked, he's shaking uncontrollably, and he's very pale. I need an ambulance here right away to take him to the emergency room."

After she answered a few basic questions about Steve, the dispatcher assured her the ambulance was on the way. She called the front desk and alerted them to the situation before she helped Steve into a jacket, socks, and shoes. February temperatures in Houston were mild, but his high fever made Steve feel like his body was freezing. In his condition, the chill of the evening air could cause his fever to go up even more.

Once they had him loaded onto the gurney, the paramedics wheeled him out of the luxurious hotel and into the back of the ambulance. Sara rushed to their car to meet them at the emergency room. At one point, she reached for her cell to inform Noah, Chaise, and Silas, but a quick glance at the clock stopped her. Eight minutes after three o'clock in the morning in Houston would be just after four o'clock in Miami, way too early to wake her kids until she knew more about the severity of his condition.

She racked her brain trying to remember all the side effects Dr. Stanton had warned them about, especially which ones were potentially life-threatening. Erring on the side of caution, she decided to call the answering service to at least report that Steve was en route to the hospital.

"Can I put you on hold for just a minute, Mrs. Steele? Dr. Stanton prefers to talk to his patients and their families directly," the young lady with the answering service explained.

"Of course. Thank you," Sara replied, relieved she could talk to someone—anyone—at that moment.

After a couple of minutes, the hold music abruptly quit, and a slightly groggy male voice filled the line. "This is Daryl Stanton. What's going on with Steve?"

"He was so warm and shivering so hard, he woke me up from a dead sleep. He's hot to the touch, but he's just so pale. I didn't even take his temperature before I called 911 because just seeing him in that condition rattled me so badly. I can't think straight right now, Dr.

Stanton, so I can't remember when you said to get immediate help. But he scared me bad enough that I would've made him go to the hospital regardless," Sara rambled.

"You did the right thing. It's not uncommon for people to have a high fever while on chemo. It effectively destroys your immune system, so even a common cold can turn ugly very quickly. We'll do some bloodwork to rule out a systemic infection, but this could very well be a side effect of his treatment. Either way, we can make him more comfortable and get his temperature down to a safe level. I'll meet you both in the ER."

"Thank you," Sara breathed her reply, the gratitude thick in her voice.

When she was finally by Steve's side again, he was resting in a darkened exam room. The bandage on his hand made her heart rate quicken because she realized the IV had been placed in his forearm. She'd seen that happen before when he was too dehydrated for the medical personnel to hit the vein closer to his wrist. She refused to listen to the inner voice that tried to issue a dire warning concerning the sudden onset of his symptoms. She couldn't even entertain the thought of Steve succumbing to the devastating disease.

"Hi, Sara," Daryl called softly from the doorway. "I've already ordered a complete blood count, and the preliminary results should be back from the lab within in the hour. Once I get that report, I should have a better idea of what's going on. Until then, we're hydrating him, and we've started him on medication to bring his fever down. It was quite a bit higher than we like to see in chemotherapy patients, so I'm sure he was feeling pretty rough."

"It was so sudden, Dr. Stanton. He didn't say anything about feeling bad last night. But then, he still likes to think he's invincible."

"That's because I'm made of Steele," Steve mumbled his witty retort but managed to give Sara a half smile.

"Did you know you were getting sick when we went to bed last night?" Sara asked.

"I wasn't sick like this, but I did feel a little off. I didn't realize it would progress to be this bad, though. Now I know what to watch for so I can stop it before it gets too far gone."

"Absolutely," Daryl agreed. "Every symptom won't be a classic, textbook example. We'll do the best we can to manage them so you're not too miserable. I'll be back when the lab results are ready, but plan on staying for at least a day or two. You should both try to get some rest now."

Steve patted the bed beside him, so Sara crawled in and rested her cheek in the crook of his shoulder. With their arms wrapped around each other, they slept until Daryl returned with the results of his blood count. The grim expression he wore did nothing to calm Sara's fears.

"Your white blood cell count is significantly low, Steve. We're going to keep you, start you on a broad-spectrum antibiotic to help your body fight off any infection, and monitor your counts to make sure we start seeing some improvements. From the date of your last chemo round, this isn't entirely unusual, but we may need to help kick-start your bone marrow so it produces more white blood cells."

"How long will I be here this time?"

"You know the rules, Steve. We take it one day at a time," Daryl replied. "Let us finish this paperwork, and we'll get you moved to a more comfortable room."

"Sara," Steve called her name softly when Daryl had left the room. "We'll eventually have to talk about it."

"Not now, we don't. You're not giving up over this...this... It's not even a setback. It's no more than an inconvenience. If you were healthy and caught the flu, you wouldn't throw your hands up in surrender."

He knew her anger and dogged determination masked her fear of what their future may hold. He wanted to assure her he'd be fine. He wanted to soothe her frayed nerves and promise he'd kick cancer's ass. For her, he wanted to be invincible and live forever. But he couldn't promise her any of those things. Instead, he just held her close to his heart and kissed the top of her head.

When he'd been quiet for too long, she prodded him again. "Steve, promise me you're not giving up."

"I'm not giving up, babe," he whispered.

Before he drifted off to sleep again, he felt the warmth of her tears soak through his thin hospital gown.

"How's my favorite patient in the world today?" Heather asked as she entered Steve's room. "Even though I've missed you, it's really not necessary for you to keep pretending to be sick just to come see me."

"But I have to keep you guessing. You never know when I'll be here and when I won't," Steve joked.

"Well, to be honest, I'd much rather you show up with some food! Breakfast, lunch, snacks—it doesn't matter what it is." Heather laughed as she took a seat next to his bed.

Sara sat on the other side and watched as the two of them playfully picked on each other. With all the time they had spent in and around the oncology floor, they'd formed a special bond with Heather because of the way she cared so deeply for others. Her warm personality was genuine, but they'd also witnessed her stubborn, take-charge side. She was an advocate for her patients as much as she was their cheerleader. She'd bravely correct an intern for giving incorrect information just as she'd forcefully demand that her patient had to keep fighting until she gave them permission to give up.

Sara had also witnessed Heather handle that very painful situation with finesse and grace. A woman held on to life with every ounce of willpower she possessed while she waited for her son to arrive at her side. The lady was obviously suffering, painfully struggling to hold on until she'd heard that last goodbye from her loved one. Though her son was on his way, his trip would take too much time, and Heather realized there was no way her patient would be able to rest in peace under those circumstances.

Heather leaned in close to the lady, kept her voice low, and spoke soothingly to her.

"You carried him for nine months. Fed him, nurtured him, cared for him, loved him. Jordan knows how much you love him, sweetheart. I'll tell him how hard you fought to have him close to you just one more time. I'll tell him how much you love him. You don't have to suffer anymore. You can let go now."

Sara watched from the hallway, mesmerized by how the woman responded to Heather's words. Her labored breathing became calmer. Her clenched fists relaxed. Her face, distorted with pain, became peaceful. Then she did exactly as Heather instructed and let go. And Sara's heart broke as she watched Heather sob uncontrollably when it was all over.

The playful banter between Steve and Heather pulled Sara from her inner thoughts. Steve already seemed so much better than he was just a few hours before. As long as Heather instructed Steve to fight, Sara held on to the hope that he would be completely healed of cancer.

"I'm going to step out in the hall and call Noah. Do you need anything, Steve?"

"No, babe. I'm fine. Tell all of our kids I love them."

Sara closed the door behind her and drew in a deep breath. The daily roller coaster rides of emotions drained her mentally and physically. She knew if it affected her that much, the impact on Steve had to be so much worse. If she was considered selfish because she wanted her husband to live, and willed him to keep going regardless of how tired he was, then she'd wear the label with pride.

At the end of the hall, she pulled her cell out of her pocket and dialed Noah's number. When he picked up, she decided it was time for her to be blunt about Steve's health status. Playing down the symptoms wouldn't make them go away.

"Hey, Mom. You're calling earlier than usual. Are you and Dad all right?"

"Hi, Noah. I thought you'd want to know your dad was admitted to the hospital early this morning. He's feeling a little better now, but he had a high fever in the middle of the night. With his low white blood cell count, they're keeping him here for IV antibiotics and to monitor his counts for the next few days.

"They've, uh, had to temporarily stop his chemotherapy so his bone marrow can make more white blood cells. It's a fine line to balance the need to kill the cancer cells but not kill his immune system entirely. We'll know more in a couple of days...if he can continue in the trial, with the experimental drugs."

"There's a chance they'll drop him from the clinical trial?"

"If he can't finish the program, yes. If it's weakening his body to the point his bone marrow isn't producing blood cells, there's really no reason to continue the chemotherapy. We're not there yet, and we're not giving up hope, but I can't let you, Chaise, and Silas be blindsided by it if it does happen."

"Mom, is he worse than you're telling me?"

"He's had some ups and downs lately. Nothing in particular that any other man going through chemotherapy doesn't have. It just seems to be hitting him harder, more things at once."

"How are you, Mom? Are you eating, sleeping, taking care of yourself? I wish you'd told me sooner. We would've been there with you."

"No, son. Brianna just had a baby last month. I know you've been busy with work. You have a life and a family of your own to take care of, and that doesn't include babysitting your mother."

"It's hardly babysitting, Mom. You don't have to do this alone. Chaise and Bull could've been there with you until Brianna was able to travel. Silas could've been there. We'd work it out. How do you think that makes me feel, knowing you've been carrying this weight on your shoulders alone all this time?"

Tears escaped from Sara's eyes and rolled down her cheeks. "You're such a wonderful son—and a great man. You're all welcome to come stay here with me anytime you want to. But I understand if you can't, so I don't want you to feel obligated."

"Love is never an obligation, Mom. It's a privilege."

IN STEVE'S ROOM, Heather continued her medical assessment of her patient. The clever banter and quick comebacks demonstrated to her that his mental faculties were intact. He was alert to people, time, and place—meaning he could match faces with names, he knew what time of day and year it was, and he knew where he was. His speech was clear and concise, no audible sign of slurring his words or exaggerated forgetfulness.

The main discrepancy that concerned her was the color of his skin had significantly changed since she last saw him. That could be chalked up to a byproduct of the chemotherapy, but it was significant enough to be noted in his chart. The optimist in her hoped it was simply a side effect of the nearly lethal cocktail he'd been given to stop the progression of his disease. The realist in her told her nothing good came from kidding herself.

This was the part of her job she hated, when she had to face the fact one of her patients may no longer be responding to treatment. The time when they had to have "the talk." The one where she helped the doctor convince the patient to stop focusing on the future and start focusing on the present. The discussion that inevitably left the patient with thoughts and feelings of hopelessness, because the message they delivered essentially said to give up hope that the treatments could change the prognosis.

While Steve still joked and played along with her, she sensed a distinct change in his overall demeanor. A peaceful acceptance of what will be will be, regardless if he tried to alter the course or not, had replaced the tough as nails, hard as Steele man she'd met initially. He was no longer fixated on eradicating all the mutated cells in his body. His focus was on his family, mainly his wife, who'd been by his side every step of the way.

Steve often joked that he was made of Steele, an obvious play on his last name, but when Sara was out of earshot, he openly confessed she was actually the strong one who made him keep going. Keep trying. Keep fighting. The last time he'd said those words to Heather, her initial gut reaction was Steve was preparing to face the end of his life. He kept trying, kept fighting, kept going for Sara, but when it was clear it was no longer helping, he could accept his fate as long as she held his hand.

"Who did Sara say she was going to call?" Heather asked Steve to test his cognitive skills again and to clear the morbid thoughts from her own mind.

"Our son, Noah," Steve replied proudly.

Heather stopped writing and jerked her eyes up to meet Steve's. "Your son is Noah Steele?"

"Yep, that's my boy."

"Noah Steele from Miami?"

"Born and raised."

"Noah Steele of Steele Security?"

"That's exactly right. Wait. How did you know that? How do you know Noah?"

4

CHAPTER FOUR

September 2001

Heather walked into her parents' house, located in one of Houston's more upscale neighborhoods, and headed to the kitchen where she knew she'd find her mom. The house itself was gorgeous, set on just over an acre of lush green grass, professionally landscaped sweeping gardens, and a backyard pool oasis that boasted an outdoor kitchen. Inside, every room was decorated by an interior designer who stayed booked up to a year in advance. The fine dark wood trim accented both the expansive arched windows that spanned the front of the house and the wood flooring with alternating planks of light and dark shades. Everything about the inside and outside of the house exuded opulence, but it reminded Heather of a museum more than a home.

Her childhood home where she grew up next door to Braxton would almost completely fit inside the entertainment room of their current house. Their old home may have been small, but there was so much love and so many wonderful memories in it. It was pure coincidence that most of those beloved and cherished childhood memories in the other house involved Braxton in one way or another.

Kay Greer wrapped her arms around Heather and squeezed her tightly. "How's my baby? I'm so glad you're here."

"I'm fine, Mom," Heather replied, although she was actually anything but fine. Depressed. Sad. Lonely. Despondent. Those were more accurate descriptions than "fine," but that wasn't a conversation she wanted to have again that day.

"You're so thin. You've lost more weight, Heather," Kay insisted, her tone rife with genuine concern. "You're not eating, are you?"

"I said I'm fine, Mom. That means I'm fine," Heather insisted stubbornly. "Don't start. I just got here."

Emmett silently stood in the doorway through which Heather had entered, intentionally not announcing his presence so he could listen to their exchange. "Your mother's right. You've lost weight. Sit down and eat."

Heather turned her head to look at him over her shoulder. "Don't think I didn't know you were back there eavesdropping. I'm not one of your employees you can just order around. I may be your daughter, but I'm also a grown woman. I'm married. And I make my own decisions."

"Eighteen is hardly a grown woman, Heather. You're not even old enough to buy alcohol yet. But you're definitely my daughter—there's no denying you got that stubborn, defiant streak from me. Speaking of being married, did you get the papers I had my lawyer draw up?" While he meant well as a father and a businessman, Emmett had a tendency to run over everyone else's thoughts and feelings.

"Yeah, I got them all right." She made no attempt to conceal her contempt or the challenge that her arched eyebrow conveyed.

"Did you sign them?"

"Nope."

"Heather."

"Emmett," she retorted, mimicking his stance by putting her fists on her hips and staring him down.

"What did you do with the papers?" His voice was even, showing no signs of his frustration. But she knew all too well that was just part of his tactic, an act to encourage others to lower their defenses so he could pounce at the opportune moment.

"I put them on my kitchen counter," she replied.

"Good."

"With the rest of the junk mail that needs to be shredded," she added.

"That's not funny." He was beginning to lose his composure. Tiny cracks in his armored façade were beginning to show.

"It wasn't funny when I opened the packet and saw divorce papers, either," she snapped. "No warning. No heads-up. You could've said, 'Hey, Heather, my lawyer is sending some papers for you to read over. Let me know what you think.' But no, you didn't even give me that common courtesy. I thought they were from Braxton when I first opened it. Do you have any idea what that did to me? Don't you think I've been through enough already?"

"Baby, I'm sorry. I didn't even think—"

"No, that's a lie, so don't even finish that sentence. You thought about it enough to have your damn lawyer write up a very detailed, explicit legal document that divides everything between us, right down to the couch and the loveseat. You try to control everyone and everything in your life, but I will not be controlled. Do you understand me? You will not steamroll over me and my decisions for my life."

"What are you going to do, then?"

Exasperated that he would even ask that question after the outburst he just experienced, her jaw dropped open, and she blatantly glowered at him. "Whatever the hell I want to do. That's what. I don't need your permission or your approval. Or even your support. But if you want to stay in my life, let me live it myself. You're not living it through me."

"I can't talk to her," Emmett complained to Kay. "There's no reasoning with her."

"You're exactly right," Heather replied. Emmett raised his eyes to meet hers, hopeful she had seen the error of her thinking, until she continued. "So stop trying because it's really irritating when I have to keep repeating myself."

"You're still young, Heather. It'll be good for you to start over with a clean slate," Emmett pressured. "You need to trust me."

"A clean slate?" She emphasized each word as she spat out her reply. With her pointed finger in his face, she continued. "Since you're my father, I'm giving you one chance to rephrase that and then never say it again. Because if you ever even tiptoe around the words 'clean slate' to me again, as if I should just *forget*, I promise you will regret it."

"That came out wrong, Heather. Of course, I didn't mean it like that. I'm sorry. The last thing I'd ever want to do is hurt you."

"Don't you see? That's exactly what you're doing every time you want to sweep everything under the rug and pretend it never happened. It did happen—and it happened to me. Stop trying to make it seem insignificant, like a few sheets of legal paper will make it all disappear."

"I'm just trying to do what I think is best," Emmett replied softly, humbled. "I said I'm sorry, and I mean it. Forgive me. Your mother and I were just about to throw some steaks on the grill. Do you want to stay and eat with us?"

"No, I need to go. Errands to run. I just wanted to stop by for a minute to see you."

"There's no need to run off. I promise to be on my best behavior if you stay," Emmett pleaded. "I don't get to see you nearly enough."

His eyes begged her to stay. His own pain at not being able to shield his daughter from the cruel world lay just beneath the surface.

"Okay. I'll stay for a little while longer," she conceded, though she was still mad and upset with him.

"That what I want to hear. I'll go fire up the grill and burn some steaks while you ladies handle the fixings."

Heather and Kay started pulling items from the pantry and refrigerator to begin cooking the side dishes. As they worked together to accomplish the tasks, Heather instinctively knew her mother wanted to continue the conversation, but she didn't know how to approach it without alienating her daughter.

"Just come out with it already. If you keep holding it in, you'll end up in the bell tower with a high-powered rifle," Heather deadpanned.

"I didn't know your father had our lawyer draw up divorce papers, Heather. Not until you'd already received them, and it was way too late by then. I've already told him what I thought about it, but you know how he is once he gets something in his head.

"My concern is about you and your well-being. What are you going to do, Heather? Braxton has been gone for going on three months now. How long do you plan to wait for him?"

"I'm fully aware he's been gone for eleven weeks and three days. That's exactly eighty days. One thousand nine hundred twenty hours. One hundred fifteen thousand two hundred minutes, give or take, since I don't know exactly what time he left. I only know what time I found the note.

"What you and Dad don't seem to grasp is this isn't puppy love. What I feel for Braxton isn't just young love that'll fade as I get older and realize it was just infatuation. He's been my best friend for as long as I can remember. We know each other better than anyone else does. Every dirty, rotten secret we've kept from everyone else. Every good deed we did without letting anyone else know. Our imperfections and perfections only made our bond stronger. If you and Dad had faced what Braxton and I have faced, could you simply walk away from him as easily as you expect me to walk away from my husband?"

"You're right. We've underestimated how much he means to you and how being in love at your age can be just as real as being in love at my age. Your love for him really hasn't waned in the least bit, has it?"

"No, and it won't. We're both dealing with the aftermath the best way we know how. I'm partly to blame for why he left the way he did. Not that it doesn't hurt like hell, but I have to be fair about it. Sure, there are times when I get really mad at him for leaving me. I scream, cry, make stupid threats I know I'd never go through with, try to strike a bargain with God. Then I remember how I mentally checked out for a while and left him feeling responsible," Heather explained.

"You stayed away from your dad and me for a long time," Kay said sadly. "Your dad thought maybe you came back around us after Braxton left because you'd changed your mind about being married."

"I stayed away because neither of you respected my marriage, especially Dad. I didn't come back around because Braxton left. It was because I knew how badly it was hurting you."

Kay glanced out the window and saw Emmett was busy in the outdoor kitchen, fighting with the grill and marinating the steaks with his signature mixture of steak sauces and spices. "While the potatoes and rolls are cooking, let's sit down and have a little girl talk."

As they sat at the kitchen table, Kay deliberated how to share the personal information from her youth with her daughter. "I know you've loved Braxton since you were kids, but it doesn't happen like that for most people. When I was a sophomore in high school, a handsome boy my age moved in to our neighborhood and, of course, every girl in our class had a crush on him. Including me.

"When he asked me out, I was ecstatic. Out of his pick of all the girls, he chose me. We went on several dates before he asked me to officially be his girlfriend. We were perfect for each other—we were interested in similar things, we had plans to go to the same college, our families became friends. I was so in love with him I didn't feel like I could breathe without him.

"Our senior year, we debated about going to the prom. I wanted to go because it was the last one we'd ever have. He didn't want to go because our junior prom wasn't any fun at all. But because I wanted to go, and he loved me, he gave in.

"I was so excited. It was a night to dress up in a formal gown, go out to eat, dance in the arms of the love of my life, and at least pretend to be adults. Mom took me to get my hair, makeup, and nails done. My dress and shoes were a perfect fit. Dad had the camera out, ready to take more pictures than we could ever use. All the things that seemed so important at the time were working out perfectly.

"While we waited for him, Dad took several individual pictures of me. He had me doing so many poses in so many different places around the house and the yard, I didn't realize how much time had passed. When I saw the time on the clock, I knew something was wrong. Chris knew how important that night was to me, he wouldn't have intentionally made us miss our dinner reservation time.

"Mom called his house, and Chris's aunt answered, crying hysterically. Mom had to break the news to me that Chris wasn't coming. We weren't going to the prom together. We weren't going off to college together. He'd planned to make that night extra special for us, and that's why he'd tried to talk me out of going to the prom. He had planned to propose to me, but he wanted it to be in a more intimate setting. So he'd arranged to do both. We'd spend a while at the prom, then leave and have the more romantic evening he'd envisioned.

"He had a job after school and had gotten off late. So he was late picking up his tuxedo, late getting home to shower and change, late to pick up the ring he was going to use to ask me to marry him. His car had been acting up, and I remember he'd told me he needed to check it out after work...but he was late. It broke down in the middle of the road on his way to pick me up. He had his head stuck under the hood when another car came flying up behind him on the wrong side of the road. Kids who had been drinking, having fun on their way to the prom, and not paying attention to the road.

"Chris died at the scene with my ring still in his pocket. The teenage driver of the other car was charged with vehicular manslaughter, and because he had a significant blood alcohol level, he went to prison. The others in that car never recovered from what they saw, what they felt responsible for causing. And I never forgave myself for insisting we go to the prom. Because if I hadn't, then he wouldn't have been there at that exact time.

"I understand the pain you feel, like you'll never be happy again. Like you'll never have a normal life. Like you'll never experience an entire night of sleep from now on. It won't be anytime soon, but it will get better. It'll become more tolerable because you'll learn to live with the pain, but it'll never completely go away.

"Heather, what you need to take from my experience is none of us, no matter what age, has a promise for the next breath. If you love Braxton the way you say you do, and he loves you, then you need to fight for your marriage. Not sit back and wait. The longer you go without talking to him, the more damage you'll have to repair and the more risk you run that you'll never have the chance at all."

Tears soaked Heather's face as she grabbed her mother in a full embrace. Her own grief had blinded her to the pain her loved ones felt. That included Braxton, as much as she hated to admit it. He'd been her rock for so long, she took for granted that he'd save her from this nightmare, too. She'd selfishly never considered that he may need saving just as much as she did.

"I love you, Mom," was all she could manage to squeak out.

She knew Kay was right, though. She and Braxton had to talk. They had to reconnect. There was no other way to begin to heal.

Making the decision to reach out to Braxton lifted a huge weight from her heart and gave her a reason to live again. They'd still have bad days; she wasn't naïve enough to believe it would be perfect, but they loved each other. They'd figure it out together.

She ate with her parents, feeling like part of the family again for the first time in what felt like forever. Even though she enjoyed the time they spent together, she was eager to get home and write down everything she wanted to say so she wouldn't forget a single word.

It was time for her to right a few wrongs and reconnect with her husband, the love of her life, before it was too late.

5

CHAPTER FIVE

Present Day

Noah put his phone back in his pocket and turned to Brianna. "Dad's back in the hospital after running a high fever. Mom sounded different this time, though, and I don't have a good feeling about it."

"Different how?"

"She's usually so upbeat, with her staunch belief that he'll beat this. Maybe it's just that she's seeing him as a mortal man for the first time. It's like her denial is fading, and she's finally facing the reality that he may not make it."

"I can't say I blame her, Noah. If I were in her shoes, I wouldn't accept losing you. I'd do anything it took to keep you with me."

"You know I feel the same." He leaned over and kissed her softly. "We'll see when we get there, I guess. It feels like this flight is taking forever."

"Now that we have a little privacy, it's time for you to do a little explaining." Brianna poked him with her index finger as she spoke.

"What?" Noah's smile covered his face though he tried to appear clueless. "What are you referring to?"

"Oh, I don't know. Maybe the fact that Rebel just dropped a bomb on us when he said the lady in the picture is his wife. Did you know about her?"

"Of course I knew," Noah replied.

He bit back a laugh when she turned in her seat to face him and narrowed her eyes in threat. "Are you really not going to tell me?"

"You're putting me in a really bad position, babe. It's part of my job to know everything about every man who works for me. And they know about me. But we also have to be able to trust each other with our most intimate information. Rebel really needs to be the one to share his story when he's ready to talk about it."

"But I am your wife." Her brows drew downward as she cocked her head to the side. "So you'd keep secrets from me?"

"That nosy investigative reporter is coming out in you. I don't have any secrets from you, Bri. You know everything there is to know about me. But the facts I've learned through my top secret security clearance can't be shared. I take the promise I made to protect that information very seriously. Rebel's circumstances are very personal, and I think he deserves the right to keep it to himself if that's what he chooses."

"Fair enough. Rebel is one of my brothers, too, so he must have a good reason for keeping it secret. He'll tell me when he's ready."

"Or when you use your own counterintelligence techniques against him and start interrogating him," Noah quipped.

"Right. Whichever comes first."

Brianna chuckled as she settled back in her seat. Her eyes strayed over to where Rebel sat, and her heart broke from his pained expression. His demeanor changed the instant Rashad threatened his wife. Gone was the level-headed, easygoing man she was accustomed to seeing. This version of Rebel was the one she presumed only his enemies had the misfortune of experiencing. Rashad's threat had wounded him in a way she'd never seen before. And just as a grizzly bear becomes more dangerous when it's wounded, Rebel obviously did as well.

Judging by the intensity of Rebel's stare, Rashad had just signed his own death warrant when he issued that threat.

Rebel's gaze drifted up, and he locked eyes with Brianna. She gave him a small, understanding smile and hoped he remembered through his pain and anger she loved him like a brother. His arm stretched over to the seat beside him and he patted it, asking her to join him.

Brianna nodded, unbuckled her seat belt, and leaned over to Noah. "I'll be back in a few minutes. Rebel asked me to come sit with him. Keep an eye on Amelia." Their month-old baby was sleeping soundly in the infant car seat strapped into the seat next to hers.

"Be certain you really want to know the answer before you ask a question, princess. You may not like the answer. Once it's spoken, there's no way to unhear it," Noah cautioned.

"All I'm going to do right now is offer my shoulder or my ear, babe. He doesn't appear to be in the frame of mind to take a stroll down memory lane at the moment."

Brianna moved across the spacious aisle of the Steele Security private jet and took her seat next to Rebel. Movement caught her eye, and she looked over at her vacated seat just in time to catch Noah in the act of waking up Amelia.

"Ahem." She forcefully cleared her throat.

Noah's head jerked to meet her incredulous expression. "What? I'm lonely. You've been gone a long time."

"I literally just left your side."

"Really? It seems longer than that."

Brianna's heart swelled with more love than she thought possible when Noah's muscular arms wrapped delicately around their tiny baby, held her close to his chest, and placed soft kisses on her little cheeks. With his lips puckered to steal another kiss from Amelia's baby skin, he glanced up at Brianna and quickly flashed a smile before finishing what he'd started.

Rebel's chuckle from beside her drew her attention back to him, focusing her attention on how her friend was dealing with the latest blow. Because she knew him well, she recognized the mixture of worry and anger in his eyes even though he tried to hide it.

"Being a mom looks good on you, Sunny."

"Thank you. It feels good, too. I never knew I could love someone other than Noah this much. It's amazing."

"Being a father agrees with Reaper, too." He jerked his chin toward where his friend sat. "Don't tell him I said that, though."

Brianna laughed and leaned in toward Rebel. "Don't think he doesn't already know that."

"Don't think I can't hear both of you," Noah chimed in, causing Brianna and Rebel to both laugh out loud.

"When we get to Houston, I need you to do me a favor."

"Of course."

"Sit this one out."

"What do you mean, exactly?"

"I mean do not get involved in this case. Don't try to help find Rashad, don't put yourself in danger, and don't take any chances. That's our job, one we're extremely well-trained to handle. The risks we take are calculated, with a plan for every possible scenario that may occur and the ability to modify as needed on the fly. This case just turned very personal, and the possibility of collateral damage is very high.

"Reaper brought you and Amelia along because he wouldn't be able to concentrate if you two weren't close by where he can reach you. You're his whole world, Sunny, and I know he's yours, too. But you're my little sister, and I can't even stand the thought of losing you and Amelia on top of everything else. Promise me I have one less thing to worry about."

She heard the ominous tone of his voice and saw the undeniable deadliness lurking just underneath his calm demeanor. His request was both a forewarning and a plea, one she knew he wouldn't make lightly. He'd never asked for anything in all the time she'd known him, and she couldn't deny him this peace of mind.

"I promise I'll stay out of it. I'll only get involved if he comes after me and I have no other choice."

"Thank you, Brianna. You know you'll have a full protection detail that will never leave your side. You haven't even been released from your doctor's care yet, so don't even think you'll get away with doing anything strenuous."

"How do you know I haven't been released yet?"

He tilted his head and slowly arched one eyebrow. "It's my job to know. So don't make me have to put you in a safe house until this is over, because I'll do whatever it takes to protect my family."

"I don't doubt that for one second, Rebel. After all these years, I think I know what kind of man you are. So, I can honestly say I'm blessed to be part of your family."

"And if I know my little sister as well as I think I do, I'd say she's trying to figure out how she didn't know this very important bit of information about me."

"That has crossed my mind, yeah," she replied with a hint of jest.

"I'm sorry I haven't told you about her," he started. "I just don't think I can right now."

"There's no need to be sorry, Rebel," she replied sincerely. "One thing I've always loved about you is how you don't always go with the grain, but you always weigh the pros and cons first. So, whatever you haven't shared with me about your life, I have no doubt you have a good reason."

Rebel drew Brianna into his strong arms and kissed the top of her head. "Thank you for understanding."

"I'm always here if you need someone to talk to or if I can help in any way, Rebel. Whenever you need me," Brianna assured him as she returned his embrace. "By the way, do I get to meet her while I'm locked in the hotel room?"

Rebel couldn't help but laugh at her tenacity as he released her. "We haven't driven that reporter instinct out of you yet?"

"Never." She grinned proudly in defiance.

"I'm sure you'll get to meet her. In the bomb-proof, escape-proof, underground bunker of a safe house that we lock you both in until this case is over."

"That's not funny."

"It's a little funny."

"I love the idea. Can we make it a reality within the next couple of hours?" Noah interjected.

"We don't need your help. We weren't talking to you," Brianna retorted with a smile.

Noah shrugged, showing he didn't have a care in the world. "My wife. My jet. My team. My call."

"Uh, boss, you know you have to go to sleep at some point, right?" Rebel asked, feigning worry for his friend.

"Good point. Maybe I should stay in the underground bunker with a protection detail instead of putting the ladies in there."

"You probably should. For your safety."

While the guys continued their playful harassment, Brianna took Amelia from Noah and settled in her seat to nurse her. "Did you reach Shadow, Bull, Chaise, and Silas?"

"Chaise replied to my message a few minutes ago. Those three will meet us in Houston later today. Shadow hasn't replied yet, but he will as soon as he can. He approaches every assignment like it's a deep undercover case," Noah replied.

"Did you say Shadow is deep under the covers? I'd better help him out," Liz jumped into the conversation. "I just had a very refreshing nap in the bedroom back there, so I have plenty of energy now. Let's make a pit stop in LA first."

"Houston is nowhere near LA, Liz," Noah replied, stony-faced.

"I know that. What's your point?"

Noah stared at her disbelievingly. "Should I be concerned at all that you're our nanny and have unrestricted access to my daughter?"

"Nope. Not at all," Liz replied before turning her sights on Rebel. "It's time you and I had a talk."

"What'd I do?" Rebel asked, visibly taken aback by Liz's stern tone.

"I don't mess with married men, Rebel. So I really don't appreciate how you've carried on with me the last few months."

"What? How'd I do that?"

"Oh, you know exactly what you did. Don't play games with me. All your flirting, sneaking glances, insisting on sitting close to me so you can touch me. If I'd known you were married during all of that, I would've kicked your ass. You need to understand there'll be no more of that if we're to be friends now."

"*I* need to understand there'll be no more of that?" Rebel couldn't believe what he just heard.

"I'm glad to hear you agree." Liz nodded. As she turned to sit beside Brianna, she stopped dead in her tracks. "Brianna, I don't really know how to say this. Well, actually, yes, I do. Your boob is hanging out."

"Amelia is hungry. I can't feed her with it inside my clothes," Brianna chuckled and shook her head. "It's okay, Liz."

"In that case..." Liz began to pull her shirt up from the hem.

"What are you doing?" Noah jumped up from his seat and put his hands on hers to stop her.

"Brianna said it's okay."

"That's not what she meant," Noah insisted. "It's okay for her to feed Amelia. It's not okay for anyone else to show their boobs. Are we clear?"

"We're clear that this isn't the party plane I was promised," Liz huffed and plopped in the seat facing Brianna, who was biting her bottom lip to keep from laughing. When Liz winked at her conspiratorially, Brianna nearly lost her composure. She quickly covered it with a cough. Liz continued when Noah's suspicious gaze cut toward Brianna. "Brianna, maybe you and Amelia shouldn't try to drink at the same time. You two need to take turns. One at a time, so you don't get choked again."

Noah's conflicting feelings were written all over his contorted face. On one hand, he couldn't just leave his wife and his baby to fend for themselves. That went against every fiber of his being, the code by which he lived his life, and the vows he took when he married Brianna. On the other hand, sitting with Liz for the remainder of the flight was detrimental to his mental health, and he needed his full mental capacity to stop Rashad.

Every war has casualties, he assured himself as he took a seat across from Rebel.

Feeling her eyes boring holes into his skull, he casually turned his eyes to glance over his shoulder at Brianna. Her brows were raised to her hairline as her eyes rapidly moved between his eyes and his new seat. Noah shrugged one shoulder and pointed to Rebel. "We need to cover the plan before we get to Houston. Make sure every detail has been thought of. I have to protect you, babe."

"Uh-huh."

Noah's eyes drifted to Liz, and he immediately regretted giving in to the temptation. She lifted her hand in front of her face, pointed her index and middle fingers toward her eyes, and then turned her hand toward Noah to point one finger at him. Noah slowly nodded, not completely sure of what he may be agreeing to, and slid his eyes to Rebel. "Let's go over the plan again."

When the plane landed in Houston, Noah, Brianna, and Liz drove straight to the hospital to see Steve and Sara, while Rebel coordinated protection details at the hotel with the rest of their men. The bad feeling Noah had continued to fester, and he knew he needed to see his parents before he fully immersed himself in the role of Reaper. Stopping Rashad would take his full attention soon enough, but for the next several hours, he'd focus on enjoying having his family together.

As they walked down the hospital corridor toward his father's room, he began mentally preparing himself for what waited for him once he stepped inside it. Before he opened the door, he turned to Brianna and Liz.

"Mom said Dad has been sick. I don't know what he'll look like, so be prepared for anything. I don't want to alarm him by reacting negatively to his appearance."

"Don't worry, babe. We've got this," Brianna assured him.

When he opened the door and walked into his father's room, Noah had to consciously make his feet move. He hid his shock and concern behind his smile. The breath that had seized in his lungs was forced to exhale as he spoke. The pride on his face when introducing his daughter to his father masked the uneasiness that squeezed his heart. The love Noah felt when he placed his daughter in her grandfather's arms convinced him that his father would survive this disease. Even if it was only because of Noah's sheer will to eradicate it from his father's body.

"She's so beautiful." Steve beamed. His translucent pallor even transformed to a radiant glow. "Amelia, you're my first grandbaby. I'm going to spoil you with so much love and so many toys."

Noah turned his head away and locked eyes with Brianna. Tears filled her eyes, and she fought hard to swallow them down. "Don't think her daddy isn't already spoiling her," Brianna laughed and sat on the side of Steve's bed. "You two must be conspiring against me."

Steve smiled mischievously. "It's my job to spoil any grandkids I have. You can ask Sara. I take my job very seriously."

"He does," Sara replied. "He always has to be the best, too. So prepare for a lot of spoiling competition between these two guys."

"I say we find a way to turn this game to our advantage, Sara. We need a little spoiling action out of this, too." Brianna winked.

"I'm game if you are."

"Don't you two worry. I know exactly how to handle these men," Liz chimed in. "We'll have them peeling our grapes and feeding them to us before long."

When they finally left Steve's room, it was only because he was so completely worn-out from cooing over Amelia, gently bouncing her in his arms, and singing her to sleep. When he fell asleep with her in his arms, Brianna snapped several pictures of them with her phone.

"I'll walk you out," Sara offered.

"Come back to the hotel with us, Mom. We'll grab something to eat, you can rest for a while, and you can play with Amelia when you wake up. Brianna and Liz will be there with you if you need anything," Noah insisted.

"No, son. I'm not leaving your father yet. I'll be back at the hotel tonight. You go on ahead and get them settled. I'll be fine. I've been doing this for a while now."

With a heavy heart, Noah left his mother at the hospital beside his dad. He didn't argue the point because he knew he wouldn't be any different if it were Brianna in that hospital bed. He'd be by her side for as long as possible. Knowing that didn't make leaving his mom behind any easier, though.

6

CHAPTER SIX

September 2001

Braxton,

    Today has been especially emotional for so many reasons, but they all seem to revolve around you in one way or another. It all started first thing today when I went to visit my parents, but not in the way I'm sure you're thinking right now. First, you probably think I went running back to them as soon as you left, but you'd be wrong. Second, you're probably also thinking they've turned me against you, but again, you'd be wrong.

Of course, my father started in on me as soon as I got there, trying to pressure me to file for a divorce. You know I've never had trouble putting him in his place, and today was no exception to that. In fact, I may have actually gotten through to him this time when I turned the tables on him. It seemed to finally sink into that thick skull of his that I meant what I said when I took those vows with you. I'm not filing for a divorce, now or ever.

Mom shared a heartbreaking story with me from when she was in school. Long story short, she lost a boyfriend who was very important to her, and the details of how and why it happened will always haunt her. After she told me about it, her words really hit home and made me think about you and me. She even encouraged me to talk to you, to make sure you know how much I still love you so we wouldn't lose any more precious time. She encouraged me to fight for my marriage and for you.

The second blow hit after I left my parents' house and rushed back to our apartment to pack a few things. Your parents have been very patient and loving to me. They've let me stay in your old room where all your childhood memories still live and I can still feel you. The apartment has just been too lonely, and too many memories show up in my nightmares. Now, I only go by there every few days to pick up more clothes, get the mail, or check on our belongings.

On my way back to our apartment, my sole focus was to get these words on paper as fast as I could. But as soon as I stepped inside, my knees buckled and I fell to the floor. The only explanation I have for what I experienced is how I wanted you to be there with me so badly. But I swear I smelled a faint scent of you when I opened the door. That signature scent that has always been solely yours still hung in the air, as if you'd just been there a little while before.

Maybe it was simply because I didn't notice it when I stayed there every day, I'm not sure. Or maybe it was because the apartment had been closed up for a few days since I'd been gone, so the scent was so much more pronounced. Regardless of why, the tears started, and I couldn't stop them for a couple of hours after that, so I curled up on the couch and let them all out. I haven't slept at the apartment for the last several weeks because I no longer felt your presence there. But when that scent surrounded and covered me, it was almost more than I could bear.

That long, anguished cry actually felt good. It was therapeutic to finally let it all out. I've kept it bottled up inside for so long, I'm surprised I haven't exploded like a can of Coke after it's been shaken and put back on the shelf. Missing you has taken more of a toll on me than I've realized. When you left, I know you did it for me, because you thought that would be best for me. Maybe you even thought that was what I wanted.

The final blow came when I finally sat up on the couch and turned the television on for the first time in months. I've kept myself so sheltered from the world, wrapped in my cocoon of depression, I had no clue what was happening outside the four walls I've kept myself locked in. Every channel had the news on a continuous loop, and I stared in disbelief at the planes buried deep inside the buildings as they burned, the people jumping out of the broken windows, the desperation of those searching for their loved ones.

I was scared—no, I was terrified. I was confused, and no one seemed to have any answers as to why this happened. My heart was broken for all those people, their families, my country. Then I realized something important about myself. I'd numbed myself to practically everything else since that day, the day we lost him. I'd been living in a stupor, just barely surviving one day to the next, until the moment I realized that the cowardly acts of terrorism would affect you. You're in the Army now, and the terrible acts that happened earlier were an act of war against us. You'll be called upon to answer the attack.

I don't know how to live without you, Brax. I don't know how to be me without you. We've been together for so long, you've been such a huge part of my life, I've always taken for granted that you'd be there for me, to carry me when I couldn't take another step. Beside me, holding my hand. Behind me, supporting me. In front of me, protecting me. More than that, you're the other half that makes me whole.

For you to understand my insanity, I need you to take a walk down memory lane with me. I know it's hard. Believe me, I know. But we need this, Brax. We need to do this together, and I'm so sorry it's taken me this long to realize it.

Brax, I want us—our friendship, our romance, our love, our marriage —every aspect that makes this ride through life mean something, through the good times and bad. I owe you an apology that I wish I could give you in person, eye to eye, so you'd see, hear, and feel everything I'm feeling. For now, I have to hope and pray this letter will accurately convey what I need to say to you.

Here we go.

My hands were shaking so badly when I took that pregnancy test, I'm surprised I didn't pee all over myself instead of that little stick. I already knew the results before I even looked at the little window. My period had always been like clockwork until the day it just stopped showing up completely. Morning sickness had already reared its ugly head enough that

I couldn't deny what was really happening. But I still needed the proof that little test provided before I'd accept it.

I remember walking out of the bathroom, hiding the test in case my parents were nearby, and rushing straight back to my bedroom. You were waiting for me, sitting on my bed and using my pencils as drumsticks, without a care in the world. You knew what the results would be, too. Unlike me, you were excited about the odds that I was really pregnant. But then, it was always hard to rile you up, unless some other guy ignorantly thought he could take your place by my side.

When I handed the pregnancy test to you without even looking at it myself, I turned around and put my head against my chest of drawers. You wrapped your arms around my waist and pulled my back flush against your front. Your hands lovingly snaked up my torso until your forearms crossed over my chest while you held me tightly. Your lips were against my ear when you whispered, "It's positive, Heather. We are pregnant."

At first, I didn't realize you'd said "we" instead of "you." I shouldn't have been surprised by it, though. You never would've made me feel like I'd have to face it alone. And I didn't, not one step of the way did I ever feel alone. When we told my parents, my dad threatened you by saying, "I'll cut your dick off and mount it over the fireplace."

You calmly replied, "Your mantle isn't big enough to hold my dick, so it sure wouldn't hold it with you mounting it."

I couldn't help but laugh out loud, and that's all it took to calm my frayed nerves so I could function again. After that, I put my dad in his place and showed them both my place was by your side. Though the rest of conversation wasn't pleasant, you helped me make it clear we would get married and they couldn't stop us from having our own family. Of course, then we had to pretend it was our choice to wait a couple of months until we'd both turned eighteen so we could marry without their permission.

Our wedding and reception were interesting, to say the least. My dad finally agreed to walk me down the aisle, if for no other reason than he wouldn't stand for someone else doing it instead. When the preacher asked who gave me to you, I thought he'd change his mind and drag me out of the church. But he surprised me and went through with it as planned. I've always wondered if my mom had something to do with that, whether she threatened him to make him do it.

Our reception was small but nice. Our three-tiered wedding cake was everything we could have asked for, the punch was perfect, and the candles that lit the room cast the perfect ambiance. Until Kelly leaned over to cut the cake and caught her hair on fire, that is. The flash from her hair spray igniting was both loud and bright. While the others patted her head to stop her hair from being charred, you and I were doubled over in laughter with tears streaming down our faces.

I'll never forget how you carried me over the threshold of our tiny little apartment when we finally left the reception. You refused to let me walk inside on my own two feet because you said it was your job to carry me. To you, it was symbolic of how you'd always be there to carry me, care for me, and love me. I didn't doubt your love then, Brax, and I don't doubt it now.

As my belly grew, so did our love and excitement for the future. Yes, it was hard going to school with everyone watching every pound I gained, but you made that easy for me, too. When a snarky comment was made, you either threatened to beat the guy up or to reveal an embarrassing secret about the girl if they didn't shut up. My personal bodyguard, your love and support were all I ever needed.

The day Dalton Miles Reed was born was a new experience for us both. It was the first time you were the one who'd needed consoling and protecting. You were so adorable in your panicked state—afraid something would go wrong and you'd lose me, helpless because you couldn't stop the labor pains that tore through me, and secretly dreading the gory part of the delivery. I had to keep reassuring you that I was fine, I would be fine, and you would also be fine. I think I said "fine" at least a million times that day.

Turns out, all three of us were ~~fine~~ excellent. After just a couple of days in the hospital, you took Dalton and me home to our little apartment. In our haste to move in together, we didn't consider the fact we'd need a separate bedroom for our son's things. So after my baby shower when we brought home the bassinet, car seat, bouncy seat, changing table, and all the baby clothes, our bedroom and living room were instantly transformed. We joked that our entire apartment had become one big nursery with no room to turn around in, but we were happy with it.

We had absolutely no clue about what colic was, how easily babies got their days and nights mixed up, or how to fix either issue. But we learned a lot about one-, two-, three-, and four-o'clock feedings, diaper changes, and what his different cries meant. The sleepless nights began to add up until we were beyond exhausted.

When I woke up that night, I immediately knew something was very wrong. I'd slept more than two hours straight for the first time in nearly three months. Dalton was in his crib beside our bed, sleeping well for the first time. I gently laid my hand on his stomach, just as I'd done so many times before when he slept, just to feel the rise and fall of his breath.

But it wasn't there.

There was no rise and fall. There was no warmth from his little baby body.

Only stillness.

My heart pounded in my chest, and my own breaths wouldn't come. I flew out of the bed and picked him up, careful to support his little head, but with an urgency I'd never experienced before. You felt me moving, and you also sensed something was terribly wrong. When you flipped the switch and the room filled with the bright overhead light, my heart splintered with unimaginable pain. The bluish hue of his skin and lips was unmistakable.

You took him from my arms and immediately started CPR while I dialed 911. Somehow, through my hysterics, I was able to tell them where we were and what had happened. Regardless of the circumstances and how badly you were hurting, you wouldn't give up, you wouldn't stop trying to revive him. All you wanted was to bring him back to us, and you did every-thing you could possibly do.

When the paramedics arrived and took over, Dalton still wasn't breath-ing. I overheard them talking when they were working on him in the back of the ambulance. They didn't know I was there when one guy asked the other if he thought Dalton would make it. He was hesitant to answer, but he finally said, "No, it doesn't look like it."

At that moment, I wanted to die. If I could've willed my heart to stop beating, I would've gladly done just that and died with him. It would've been better than living with the devastation that had just hit me like a speeding locomotive.

We didn't speak the entire ride to the hospital. I know I was lost in my prayers, begging for a miracle, trying to bargain with God to make it all a nightmare so I could wake up and gladly give up another night of sleep just to care for our baby. At the time, I didn't even realize you hadn't said a word. It wasn't because I didn't care. It wasn't that I was mad at you. I was just so very lost in mourning, afraid to hope, and afraid not to hope.

When the doctor came in to tell us our perfectly healthy eleven-week-old baby boy couldn't be revived, whatever was left of my grasp on reality completely and utterly shattered. I remember crumpling to the floor because I wished it would just swallow me whole and put me out of my misery. I remember your strong hands catching me before I hit the ground with the full force of my weight. You kneeled behind me, pulled me into your lap, and wrapped your arms around me.

Holding on to your arms was the only thing that kept me from completely checking out of my sanity. I couldn't tell you then because I couldn't even speak, but you were my lifeline. You were the only reason I continued to hold on and not give up entirely. I wish I'd told you then. I wish I'd been strong enough to explain everything I was thinking and feeling. But planning Dalton's funeral became another nail in my own coffin, and the deep depression soon overtook me.

Hindsight really hasn't been my friend because it so brilliantly highlights my failures. I have so many regrets. There are so many things I want to go back and do differently. Besides the obvious regret of not staying up all night with my eyes glued to Dalton to watch over our son as he slept, there are so many things I didn't give you enough credit for doing. I now realize so many things you did for me, to take care of me, that I took for granted. But I didn't do the same for you, and you deserved to have the same consideration you so freely gave me.

When I stood beside his little casket for hours without moving, you were beside me, holding my hand.

When they lowered his casket into the ground and my legs wouldn't hold me up, you stood behind me, supporting me.

When I had a complete mental breakdown after I realized I'd never see or kiss his little face ever again, you stood in front of me, protecting me. Shielding me. Putting me first. Even though you were dying inside, too.

I needed you, and not once did you let me down.

You needed me, and I repeatedly let you down.

At the time you needed me the most, I failed you. My lapses are truly unforgivable.

Yet, in your goodbye letter, you took all the blame. You're still protecting and supporting me, even though I retreated inside myself from the intense grief I didn't know how to deal with in my own mind.

Even though I have no right to ask this of you, I have to try. Please forgive me and give me a chance to make it up to you. I'm here for you, Braxton. I want to stand beside you and hold your hand. I want to stand behind you and support you. I want to stand in front of you and protect you. I want to take away the responsibility you feel for Dalton's death because it doesn't rest on your shoulders. I want to take away all the pain I've caused you in my ignorance, selfishness, and weakness.

I'll wait for you to come back to me for as long as it takes. My life is with you—it always has been, and it always will be. People say we're still young, we can still find love and happiness, we can still have a family one day. They're exactly right, Braxton. We can still find it all in each other— love, happiness, and a family. You're all I want, all I need, and I won't settle for anything less than what we already have together.

I'm waiting to hear from you.

I love you, Braxton. With every ounce of love I possess, I love you.

Your wife—until death do us part,

Heather Reed

HEATHER WALKED into the kitchen where Bryan and Jackie Reed sat at the table and held up a thick envelope. She was so grateful to them for taking her in and letting her stay in Braxton's old room. The apartment had become suffocating, and not from the small size. All the memories it held were impossible to escape during the best of times, but being there alone every night had become unbearable.

"I've written Braxton a long letter. I love him so much, and I can't go one more day without telling him exactly how I feel. Do you know how I can get this letter to him?"

"Yes, sweetheart, he gave me his mailing address while he's at AIT. I'll be glad to mail it for you tomorrow." Jackie wiped her eyes as she stood and took the letter from Heather. "We were just talking about all the attacks today—in New York, Washington, DC, and the plane that went down in Pennsylvania."

"It's so scary, especially since Braxton is in the service now. I'm worried about him. I can't lose him too." The tears had flowed so freely while she wrote the letter to him, she was surprised she still had tears to cry. But a mere fleeting thought of losing Braxton reduced her to tears every time.

Jackie wrapped her arms around Heather to comfort her daughter-in-law. "I know, sweetie. We have to be strong and believe he'll be okay, though. He needs all of us to believe in him and give him the strength to succeed."

THE FOLLOWING WEEK, Braxton was fully immersed in the Army's intelligence AIT program. When the attacks occurred, he'd insisted he wanted to be on the front lines of any imminent retaliation. But since he'd just started his job-specific training, he was stuck there until he finished it. Until that day, he vowed to keep his head in his training program and learn everything he could possibly learn.

"Reed!"

He heard his name being called and looked up from his training manual. "Yes, sir."

"Mail call. Come get your letter, princess. I don't deliver."

He took the thick envelope and eyed it warily. He immediately recognized the handwriting as Heather's. His heart dropped to his feet, and he wanted to stomp it into the ground so he'd never feel anything again. As packed as the envelope was, he assumed it must hold the divorce papers that were waiting for his signature.

"You'll have to get that divorce without my help, my love," he said as he put the sealed envelope away with his other private belongings. "There's no way I can sign those papers."

7

CHAPTER SEVEN

Present Day

Rashad Samir moved through the hospital corridor as though he belonged there, walking with purpose and a casual stride. The pretty nurse with the short black hair had continued to evade him with her cleverness and preemptive moves. At first, it only served to make him angry at her, more determined to outwit her and beat her at her own game. But after he'd had time to calm down and consider the skill it took for her to pull it off, he became impressed with her competence. Now it was a game of wills and wit to him. A way to demonstrate once and for all who would be the better opponent in the game with human chess pieces.

Dressed in clothing that closely matched the hospital's maintenance crew uniforms, Rashad blended into the background noise of the normal hustle and bustle of the hospital. Patients and their families assumed he was supposed to be there. Nurses and other hospital personnel only briefly glanced at his attire and continued what they were doing. His ball cap covered his hair, and the brim was pulled low to hide his face, completing his makeshift disguise.

As he strode past the patient rooms, he kept his ears attuned to the conversations inside for any morsel of information he could glean. He heard a man's deep laughter reverberate into the hall and immediately recognized it as belonging to the only male nurse in the oncology wing.

"Mr. Steele, you have to give Heather a break. She can't work twenty-four hours a day, seven days a week."

"No offense, Rob, but you're just not as pretty as she is."

"I can't argue with that." Rob laughed in agreement. "But I'm afraid you're still stuck with me for the next couple of days."

"I would say you could at least dress up and pretend to be her, but I'm afraid that would just make you even uglier."

The older man's voice held a blatant teasing tone. Anyone simply passing would know the two men were kidding with each other, an attempt to lighten the mood of the otherwise morose unit with their witty banter.

"You know what, Steele? Just because you've now put the idea in my head, I may just do that one day and shock the hell out of you," Rob laughed.

Rashad's curiosity got the better of him from the repeated use of the name Steele. He had to see the man's face and find out exactly who he was. He knew he was taking a huge, unnecessary risk by even stepping into the room, but he couldn't seem to stop himself. Just as he cleared the doorway, Rob the nurse turned around and looked directly at him, catching Rashad off guard.

"Hey, man. What's up?" Rob asked. He obviously knew Rashad was in the wrong room.

"I'm looking for my partner. I heard voices and thought he might be in here," Rashad lied.

"I haven't seen any maintenance guys on the floor lately except you," Rob replied. "Have you, Mr. Steele?"

Rashad shifted his gaze to the patient lying in the bed. He was obviously a sick man, judging by his color and gaunt frame. This man was older, but the similarities between him and the younger man from Miami were undeniable. Mr. Steele's hair wasn't as black or thick as the younger man's, but age and illness had a tendency of changing those characteristics. There was no denying the eyes, though. Mr. Steele's eyes had a dull sheen to them, no doubt from the cancer in his body, but they were just as piercing as his son's.

They were also just as cunning and keenly aware of his surroundings.

"No, I haven't seen any maintenance guys up here today," he confirmed, keeping his eyes locked on Rashad's. "And my door has been open the whole time."

"Okay, I'll keep looking. Thank you both."

Rashad left the room, cognizant of the fact that Mr. Steele wasn't completely buying his act. He didn't even attempt to hide the suspicion in his eyes or in the inflection of his voice. Rashad had no doubt that the elder Steele would call the younger one as quickly as he could reach for the phone. He realized he'd made the same impulsive mistake his brother, Turan, had once made.

In his quest to outwit the others and prove his superiority, he'd taken unnecessary risks that could've jeopardized his entire operation. The others he worked with, and those who worked for him, wouldn't hesitate to take his life over his foolish decisions. But they wouldn't give him as many chances to redeem himself as he'd given his brother before he finally killed Turan.

"No matter," he muttered to himself. "Maybe there's a way I can use this to my advantage, after all."

Armed with the confirmation that Heather wouldn't be at work for a few days, he knew the printed work schedule he found in the nurses' break room was accurate. While keeping his face down as he left the hospital, he carefully avoided the security cameras strategically placed around the campus and parking area. He'd done his homework, changed vehicles he used to visit the hospital, and altered his appearance to blend in, but the plan was far from over.

As he drove away, his smile covered his face when an extended plan formed in his mind. The scenes played out with expert precision as he visualized the fall of the prideful soldiers who'd invaded his childhood home. The one who'd taken his father's life would suffer first. The looks on all of their faces would be priceless when they realized how epic their failure was in the end, just before he killed them, too.

He stopped at the large merchandise store before heading back to his rented house. The magazines he was forced to buy in order to implement his plan were beyond embarrassing and insulting for a man of his caliber to have in his possession. If anyone in his group had witnessed the abomination, he would've been excommunicated and publicly disgraced when his body was returned to his homeland. But they were necessary to carry out his genius plan, and he would execute it to the fullest extent.

With the pages torn out of the numerous magazines scattered across the floor of his den, Rashad began the arduous task of cutting out individual letters. It was crass, it was obvious, and it was brilliant. Threatening notes made from the various sizes and colors of letters and words cut from magazine pages and glued to a plain white sheet of paper screamed "amateur."

"The simpleton approach will give them a false sense of security and superiority. Their foolish pride and misguided bravado will lead them directly into my trap. They won't know what hit them until the exact moment I want them to know," Rashad remarked to himself.

When the first letter was finished, he held it up in front of him to admire his handiwork. "It's really too bad Turan isn't here with me. He would appreciate this approach."

Thoughts of his brother had him picking up his laptop to perform the basic searches for information he knew how to do. With Turan's computer abilities, Rashad could've accessed even the minutest of details to help tip the scales in his favor. Without Turan, he could only find the information that was available to the general public. There were others on the team who could help, but they wouldn't. Not with this personal vendetta. Not with his personal chess game.

The names of the other soldiers were still hidden from him, locked away on a computer that was inaccessible from anywhere except onsite. In a highly secure, secret building. In a room necessitating above top secret security clearance to enter, behind an armored door that required a unique passcode and biometric identification.

Protected by some of the deadliest men in the world, who would shoot first and ask no questions later if any unauthorized person attempted to enter.

When Turan had been an active member of his team, he'd installed a facial recognition program on Rashad's laptop that scoured social media sites for possible matches. With a few clicks of his mouse, he could upload a photo and the program would automatically locate anyone whose characteristics met enough distinguishing points. Not that anyone as skilled at being covert would be so foolish as to have a profile on the popular sites, but distant relations and long-lost friends could always be counted on.

That was the only way he'd been able to find Heather. The program ran day and night, scouring through millions and millions of photographs uploaded on a daily basis, looking for any connection to Rebel through her. It was as if fate herself smiled upon him, because the program finally located one potential match out of all the pictures on social media sites. The proverbial hidden needle that was lost in the haystack, the program indicated the youthful, carefree face that smiled at him from his computer screen had enough facial feature matches for an eighty-nine percent certainty the man was Rebel.

The class pictures were connected to a high school reunion in Houston, posted by someone who was very blatantly not Rebel. Heather and the unnamed young man posed together in this particular picture, smiling and very much in love. But the young man's face wasn't tagged, his name wasn't mentioned in any of the comments, and Rashad knew that for certain because he'd painstakingly checked each one. But Heather Greer's maiden name was listed, along with her married name. Rashad was able to find her fairly easily since she was a nurse and her license was on display in the state database. Unfortunately, every shred of information about her wedding—including the groom's first name—had been removed from public records everywhere. When he snapped the picture of Heather Reed and sent it as a threat, he'd played a wild card he'd only hoped would pan out.

But Noah Steele's name and information were more readily accessible because he was the owner and operator of Steele Security out of Miami. Once Rashad found the initial information on Noah, he was able to expand the search to include Noah's known family members. The demographics he found on one Mr. Steve Steele appeared to match the man he'd met earlier at the hospital. It at least gave him enough information to call the hospital and verify what he'd found.

After going through the information desk to reach the oncology unit's nurses' station, he waited patiently as the phone rang several times.

"Oncology. How can I help you?"

"I'm trying to reach a patient's room, but the phone just rings repeatedly. Is there any way you can go check on him for me? He may be sleeping, but I just need to know he's okay."

"Of course. What's the patient's name?"

"Steve Steele."

"Just a moment, let me check the census for tonight. Here he is. I'm going to put you on hold for a minute while I go check on him."

"Thank you so much. You have no idea how much I appreciate your help."

After a few minutes, she came back on the line. "He was asleep and said he didn't hear the phone ringing. He's awake now if you want to call his room again. Or I can transfer you."

"I'll just dial his room directly. You've already been so helpful. Thank you for checking on him."

"My pleasure."

With that, they disconnected, and Rashad smiled at his own cleverness. With the privacy laws, the information desk wouldn't give out patient statuses or even if the person was actually a patient there. But the caring and helpful nursing staff could always be counted on if a patient's health and well-being were in question. Going off a gut instinct and following his hunch, he got lucky in confirming his suspicions.

"Why stop at his dad, though?" Rashad laughed sardonically as he finished the cartoonish letter to threaten the elder Steele man. "Let's make it a family affair."

Going through the extended family information, he located Brianna's name. From there, it was relatively easy to find more information on her than he needed. Her time as an investigative reporter gave him plenty of ammunition to use against the entire Steele family, naming Noah's wife directly in his threats. She'd be the main topic of the next letter he created, maybe even followed by Noah's mother and then his sister.

But Heather would be the initial focus, the spark that would ignite his plan and draw Rebel out first.

"I'M SO glad you decided to come back to the hotel with us, Sara." Brianna put her arm around her mother-in-law's shoulders. "You needed a break from the hospital, and Amelia needed to spend time with you."

"I think I need her more than she needs me. She's such a good baby."

"We've been very fortunate. She still wakes up at night to eat, but she goes right back to sleep. Of course, Noah and I sitting up longer every time just to hold her and rock her probably doesn't hurt either," Brianna laughed. "We just can't seem to get enough of her."

"You've had a long day. If you want to take a nap, I'll be glad to watch her," Sara offered.

"You've had a long day, too, Sara. In fact, you've had a long, hard few months. We talked you into leaving the hospital so you could get some rest."

"I'll have plenty of time to rest later. While you're here with my granddaughter, I want to spend time with her," Sara insisted.

"Okay. I'll go unpack all of our suitcases while Noah's on his way back to the airport to pick up Chaise, Bull, and Silas." Brianna kissed Sara's cheek and Amelia's forehead before she walked toward her bedroom.

"What about Shadow? Where's he?" Liz asked, stopping Brianna.

"He's still in LA. He'll contact Noah as soon as he can. They have specific times they're required to check in when they go off on their own, and he hasn't missed it yet."

"Well, he'll meet us here, won't he?" Liz demanded rather than asked.

Brianna hid her smile at Liz's infatuation with Shadow. "That depends on what he's found in LA. We may want him to stay there more than we want him to come here."

"There is nothing that could happen in LA that would make me want him to stay there more than I want him to come here," Liz retorted. "There are tricks of the trade he needs to teach me. He's withholding information from me."

"I don't doubt that at all, Liz."

Brianna smiled after she turned to leave the room. Liz's fascination with Shadow had more to do with his undercover spy skills than with his looks. But she also enjoyed the playful exchange of teasing and razzing the two of them engaged in. She'd lived alone for so long. After her children moved to different states and her husband died, she'd never allowed herself to hope she'd have a family again. She found a new fervor for life when they'd adopted her into the Steele family.

"Liz, let me know if you want me to help you unpack, too," Brianna offered.

"I know you think you're supermom and superwife, but you just had a baby a few weeks ago, little girl. I'll do the unpacking, and you relax in here with Sara and Amelia," Liz insisted.

"Yes, ma'am," Brianna agreed. When she took a seat, she looked at Sara and loudly whispered, "She's so bossy."

"I'm not bossy," Liz corrected. "I *am* the boss. There's a big difference."

Brianna and Sara smiled at each other as Liz continued into the master bedroom. "I hope I don't find any of those crazy sex toys in your suitcases. Blow-up dolls and such. That'd be embarrassing for

Noah, because I'd blow it up and have it sitting on the couch when he walks in."

Sara and Brianna both busted out in laughter at Liz's suggestion and the way she giggled diabolically at herself.

"You don't have to worry about any of that, Liz," Brianna called out to her.

"It could be fun to get one and mess with Shadow, though," Liz replied thoughtfully, as if she were already calculating a plan.

Brianna and Sara locked gazes, each secretly hoping Liz would be successful in her endeavor, while also fearing that very thing. "Never a dull moment," Brianna quipped.

A couple of hours later, Noah, Chaise, Bull, and Silas arrived at the hotel. Chaise was the first one to join Brianna and Sara in the living area. The three-bedroom luxury suites Brianna's father, Evan Tate, had secured for them had every amenity they could possibly need. He insisted on the best for his granddaughter, plus that particular floor was inaccessible to anyone without a keycard that had been specifically programmed for it. For Noah and Brianna's suite, he'd also made sure the staff provided a crib beside the bed in the master bedroom.

There were four identical suites on the same floor that Evan had also reserved for the others in the Steele clan. If anyone who didn't belong on the floor showed their face, they'd be immediately spotted by the security team. Brianna knew the added protective measures her father had put in place for his family helped him sleep better a little better at night, even though he'd worry about them regardless.

Brianna stood to hug them as they walked into the suite, pulling Chaise into her embrace first. "Hi, Chaise. Did you go by to see your father first?"

"Yes," Chaise replied as they released each other. "He looked well rested when we got there. Noah said he was pretty worn-out by the time he agreed to let go of Amelia."

"Yes, he was. But it was his own fault," Brianna chuckled. "Where are the guys?"

"They're out in the hall having a secret decoder ring meeting."

Chaise rolled her eyes. "They received a call while we were at the hospital. They wouldn't tell me what's going on, but it has to be something big about Rashad and his cell with the way they're acting all secretive about it."

"That's rude."

"They said something about it being a matter of national security. It's top secret, it's their job, blah, blah. Like we're not eyeball-deep in this case with them. Don't worry, I'll get it out of Colton later. None of his training prepared him for the torture I can inflict on him." Chaise smirked knowingly.

"It's like they don't know us at all." Brianna teasingly rolled her eyes.

"You need information out of those men? I can get it out of them," Liz added. "I'll have them singing like little girls and begging to tell me all their secrets. The trick is all in how you flick your wrist. Get a good hold and just flick it. Works every time."

"There will be no holding and flicking going on around here," Bull announced as he strode into the room. "Especially from Liz."

Noah and Silas walked in and stood behind Bull. Brianna immediately recognized the seriousness of Noah's expression and the fighting stance he innately reverted to when danger was imminent. His eyes swept around the room until they landed on hers, and for the first time since she'd seen him on a mission, there was a hint of something else in his eyes. He crossed the room, making a beeline for her, and wrapped his arms around her.

"What is it, Noah?" she murmured in his ear.

He shook his head lightly. "We've received our new orders from the top. We were also briefed on new intel about our target."

When Noah released her, she saw Sara had her arms wrapped around Silas's waist. "How's my oldest child?" she asked as she squeezed him. "I've missed you so much."

"I've missed you, too, Mom. But I'm here now, and I'm not going anywhere else," Silas replied and protectively squeezed his mother to his side.

Brianna felt Noah staring at her before she glanced up at him. "It's bad, huh?" she asked, although she already knew the answer.

"More of his team has moved into the Houston area. They haven't identified the exact target yet, but they know from the chatter that he's managed to infiltrate whatever it is they're planning to attack."

8

CHAPTER EIGHT

December 2001

"Surprise!" Braxton called out to his parents as he walked through the front door. "I'm home for Christmas!"

"My baby is home!" Jackie squealed and ran into his outstretched arms. "Why didn't you tell us you were coming home?"

"Because I wanted to surprise you. Besides, I wasn't sure what exact day I'd get here until the last minute."

"How long are you home, son?" Bryan asked before he pulled Braxton into a fatherly embrace.

"I get two weeks off for Christmas Exodus then I'm headed back to Arizona for more training."

"Isn't your AIT completed by now?" Bryan asked.

"I just completed the intelligence analyst training course. It was pretty grueling, but I aced it. With everything that's going on in the world right now, we need more intelligence officers. I've been offered a chance to attend counterintelligence training next. If I complete it as well as I did this one, they'll advance me up to a sergeant sooner than most."

"How'd you get picked for that?" Jackie asked suspiciously.

Braxton shrugged, giving the appearance the answer was boring and unimportant. "I guess I did pretty well during the first round of training. They said my ASVAB and test scores were high. My marksmanship is one of the best.

"Plus, I've decided to make a career out of the Army. I'm signing up for every type of advanced training I can get into. Jump school will have to wait a little longer, but I'll get there. I've been accepted to a college near the base, so I can get a degree and move up to an officer."

"Son, you're taking on way too much all at once, don't you think?" Bryan's concern for his son was written all over his face.

"Might as well do all I can while I'm young, right?"

"You won't have any spare time, Brax. You'll spend every waking moment training, going to class, or studying," Jackie warned.

"That's the point, Mom," he finally revealed. "It'll keep my mind and my hands occupied. I won't have time to think about anything else. I'm actually looking forward to it."

"You'll probably be stationed somewhere else after you finish this training, though."

"I'll just transfer and keep taking classes at a college near the base. It'll be okay, Mom. Quit worrying about me so much." Braxton put his arms around her in an attempt to reassure her.

"Brax, you're my baby. I'll never stop worrying about you as long as I'm alive."

"Are you worried that I'm hungry? Because I'll let you worry about that all you want every time I come home."

Jackie released him and rolled her eyes exaggeratedly at him. "Of course, you'll let me worry about that. Come on, I'll feed you."

"Okay. I'm going to put my stuff in my room first. I'll be right there."

When he opened the door to his childhood bedroom, the past rushed over him in much the same way a tsunami crashes onto land and obliterates everything in its path. Memories of Heather filled the room—from their friendship as kids to their first time as lovers, these four walls had seen it all. The crushing weight of his past failures settled on his chest and threatened to choke the life out of him.

Dumping his duffel bag on the floor by his bed, he quickly retreated back to the kitchen.

"How am I supposed to sleep in there?" he murmured to himself as he walked back down the wall.

"Brax, while your mom is cooking, I'm going next door to help Frank with his car. I'll be back in a little while."

When Bryan was out the door, Brax looked at his mom and smirked knowingly. "That wasn't obvious at all."

"What?" She feigned innocence, knowing exactly what he meant.

"Dad rushed out to help Frank with his car, but he didn't ask me to help, too? Come on. I've known him all my life," he deadpanned. "So, what is it you want to talk to me about? Let's have it."

"Okay. But just remember you asked," Jackie began. "Why haven't you answered Heather? You've kept her waiting for months now."

"Why do you think I'd answer her, Mom? If that's what she wants, she can do it without me."

"Do what without you?"

"Divorce me," Braxton bellowed. "I'm not signing those damn papers. There are other ways she can get it without my consent."

Jackie shook her head and gave him a sad smile. "Why would you think she sent you divorce papers?"

"Because I saw them myself," Braxton replied sadly. "I went back to the apartment before AIT to talk to her. They were on the kitchen counter, ready to dissolve our marriage. All they needed was our signatures."

"Oh, my baby boy." Jackie put her hands on his shoulders and shook him gently. "You didn't even open the envelope, did you?"

Braxton shook his head from side to side.

"She didn't mail divorce papers to you. Do you still have the envelope?"

"Yeah. It's in my duffel bag. I was going to leave it here with you."

"You need to go open it. I promise it's not divorce papers."

Suddenly, Braxton couldn't wait to get back to the very room he'd just left. Question after question flashed through his mind in the few steps he took toward his room.

If she didn't send the divorce papers, why did she have them?

The envelope was very thick. What else could she have sent?

Is it something I even want to read?

Dumping all of his neatly folded clothes out of his bag onto the bed, he rifled through his belongings until he found it. With his heart beating wildly against the side of his chest, he absently sat down at his old desk and slid his finger under the sealed flap. His eyes were fixed on the contents of the envelope as he gingerly removed the papers inside. After inhaling a deep breath, he held it as he unfolded the letter and began reading the words Heather had poured from her heart onto the pages in front of him.

He allowed himself to feel the emotions her words invoked. As she moved through their time together, the memories resurfaced in the form of tears flowing down his cheeks. The good and the bad times, they were all still right where he left them, and he felt them one by one all over again. Only this time, he was reliving them through her eyes, through her words, all in exactly the way she'd perceived the events as they unfolded. Thoughts and feelings they should've shared with each other, only they were blinded by youthful inexperience and their self-imposed confinement in a hellish prison.

She didn't blame him, she didn't hold him responsible, and she didn't hate him. She actually still loved him. Nothing that had happened changed or lessened her love for him, and she wanted their marriage to last. At least, she'd felt that way when she wrote the letter a few months before. His mind worried that she would've given up on him by now because he never answered.

His heart told his mind to shut the hell up because Heather would never do that.

Jumping up from his seat, he tore out of his room and ran back to the kitchen.

"Mom—"

She was waiting for him with her car keys in her opened palm. "Go, son."

After kissing her cheek and grabbing the keys from her hand, Braxton rushed out to the car and sped all the way to their apartment.

He mentally berated himself for not getting more information from his mom before he left. Heather said she'd been staying in his room. For how long? When did she stop? Did she move back in to their apartment, or was she at her parents' house now?

Since it was the week before Christmas, she may not even be home. She could very well be visiting other family members. If that was the case, he didn't know what he'd do, other than wait for her, however long it took. The undeniable truth was they were made for each other. They were one of the rare couples who'd always known their union was meant to be and their hearts would never be satisfied with anyone else.

The tires skidded to a stop in the parking space, and he rushed up the flights of stairs as fast as his feet could carry him. Standing in front of the apartment door, his chest heaved forcefully from the emotion that welled up inside it. He raised his fist in the air, poised to knock on the door, but it swung open widely before his knuckles could connect.

Heather stood in the doorway. Her eyes were wide open, her mouth ajar in a silent gasp, and her muscles were tensed. She was still the most beautiful girl he'd ever seen. She was still the best friend he'd ever known, and she was still the person he loved most in the world.

She was still his wife.

Recognition that it was actually Braxton who stood before her took a few seconds to register in her shocked state. He knew the very second she realized who he was—the expression in her eyes instantly changed from slight fear to passionate love. As if to further validate their connection, they spoke at the same time.

"Heather."

"Braxton."

Desperate need for the other overtook them, their bodies collided and melded into one as their arms encircled each other. When their lips met, time and troubles melted away until there was nothing left except their love and need for each other. Lips crashed together, teeth collided, and tongues caressed with a heated fervor.

Though it took all of his restraint, he slowly halted their passionate embrace.

With their foreheads touching, Braxton lovingly caressed her cheek with his thumb while keeping her held tightly against him with the other hand. "Heather." He whispered her name with such reverence, such devotion, it was as if her name had become his prayer. "I've missed you so damn much."

"Braxton, where have you been?" she implored. "I've waited so long for you to come home."

"I'm here, and I'm so sorry I've kept you waiting. I just read your letter this morning, and as soon as I finished reading it, I rushed straight over here to you."

"You only read it today? But I mailed it months ago." The confused look on her face was endearing and heartbreaking.

"Can I come in and explain?"

She smiled bashfully. "Of course you can come in. It's your home, too."

Those four words coming from her meant more than she'd ever know. He walked her backward into the apartment while not letting go of her and closed the door behind him. "Were you going somewhere?"

"Nowhere important."

"Good. Because I've been away too long, and I don't want to share you with anyone else for however long I can keep you locked away."

"What took you so long to read it?"

Knowing he put the uncertainty in her eyes cut him to the quick. *She thought I quit loving her,* he thought.

"I came by here to see you on my way to Arizona. Took the long way and rushed over here on a layover, but you weren't here. When I was looking for something to leave you a note on, I found the divorce papers on the counter. So when I received the envelope, I assumed it was the papers for me to sign."

"So if it had been those papers, you wouldn't have signed them?"

"Not a chance in hell."

"Brax, I promise I didn't want them. I've never wanted that. They were actually in with the papers I needed to shred. My dad pushed it for a while, but he knows better than to do that now."

"There are a lot of things we need to talk about, Heather. We've both been guilty of letting our misconceptions and assumptions rule us. We've been apart for way too long already."

She led him to the couch, where they sat together and talked for hours. Through their tears, they discussed the events that led up to their separation. By laying their feelings out on the table to examine, they exposed every vulnerability and made their relationship stronger.

"I never blamed you, Brax," Heather said through her tears. "My world revolved around you and Dalton, and I never doubted that your world revolved around us. The last thing I'd ever do is blame you for his death, but I understand why you'd think that. I blamed myself for not waking up to check on him earlier. Part of me just assumed you blamed me for that, too. It wasn't a conscious thought, though. In my mind, it was just a given that it was my fault."

He shook his head from side to side. "No, baby. It never occurred to me that anything was your fault. Now I have to get past the fact that I put even more pain on you when I left. At the time, I obviously wasn't thinking clearly, but I honestly thought it would be easier on you without me."

She sighed heavily and placed her palm on his cheek. "Aren't we a pair, Brax? Losing Dalton sent us both into a tailspin. One neither of us had a clue how to handle. I should've told you that your mere presence grounded me. Your love carried me through many dark nights I wasn't even sure I'd survive while we were going through it. The only thing I was sure of was you."

"Promise me something."

"Anything."

"No matter what happens in the future, this is how we talk about it. No matter what it is, no matter how hurt, mad, depressed, or confused we are. Two heads are better than one. Facts are better than assumptions."

"I promise this is how we'll talk about everything. I've been going to a therapist the last few months, and she has really helped me. I've told her everything that's happened, and she had an interesting observation."

"Yeah? What's that?"

"First, she's very impressed with our commitment to each other. I explained that we started out as best friends first and how our love and loyalty have never been in question. She doesn't think we've had a chance to develop as individuals. We went from friends to lovers to a married couple to parents, on top of being so young. She suggested we use this time apart to grow as individuals, so when we're reunited, we'll be stronger as a couple."

"How long do you plan to stay apart from me?"

She smiled at him lovingly and stroked his jaw with her fingers. "I don't plan to stay apart from you at all. But you've joined the Army now, and I don't really know how that works. Are you still in training? With everything that happened on 9/11, will you be sent away to fight? If not, where will you be stationed, and can I go with you?"

"Okay, I get your point," Braxton chuckled. "I can only take things a day at a time right now, except over the next two weeks while I have a break over the Christmas holidays. I'm finishing up my first round of individual training, but I've been selected to go for a second round with a group of handpicked soldiers. I'll be away another four months for it. After that, I have jump school in Georgia and hopefully Ranger training after that. Those two trainings will add at least another three to four months, depending on timing."

"So, almost another year of you being away, traveling and training," Heather replied.

"That was my original plan, to make the Army my career and see how far I can go with it. Heather, if you want me to take a normal Army job and settle at one base so we can be together, I'll do it. Nothing is as important to me as you are."

"No, I can't let you do that. It wouldn't be fair, Brax. Of course, I want to be with you, but I haven't seen your eyes light up when we've talked about the future for so long. But that spark was there just now when you were describing the path you want to take. I've also decided what I want to do, what I want to be."

"What do you want to be?"

"A nurse. I want to help others. Being there for them when they need help the most, being able to help them, that makes me happy. It makes me feel like my life means something. I've applied to UT for the Bachelor of Science in Nursing program."

"So four years?"

"Yeah, but I'll be able to travel to see you on the weekends, holidays, and breaks. Or you can come here. During the summer, I'll live wherever you're stationed, unless you're out of the country. We can make it work, Braxton. Don't give up on us."

"I'll never give up on us, baby. I'm all for your plan, I think it's a great idea. You'll be a wonderful nurse, and the patients will be lucky to have you. I guess that homeschooling our guidance counselor insisted on at the end of your pregnancy really paid off, didn't it?"

"Yes, I'm so glad she didn't let me get away with not finishing just because I was trying to be lazy," Heather chuckled. "I'm really excited about going back to school."

"So am I."

"You're going back to school?" Heather asked excitedly.

"I guess I left that part out. When I left for basic training, I admit I thought that was my only option at having any kind of future. But once it started, I realized it's much more than a last resort. This can be my career, a way for me to make a difference and leave my mark. With what I want to get out of it, I need a college degree, so I've decided to go for Criminal Justice."

"I'm so proud of you, Braxton."

"I love you, Heather. So damn much. It's always been you—it's only ever been you."

She moved to sit in his lap, and his arms curved lovingly around her. With one arm around his neck and the other hand resting on his chest, she felt his heart racing under her touch. "I love you, Brax. Only you—forever. And I've missed you more than you can imagine."

He watched with hooded eyes as she leaned forward and crushed her lips to his. Her hands roamed across his body. Her fingers felt each bump and ridge of his finely developed muscles. The intensity of the kiss she initiated increased markedly, conveying her need for him just as when they'd been together before their worlds crashed and burned. But in the ashes, they found the embers of a love that, once fanned, would again become white-hot and uncontainable.

He weaved his fingers through her hair, removing his lips from hers only for the split second it took to tilt her head to deepen the kiss. His tongue caressed her lips before forcing them to part. He claimed her mouth, matching and exceeding her tenacity and vigor while savoring the sweet essence that belonged only to Heather.

She broke off the kiss first but kept her lips a breath away from his. "Braxton, it's time to re-consummate our marriage."

"If that's what my wife wants, how can I deny her?"

Holding her securely in his arms, Braxton rose from the couch and carried her to their bedroom. Placed her on their bed. And showed her in every way that their marriage couldn't be bound by any type of measurement known to man. With their lips joined, he told her no amount of time would lessen his devotion. With their eyes locked, he promised his loyalty wouldn't wane with the distance between them. With their bodies joined as one, he vowed his love couldn't be measured because there was nothing that compared to its vastness.

9

CHAPTER NINE

Present Day

The first day off after a long stretch of twelve-hour work days didn't allow much downtime. After Heather's intense workout first thing in the morning, she spent the rest of her day off running errands. By the time she'd had her car serviced, her hair styled, and bought groceries, she was ready to collapse on the couch and pass out in front of the television. Staying on high alert and diligently watching her surroundings every second, thanks to her would-be stalker, had only added to her fatigue.

Once she was hidden behind her garage door, she released a sigh of relief. She loaded her arms with the plastic grocery bags to avoid making a second trip and managed to unlock the door. She released a loud grunt of frustration when she finally reached the table and let the bags slide off of her arms. She inhaled a deep, calming breath, closed her eyes, and slowly released it as her chin dropped to her chest.

"I know you're in here. You're not fooling me, so don't even try to hide. You have about two seconds to show yourself." Her voice held conviction and authority as she issued her directive.

Her unannounced visitor stepped out of the darkened living room and into the kitchen directly behind her. His thick arms slid around her waist, and she willingly stepped into his embrace. "How do you always know when I'm here? I can't ever surprise you."

"I could tell you, but then I'd have to kill you," she teased.

"I've missed you so much. It's been too long since the last time I saw you." Rebel placed a kiss just below her ear, then let his lips and tongue glide down her neck.

"Mmm," she purred and her skin prickled with yearning. "I completely agree. Even though it was technically just a few weeks ago. The last time my week off came up in the rotation."

"A few weeks is weeks too long, Heather. I'll help you put away the groceries, and then we're spending the next several hours in the bed."

"You know I love it when you get all demanding on me. Well, demanding in the bedroom, anyway."

Rebel chuckled softly against her neck. "Yeah, I know. If I tried to tell you what to do in the kitchen, I'd end up with a butcher's knife thrown at my head."

"You know me entirely too well, Brax." She turned in his arms and wrapped hers around his neck. "I'm so glad you're here. But since you're early, I have a feeling it's because someone has been following me."

One side of Rebel's lips quirked upward, and he shook his head lightly from side to side. "You already knew?"

"Of course, I knew. How long have we been married? You know, I have learned a thing or two from you over the last fourteen years."

"You've been watching me, huh?"

"I watch your every move, babe," she confirmed.

He bowed his head and captured her lips with his. A warm, welcome kiss quickly turned into a passionate, uncompromising need to consume her, reclaim her as his. Using one arm to clear the way, he easily lifted her with the other and placed her on the table directly in front of him. He gently pushed her shoulders until she lay flat on the table. His fingers gripped the sides of her yoga pants and began inching them over her hips.

"Did you forget about the groceries?" Her words reminded him, but the inflection of the desire in her voice told him her mind was on something else.

"Nope, not at all. I'm starving. I was actually hoping there would be some whipped cream in here I can use," he murmured seductively.

"If I'd known you'd be here when I got home, I would've picked some up."

"It's not a big deal. I'm here with you and that's all that matters. I miss you that much and more every day, Heather."

"I know," she replied softly. "I miss you too. So much."

"You know how we can permanently fix this problem," he reminded her as he lifted her from the table.

"I know exactly how to fix it." She gave her standard reply. "We can move your stuff out of that crappy little apartment and into our home where you belong."

"Let me take you to our bed and see if I can convince you to move to Miami with me."

"Fine by me. As long as you know I'll be trying to convince you to stay in Houston with me."

"You are so stubborn," he chuckled as he sat her on the edge of the bed.

His fingers skimmed across her chest as he removed her shirt. The length of time they'd been apart made him want to rush through the motions, but the limited time he had to spend with her forced him to take it slowly.

When she reached for him, the sensation of her fingertips against the sensitive skin of his lower abdomen was all it took for her to completely own him. In a flash, she had removed all of his clothes, and they stood bare in front of each other. When she reached for him, he gritted his teeth, leaned his head back with his eyes closed, and savored her touch.

Effortlessly, Rebel lifted her from her position in front of him to instantly lying on her back on the bed beneath him. One swift move had them joined until there was no way to tell where he ended and she began.

"You feel so good. I can't get enough of you," he murmured.

He spoke in clipped statements, barely able to speak the words.

"I'd love to keep you right here."

"In this bed."

"Screaming my name."

"Over and over."

"All damn night."

With their bodies slick from sweat and breathless from exertion, they reached the summit of pleasure together.

Rebel rolled over to his side, swiveling Heather to face him as he moved. "Is this where you try to convince me to move back to Houston permanently?"

She gave him a small smile, but he detected a sense of sadness in it. "If I honestly asked you to stay here with me for good, would you?"

"Yes," he answered immediately.

"No hesitation?"

"None. I'd be here with you in a split second."

"Why now?"

"It's not something new, babe. You've always loved your independence. Maybe because you didn't have a lot of choice during all the years I was in the service. While I was on assignments all over the world, you built a life and friends here, so I understood when you didn't want to just up and leave it when we started the business in Miami. You're the one who suggested our current arrangement, but if you need more of me, all you have to do is say the word, and I'm here. I always need more of you."

"You're right, I did suggest this setup, with one of us traveling to the other so we could spend time together and still have our careers, our friends, our lives. But now I feel like we're missing out on a life we can build together," she admitted.

"So it's my turn to ask you. Why now?"

Her eyes flicked back and forth between his, telling him she was searching for the words to convey what had shaken her independent resolve.

"One of my patients recently really got to me. She was younger than me, only twenty-nine, and she had stage four breast cancer. Her biggest regret was putting so much focus on her career that she gave up the man who was her one true love. He'd wanted to get married, have kids, move to the country where they'd only have each other, no neighbors. He wanted them to build a life where their relationship was their main focus. She died without ever knowing what that life would've been like. All she knew was her job and the few friends who stayed by her side until the end.

"I feel like our time to have that kind of relationship is slipping through our fingers. And it's not even like sand where we can hold on to some part of it. It's more like trying to hold on to flowing water. Brax, I love you, I've always loved you, and I want a real life with you now. But I feel guilty because that would take you away from your friends, your brothers, and the commitments you've made to them and the business."

"You are my commitment, Heather. First and foremost, above anything else. You're my wife, and I love you more than anything and anyone else. I've been temporarily reactivated as an operator, so right now it's out of my hands because of national security. But when this case is over, I'm all yours."

"Can we start a family then?" She blurted the question out before she could stop herself, but she had an intense need to know if he was on the same page with her. She could no longer deny the two things she wanted most were to have her husband and to have a family.

"I'd love nothing more than to make a family and a full life with you, wifey."

It had always been her touch that drove him, her kiss that fueled him, and her love that invigorated him. They drifted off to sleep wrapped in each other's arms, their legs intertwined and hearts full. They'd spent long stretches of time and distance apart, but their reunions had always made up for it. This time was no different, even though it was under different circumstances.

THE STREAMS of light filtering in through the blinds woke Heather from a deep sleep. She reached across the bed for Rebel but found only a cold, empty space. At first, she questioned if she'd dreamed the whole thing. He'd been on her mind so strongly, and so often, she could barely make a move without thinking of him. She rolled over and grabbed his pillow, hugging it closely to her, and his scent enveloped her.

A dip in the mattress beside her startled her, and she jolted up on one elbow. "Braxton," she sighed with relief. "You're really here. It wasn't all a dream."

He smiled lovingly at her. "Well, I don't know if you're dreaming about me, but I am really here. It wasn't a dream when I ravaged your body last night. And it won't be a dream when I do it again in the shower after breakfast. Or later today in the car. Or tonight, somewhere else in the house that's to remain a surprise.

"But first, here's your coffee. Breakfast is almost ready. Get up and come eat," he demanded playfully and smacked her bare ass.

As he moved toward the door, she replied softly. "You said you'd give up everything to move here with me."

He stopped and turned his head to look at her over his shoulder, his eyes locked on to hers. She held her breath until he replied. "I did, and you know I meant it."

The look of pure, unabashed love that emanated from his eyes was solely for her. She'd never doubted him or his devotion to her, and she knew he'd never give her a reason to. "Thank you, Braxton. I'm so excited and so ready to start this new chapter of our lives together. I can't wait."

"Neither can breakfast. Come eat while it's hot."

He winked and continued back to the kitchen. She retrieved his shirt from the floor and pulled it over her head. With her steaming coffee in hand, she quickly followed him and sat at the table. She glanced around the kitchen and noticed the groceries from the night before were missing.

"You put the groceries away for me?"

"Yeah, I got back up after you fell asleep last night and put every-thing away so it wouldn't spoil." He set her plate full of her favorite breakfast foods down in front of her.

"This looks delicious. Thank you. I love having you home. You spoil me."

"It's my pleasure."

"Speaking of, you distracted me last night, and I didn't get a chance to interrogate you about why you're here early. It has some-thing to do with the guy who's been following me, doesn't it?"

She watched as he took a bite of his bacon and intentionally held her gaze as he chewed, deciding what information to share and what to hold.

"Don't do that, Braxton," she warned.

"Do what?"

"Withhold information from me."

His smile crawled slowly across his handsome face. "I would never do that, babe. I was just testing your skills, making sure you're still quick on the uptake."

"You can quit stalling now, too."

He threw his head back and roared with laughter. "There's my girl. I'm afraid I've taught you a little too much over the years. By the way, Liz is with us, and she's still waiting for Shadow to teach her all of his secret spy tricks. Don't let her know that you're trained, or she'll never leave you alone."

"I can't wait to meet Liz." Heather beamed. "Actually, I can't wait to meet all of the ladies. So who's the guy following me?"

While they ate breakfast together, Rebel briefed Heather on the recent events that prompted his early return to Texas. She already knew much about the case the team had been working and why Turan had wanted to kill Rebel. During their many phone conversa-tions, he'd kept her apprised of how the case was unfolding. When he reached the part about the picture of her being sent to him, Heather nodded in understanding.

"I knew I was being watched. All the hairs on the back of my neck were standing at attention in the parking garage. I never saw him, but I knew someone was there, so I watched my rearview mirror for a tail on my way home. Spotted him immediately. He's not very good at being covert."

"He most likely underestimated your cool ninja skills, babe."

"Yeah, he did. Then he spent a long time driving around the subdivision looking for my car. So I've been driving the Land Rover and parking in different places around the hospital when I go to work. Using different doors to enter and exit. I'm off for the next week, though. Makes it easier for you to guard my body every day."

"I will absolutely guard your body, several times a day." His heated stare expressed the true meaning behind his words. "Can you take off more time, just in case?"

"I'd have to contact Becca immediately so she can get my shifts covered," she replied, her mind drifting to her patients and how much longer she'd be away from them. "Do you have a picture of this guy I can give to security in case he shows up there?"

"Reaper has it in the file. We'll make sure it gets to them as soon as possible. But for now, it's time for you to take my shirt off. We have to take our shower so I can guard your body for the first time today. It'll take at least the next hour and all the hot water."

She slowly rose from her seat, drew his shirt over her head, and dropped it at her feet. As she stood completely naked before him, she flashed him a challenging grin. "This body? Is this the one you want to guard?"

Rebel sat back in his chair and pushed it back from the table. Arching his eyebrow in a responding challenge, he nodded slowly while his eyes raked up and down her body.

"You'll have to catch me first." She shrugged nonchalantly before taking off running at full speed toward the hall. Before she reached it, she squealed with playful laughter as she flew through the air and landed on his shoulder.

"Challenge accepted, little lady. But don't act like I didn't catch you many years ago," he chuckled as he carried her to the master bath. "You've always been mine, and I'm about to remind you why."

10

CHAPTER TEN

"Where did you park?" Heather asked as she and Rebel climbed into her Land Rover. "There wasn't a strange car in any of the driveways on my street."

"It's good to know I can still be invisible when I need to be." Rebel winked. "I scouted the entire neighborhood yesterday while you were out running around—at your workout, getting your hair done, buying groceries. There's a vacant house on the next street over, so I made a few calls, and it's now our command center. My rental car is parked in the garage over there."

"Were you following me yesterday?" She turned in her seat and faced him, cocking her head to the side and purposely letting her mouth fall open. Her narrowed eyes were the dead giveaway she was not pleased with the answer she already knew.

Rebel shifted uncomfortably in the driver's seat. "Babe, you know I had to follow you. I wasn't checking up on what you were doing, though. It was only to find out if anyone was tailing you."

"And?"

"No one besides me tailed you yesterday," he confirmed. "You didn't see me, though. Did you?"

She turned to sit straight forward in her seat and crossed her arms over her chest. "No," she finally admitted.

Rebel laughed, knowing that it killed her, with her fierce competitive streak, to admit that to him. "Don't be mad. I'm trained to be invisible, and I've been perfecting my technique for years and years."

"That doesn't make me feel any better," she huffed. "Maybe I should have a long talk with Liz, after all. Seems there are a few things she and I both need to learn to do."

"Don't unleash Liz on me. She's already threatened to kick my ass and accused me of leading her on."

Heather burst out laughing at the visual. "I hate that I missed seeing that in person. Liz sounds like my kind of people."

Though she'd never met Liz, Rebel had described her to a T during their nightly conversations. Since Rebel had returned from active duty, they hadn't skipped sharing the events of their day, regardless of how mundane, for even one single night. The people in Rebel's life were as important to Heather as they were to Rebel because they kept him company, they kept him sane. They kept him alive. They were like family to her, even if not all of them knew she even existed.

"They broke the mold when they made Liz. And we're all very thankful for that," he chuckled. "She's really a great woman. Regardless of how eccentric she acts sometimes, she's as good as gold. We all know she'd do anything for us, without hesitation. The way she's taken care of Brianna, Reaper, Amelia, and Reaper's parents...we couldn't ask for more."

Heather's responding silence concerned Rebel and prompted him to cut his gaze toward her. The profound sadness he saw on her face struck a chord deep inside him. He took her hand and gently squeezed it. "What's wrong, babe?"

"You'll think I'm crazy."

"I already do, so there's really no danger in telling me what's on your mind."

She smiled because she knew all he wanted was to cheer her up. "Fair enough. It's irrational, but I'm jealous of the time they get to spend with you. I'm jealous of what you experience with them, and I'm kicking myself because those memories aren't with me."

"Heather, whether you're physically with me or not, you are in every memory I have. Everywhere I go, everything I see, every emotion I feel, you are at the center of it. I understand exactly what you mean because I feel the same way when you tell me about things you do with Becca and your other friends. One reason why I share everything with you is so you'll feel like you're a part of it, too."

"I know, and I do the same with you. I told you it was irrational. It's mostly because I miss you so much. And because hindsight is twenty-twenty. There are so many things I'd do differently if we could just go back and start all over again."

"All we can do is make it the best it can be from now on."

"You're right. And we will."

He pulled into the valet parking area of the Sterling Luxury Resort and handed the keys to the attendant as he got out. When he stated the room number, Heather's head jerked in his direction and her brows furrowed, but she remained silent. Rebel led her inside, his hand possessively on her lower back, and into the elevator. He retrieved the keycard from his pocket and slid it into the reader before pressing the floor number.

When the doors closed, Heather turned to him. "You have a room here?"

"We have a room here, if we need it. It's on a secure floor that only we can access. If I need to pull you out of harm's way, you can stay here with Brianna, Chaise, and Liz. Sara will be in and out since Steve is still in the hospital."

"I didn't put two and two together when I first met Steve. He's my patient, but it was just recently that I learned he's Noah's father. I probably sounded like a lunatic when I realized it," she laughed. "This is a very elegant hotel. So, Brianna's family owns it?"

"Yes, her father built a luxury hotel empire from the ground up. He reserved this entire floor for us. There are several three-bedroom suites at our disposal."

"And the house in my neighborhood?"

"We'll use it to coordinate our activities and keep the focus away from this hotel. The more we come and go from here, the more dangerous it makes it for everyone staying here. It's too likely that someone from Rashad's cell will see us and use the hotel customers to get their point across."

The elevator doors slid open, and Rebel took Heather's hand in his as they strode to the door of one of the suites. They could hear the voices coming from inside—the laughter, the teasing, the sounds of friends and family enjoying the company they were in. Their eyes met, and they each knew what was in the other's thoughts.

"You're a member of this family, Heather." Rebel inclined his head toward the door. "When you meet Brianna, Chaise, and Liz, you'll see it doesn't matter that you didn't know them before now."

"Okay. I'm ready."

He opened the door and walked through with Heather in tow directly behind him. "Here she is, everyone. Say hello to my wife, Heather."

Before the door closed behind them, Brianna, Chaise, Liz, and Sara had surrounded Heather in a flurry of excitement. The ladies made their introductions while Rebel joined the guys at the table, reviewing the assignments and the information they'd been provided from their contact. The only one who was still missing was Shadow.

"I'm so glad you're here with him, Heather," Bull called out across the room. "You have no idea how pissy he gets when you're not around."

"I can't believe you've all kept her a secret from us all this time. What the hell is that all about?" Brianna retorted. "Every one of you knew about her and never said a word."

"I'm afraid that's partly my fault," Heather admitted.

"It's mostly mine, though," Rebel corrected as he moved back to her side. "We were already married before I joined the service. One training led to another, one mission led to the next, more dangerous mission. When I graduated college and became a Green Beret, there was just too great of a chance she'd become a target while I was out on assignment somewhere. Keeping her off the record was the best solution at the time."

"And when you left the service?" Brianna put her hand on her hip and raised her eyebrows at him.

"By then, we were already set in our routines, and we were both protective of our relationship." Rebel shrugged. "And I knew you'd give me a hard time and tell me what an idiot I've been."

"You're damn right, I would have."

The room erupted in laughter, including Brianna, and Noah wrapped his arm around his wife's shoulders. "Cut them some slack, babe."

"Braxton is covering for me," Heather replied with a sideways smirk at Rebel. "I'm a little headstrong at times, and I insisted on keeping my independence. My family and friends have always been here in Houston. He was gone on assignments a lot, especially in the early years when he was a Ranger and then a Green Beret. His deployments were shorter but more frequent, and I was in nursing school, so it's not like I could just up and move anywhere. By the time his missions slowed down enough, we were both used to it. It's just the way it has always been."

"Maybe we should've nicknamed her 'Rebel' instead of you," Bull teased.

"Rebel One and Rebel Two," Noah joked. "Heather, you haven't met my brother before now. This is Silas Steele."

"Now that we've met you, don't expect us to just let you go," Chaise asserted. "I've never believed a long-distance relationship could work, but you two have made a believer out of me."

"Don't go getting any ideas," Bull warned. "I'm not sleeping without you every night."

"So you're the one, huh?" Liz spoke up at last. "You should probably come around more, my girl. I've had to call this one down a time or two for flirting with me."

"He has told me all about you, Liz." Heather smiled broadly. "And believe me, I've already given him a piece of my mind for his antics with you."

The mischievous gleam in Liz's eyes was unmistakable. "You and I are going to get along just fine."

"As much as I'd love to continue this conversation, we need to get to work and catch this asshole as soon as possible." Rebel stopped the conversation before it got out of control.

Rebel turned and walked to the table without checking to see if the others had followed. He began reviewing the original case file and the latest intelligence Silas got from his contacts on Rashad and Turan. "Heather, come here for a minute."

When Heather reached him, he handed her a picture of Rashad. "Have you ever seen this man before?"

"Yes. At the hospital. He's been on my floor a couple of times in the past week. Is this the one who's following me?"

"That's him. His name is Rashad Samir. His brother wanted to kill me because I'm the one who killed his father in a raid on his compound ten years ago. They were just kids then. Rashad will try to take the opportunity to exact revenge on behalf of his brother."

"But based on our latest intel on Rashad, he and Turan were complete opposites in the way they work, like day and night opposites. Turan was a socially inept techie who could make a computer dance on a stripper's pole. He was dangerous as far as the havoc he could create through the internet, but he didn't offer much in the man-on-man category.

"Rashad is the polar opposite of his dead brother. He's not a tech expert in any sense of the word, but what he lacks in computer skills, he makes up for in explosives. This guy could teach one of our explosives experts a thing or two. He considers it a form of art and prides himself on finding new and exciting ways to blow shit up," Silas explained.

"Great news," Rebel deadpanned. "So we'll get to see a fireworks show up close and personal."

"It's far too likely to happen with his training and background," Silas confirmed. "We can't take any chances."

"Heather, you'll have to stay away from the hospital until this is over. With his profile, he wouldn't hesitate to take out as many patients as he can in his quest to hit us. We'll have to plan this just right. We have to let him know you're taking time off without him realizing we're feeding him the information. You've already been avoiding him, so it would raise too many red flags if you just suddenly went back to your regular routine," Rebel explained.

"So, I need to go back to work one day, let him see me accidentally on purpose so he can hear me while I tell Becca I need to take time off. Is that about it?"

Noah smiled knowingly, immediately picking up on her no-nonsense wit. "You got it. What do you need us around for?"

"For the eye candy and the company," she quipped. "I have everything else covered."

"Oh, yeah. You'll fit right in with this bunch. No doubt about it," Noah laughed.

The pride and admiration that shone on Rebel's face was reserved just for her, and she knew it without question. Guilt filled her, squeezing her heart like a heavy vise and virtually paralyzing her lungs, making it hard for her to breathe. She hid the pain of her regret behind her smile, but the ominous feeling that she'd realized what was important far too late wouldn't go away. If anything, it was multiplying with each tick of the second hand.

It felt as if she was watching a timer on a deadly bomb count down, but she was powerless to stop it.

Please don't take Braxton away from me now, she prayed silently.

"Do you need me anymore?" she asked.

"Always," Rebel replied. "But you can go get to know the ladies while we finish going over these files if you want."

"Okay," she replied softly. "You know where to find me if you need me to take over and show you boys how it's done."

Rebel chuckled and pulled her close to him, his arms wrapped around her waist, the adoration glimmering in his eyes. "You can show me how it's done all night. For now, I need to figure out how to stop the bad guy."

Amelia's cries broadcasted throughout the spacious room from the speaker of the baby monitor. In her peripheral vision,

Heather saw Brianna rise from the couch and rush toward the bedroom to soothe her newborn. But the connection between Heather and Braxton held their eyes firmly locked on each other, to both comfort and share whatever strength they could muster for the other. No amount of time could lessen the loss they felt, but it did give them both time to learn to handle the pain.

"I love you," Rebel mouthed.

"I love you more," she mouthed in reply before releasing him.

He watched as she strode across the suite and sat beside Brianna to coo over Amelia. When Brianna offered to let Heather hold the baby, Rebel watched with amazement as his wife took the tiny baby in her arms, held her close to her bosom, and softly kissed her little pink baby cheeks.

Silas, Noah, and Bull began talking about the contents of Rashad's file and pulled Rebel out of his thoughts, back into the conversation. While actively participating with his team, he kept one ear attuned to Heather's conversation with the other ladies. They were dying to pry into the more intimate details of their married life, but socially acceptable decorum kept them in check. When he realized not even Liz had blurted out the questions she wanted answered, he knew Reaper must have warned them before they'd arrived at the hotel.

During a lapse in conversation at the table, Rebel looked up at Reaper. "Thanks, man."

"For what?"

"For whatever threat you issued that's keeping the ladies from bombarding Heather with questions about us."

Reaper tried to hide his smile at first, but it was pointless. "I just told them if they pushed too hard, Heather may never come around again. She's stayed away all these years, so they have to make her want to be around them."

"I always knew there was a reason why I liked you and kept you alive. You've earned your keep today."

"Good to know I'm useful for something."

"Try being useful for this case now. Where's Rashad hiding out? What's his ultimate plan? He's here for more than Heather."

"Babe?" Heather called out. "Becca just sent me a text. She said a letter was left for me at the nurse's station. It's marked personal and urgent, so I'm going to tell her to send it over here by private courier. They can have it here in a few minutes."

"There's no other name on the envelope?" He was on instant alert, knowing the courier could be followed and their location could be compromised.

"She said it only has my name, and the personal and urgent is written in capital letters under my name."

Rebel and Reaper exchanged glances, unspoken words passing between them. "Heather, have them send it to me here at the hotel." Turning to Rebel, he continued. "I'll increase security around the hotel. Extra men can be here within the hour." Reaper stepped away from the group to call in the additional contracted surveillance teams.

Within twenty minutes, the suite phone rang, making the four men turn their heads and stare at it guardedly before Reaper picked it up.

"Steele."

"Mr. Steele, a letter addressed to you has just been delivered to the front desk. Would you like me to have it delivered to your room, or would you prefer to come to the lobby to pick it up?"

"I'll come down. Who delivered it?"

"A local courier, one we've used frequently. I can give you his name and company information if you need it."

"Yes, if you can write it down for me, I'll be down in a minute to pick them both up."

After a quick trip to the lobby, Noah returned to the suite with the letter in hand. He nearly succumbed to the urge to open it in the elevator, but he knew he'd never hear the end of it from the rest of the team if he did.

Once inside the suite, he laid the letter out for everyone to read.

"What the fuck?" Rebel exclaimed.

"Dickhead is playing games. He thinks he's funny, doesn't he?" Bull replied in disgust.

Spelled out in letters cut out of magazines in different sizes, colors, and fonts was a letter addressed to Heather.

> *You're so good with syringes and starting IVs.*
> *You stick them in others while you roam free.*
> *But your turn is coming, the time is so near.*
> *When you'll get your own stick, it's almost here.*

11

CHAPTER ELEVEN

"What the hell is he up to?" Rebel asked calmly, masking the anger that welled up inside him. "It's definitely a direct threat, but what's his plan?"

"The part about her roaming free could mean he plans to snatch her," Bull reasoned. "He could be planning to drug her and take her. But the part about the stick could refer to different things. A stick in the way he started the letter, meaning he'll inject her with something. A stick of dynamite, meaning he'll blow up something. Or it could be neither one, simply meant to throw us off."

"With his background, we have to assume he's referring to bombs. Her turn is coming soon, he sent pictures of her to Rebel, and he's been following her. Left this at her nursing station, so he knew she wasn't there. But he hasn't found her house yet, or he would've left it there." Noah met Rebel's gaze dead on. "A bodyguard will be on her at all times. That's not negotiable."

Rebel nodded. "I guard her body just fine, but thanks for asking."

Noah smiled, understanding exactly how he felt. "You can't stay awake and alert for twenty-four hours a day, seven days a week until this is finished. She'll need a protection detail, even if they never touch her body."

"If they value the protruding parts of their bodies, they'll keep their hands off of her."

"Can't say I'd be any different," Noah replied.

"Hell no," Bull added. "The body would never be found if one of them touched Chaise."

"You're all pussy-whipped men," Silas sighed. "What happened to the badass Delta Operatives the three of you used to be? You know, before you traded in your man cards for women's purses."

"I'd just like to point out that I've been a badass Ranger, Green Beret, and Delta Force operative all while being married. I can carry my wife's purse better than any man, while still whipping your ass." Rebel arched a single brow at Silas in a silent mock threat.

"No need to get your girly panties all in a wad." Silas grinned.

"I'll assign the protection detail shifts to Blake, Roman, and Alex, and get Brad to start his computer magic to help find Rashad using the limited information we have so far." Bull picked up his cell phone and walked away while issuing the new orders to the other men of Steele Security.

"Rebel, I got the official word from our commander in chief while you were doing surveillance yesterday. The airwaves are full of chatter that Rashad's cell is planning something on a large scale."

"How large?"

"To rival 9/11."

"What are our orders?"

"Take no prisoners once we're sure of their plans."

"I know for a fact they won't take prisoners. While I was undercover investigating his cell's activities, the low-level guys I was allowed around couldn't wait to be promoted so they could take out as many of us as possible," Silas added. "I'm glad to hear we're ordered to take them out."

"I thought you left the CIA?" Rebel asked Silas.

"I did. Just like you left Delta Force," Silas replied.

"Delta Force doesn't even exist. I thought you spooks were smarter than that."

"And the CIA doesn't operate on American soil. So neither of us actually exists."

"Fair enough," Rebel chuckled. "Do you have any suggestions on where we should start looking for him? Or how to draw him out to us?"

"Rashad sets himself up on a pedestal, so he'd want to stay somewhere nice. His minions are more likely to be in a rat-infested motel while he stays in a suite like this one. But with what the intelligence says he's planning, he'd need somewhere with complete privacy. So I'd say he has a house here, whether it's rented, borrowed, or owned," Silas answered.

"Well, that narrows it down," Bull deadpanned.

"Exactly. Let's start narrowing it down," Noah replied. "Have Brad start searching for shipments of the most common ingredients these suicide bombers like to use. Who's moving the most paint remover and industrial-grade hydrogen peroxide? Or ammonium nitrate and diesel fuel? Cross-reference the addresses and materials. They may be splitting up deliveries of the ingredients to avoid detection."

"On it," Bull answered. "I'll have him include businesses around here, too. They may be ordering shit through an employer to hide it, too. Or stealing it."

"I'm going to take a closer look at his uncle's finances and see if anything jumps out at me now. We know there's still a connection there, but with him having immunity as an ambassador, we haven't been able to do anything about it," Rebel added.

"Let me don my disguise, and I'll go shake some local trees and see what the word on the street is." Silas stood up and turned to find Heather looking at him quizzically.

"Disguise? Shake some trees?" she asked.

"Yeah, with all of us being in Houston, the chances of being seen are just too great. I was undercover with Rashad's cell for a while, with the lowest level guys who didn't know enough to tell me anything. So, I'm going to go locate my confidential informants and find out what the word among the criminals is."

"Alone? Aren't you taking backup or anything?"

Silas smiled at her concern for his well-being. "No, I don't take backup out with me. This is what I'm trained to do, and it's best that I talk to them alone. Informants tend to clam up when people they don't know start asking them questions. Don't worry about me. I'm a big boy."

With that, Silas left the group to prepare his disguise. When he emerged again, he was unrecognizable as the handsome, fit man who'd just closed the door behind him not fifteen minutes before. He appeared heavier, his hair was shorter and light brown. His eye color had changed from the deep blue that matched Noah's to a chocolate brown. His eyebrows were bushier and matched the color of his new hair. It was the obvious changes to his face with latex prosthetic makeup that completed his transformation, making him unrecognizable as Silas Steele to everyone else.

"Who are you?" Brianna asked her brother-in-law.

"Charlie Murphy, street corner sales professional," Silas replied with a sneaky smile. "Otherwise known as a drug dealer."

"Even your teeth have changed. Are you wearing dentures?" Brianna leaned in closer to get a better look.

Silas smiled widely, giving her an opportunity to get a good look. "I sure am. These are Charlie's teeth, so I have to wear them."

"That is so cool," she replied with amazement.

"You and Shadow are keeping all the good stuff from me!" Liz stomped her foot and put her fists on her hips. "I've been asking for this for a long time now. When you get back, you're going to put some of that makeup on me and let me help with this investigation."

Silas glanced around the room, waiting for anyone to step in and act as the backup he'd just asserted he didn't need. "I'm not so sure about that, Liz. It's really too dangerous for you."

"You know what's dangerous, Silas?" Liz shifted her weight from one leg to the other and crossed her arms.

"What?" he asked tentatively.

"When you're sound asleep in your bed..." She paused for emphasis. "And I'm in the same room with you."

"One spy makeup tutorial coming up," he conceded. He made a

long trip around the room for the sole purpose of looking each man in the eye as he muttered "traitor" under his breath when he passed by. Silas left the suite to begin tracking down his informants, ignoring the snickers that turned into full belly laughs when the door closed behind him.

The neighborhood Silas had to venture into was in the worst part of town, with the highest crime rate. Charlie Murphy looked as if he would not only fit right in, but it was more likely he was there to take over. His dark brown eyes were menacing and calculating as he scoured the neighborhood. He made it a point to look directly at each person he passed, leaving the distinct impression anyone who fucked with him would regret it. His confident swagger coupled with the obvious outline of the gun lying just under his untucked button-down shirt ensured others moved out of his direct path.

His appearance and demeanor perfectly fit the part of a dangerous lowlife to everyone around. Little did they know how deadly he actually was. Trained to blend in anywhere he was placed, and to also get out with the exact opposite of any identifying traits, Silas had no qualms about running into anyone in a dark alley. He knew which one of them would be walking back out on his own two feet—and which one would be wheeled away on a stretcher.

With three raps on the door in quick succession, he listened intently to the muffled sounds coming from inside the dingy, run-down apartment. Though the inhabitants attempted to be as silent as possible, hoping the person on the other side would think no one was home, they'd already made too many mistakes to pull that ruse off.

"Open up!" he commanded from the dimly lit hallway. His stern tone left no doubt he'd kick the door down if he had to tell them twice.

"Who is it?" a woman's trembling voice called back.

"That's a new low, man. Do you have any idea what kind of bad things could happen to a woman home alone in this place?"

The doorknob slowly turned, allowing the door to open only by a small crack as an eyeball peeped out.

"Pay the five dollars and install a fucking peephole. You really think that flimsy chain and your measly foot could stop me from busting in if that's what I wanted to do?" Silas asked incredulously.

The door shut softly, the ring bolt slid across the metal guide, and the chain fell against the doorjamb. Silas pushed lightly on the door, and it swung open with ease. On the other side stood Joe, the CIA agent who'd disappeared from Miami, with an overall countenance of complete deflation. His shoulders slumped, his face was crestfallen, and his eyes were lackluster.

"We don't have anything you can steal, and we can't get anything that could be of any worth to you. My wife is sick, and I've been out of work for months. What could you possibly want with us? We mind our own business and stay out of everyone else's business," Joe rambled on and on.

Silas walked in, fully aware that Joe hadn't recognized him under his disguise, and closed the door behind him. Even with Joe's down-on-his-luck demeanor, the training he received at The Farm was ingrained in his every cell. He watched Silas's movements with the precision only his years of service could provide. Once the door latched, Silas intentionally stepped out from in front of it, out of the line of fire of anyone who may show up on the other side. Joe's gaze shot up and met Silas's knowing smirk.

"Who are—?" Joe started to ask but stopped short.

"You and your *sister* need to come back with me. You're not safe here. Besides, this place is a shithole. If she's not already sick, she will be soon just from living in this dump. How do you know you haven't already contracted typhoid fever?"

Joe stared at Silas, or *Charlie*, for several long seconds. "How'd you find me?"

"Come on, Joe. You're not seriously asking me that, are you?"

"I've been very careful with every move I've made."

"Ever considered that's your problem? You're too careful, and that makes you too predictable. That'll get you killed in this job."

"I thought you quit the CIA." Recognition dawned in Joe's glare at last.

"Have you ever known anyone who actually quit? Enough with

the stalling. Grab anything that could identify you, and let's go. Your sister will have a luxurious, safe place to stay, and she'll have the best company in the world."

"And where will I be?" Joe asked skeptically.

"With my brother, his team, and me. I know you took off for a reason, but now it's time to man up and make a stand."

"You don't think I tried? Too much planted evidence appeared to point at me, and I couldn't undo it."

"We know Bill was the dirty one, not you. Rashad took him out, so it's probably best that you got out of Miami. But Rashad is now in Houston, and we need to go hit up a couple of my CIs to find out the word on the street."

The color drained from Joe's face, and his eyes found his sister's worried expression. "I knew he'd end up here sooner or later. It's time to go, then. Emily, you know what we have to do."

She nodded, walked into the bedroom, and pulled the small suitcase from underneath the bed. Joe followed her, and they began filling the bag with their belongings. Silas heard Emily whisper to Joe as they packed. "Who is he? Can we trust him?"

"He's Silas Steele with the CIA. And we don't have much choice but to go with him if Rashad is here," Joe whispered back.

"Stop whispering about me. I can hear you both," Silas called. "In fact, this place is so small, I can still see you."

Emily turned her head and met Silas's knowing gaze in the mirror hanging on the bedroom wall. "I'm sorry. I'm just not cut out for all of this."

"I understand, Emily. You'll like it much better where I'm taking you."

Once in the car, Silas called Noah as an advance warning that he was bringing someone by the hotel. "Hey, little brother, I have a surprise for you."

"You know how I feel about surprises. What is it?"

"We need to make room for one more couple, one of them in the hotel and the other in the house. I'm on my way back to the hotel now to drop Emily off. Can you have Chaise come down to get her?

Joe and I are going back out to get information, but it's not safe to take her with us."

"Of course. I'll let the ladies know to expect her soon. If it's the same Joe I think it is, I can't wait to hear this story, big brother."

The rest of the ride back to the hotel was quiet. Silas left Joe and Emily with their thoughts, knowing they were scared for their own safety, not quite convinced they could totally trust him, and fully aware of the havoc Rashad could rain down on their lives. In the grand scheme of things, Joe viewed Silas as the lesser of the evils he and his sister faced. Silas couldn't blame him for being concerned, but they needed Joe's help to stop whatever Rashad had planned.

When they reached the hotel, Bull and Chaise were waiting to escort Emily up to the secure floor. Noah jumped in the front seat of the car and turned to give Joe a menacing glare. "Well, well, who do we have here?"

"I believe you two have met," Silas chuckled.

"It can't be Joe Brown. The very same Joe Brown I met in Miami and who then disappeared into thin air in the middle of a national security case," Noah retorted.

"Just what I need. Two Steeles in my life. This should be fun," Joe deadpanned.

"Why'd you desert us, Joe?" Noah demanded.

"I found out Bill was dirty. I'd suspected for a while, but I couldn't get anything concrete on him. Then he started getting sloppy, blatantly prideful. I knew he'd end up getting us all killed with his arrogance. I had to get my sister away from everything. Rashad will do worse than kill her, and she's the only family I have left."

"Has he threatened her?" Noah asked.

"Yeah." Joe nodded, his eyes downcast. "He threatened to take her back to his homeland and sell her to the highest bidder. The thing is, that isn't just an idle threat. It's not his main focus, but he's done it before, and he'll do it again. Especially if it's a way of getting revenge on someone who has defied him."

Both of the back doors of the car opened simultaneously, and Rebel and Bull slid in, forcing Joe to move to the middle as they flanked him. All four men stared Joe down with their eyes lethal but their faces expressionless. Joe shook his head, resigned to being the outsider until he'd proven his allegiance to them after abandoning them before. "Let's take this bastard down," Joe finally stated resolutely.

"Let's do it. Did you girls say goodbye to your ladies?" Silas joked.

"Yeah, yeah. We're ready to go to the command center," Bull replied. "Let's get this motherfucker so I can get back to Chaise. He's being a serious cockblocker."

"Bull. Seriously." Noah cut his deadly gaze toward his friend. "That's my sister you're talking about. How many times do I have to tell you I don't want to hear that shit?"

Bull's only reply was to flash his best friend a shit-eating grin.

"I kind of feel bad for all of you pansies since I'll still get to sleep with my wife every night. Not bad enough to give that up, though," Rebel chimed in. With a round of threats to Rebel's manhood, Silas set out for the shadier side of town to start gathering more information on Rashad's plans.

"Our informants will no doubt be thrilled to see all of us coming for them," Silas laughed.

12

CHAPTER TWELVE

The view of sprawling greenery of the ninth fairway was one of the most coveted in the uber-exclusive gated community, but it had nothing on the expansive Mediterranean mansion Rashad presently called home. Through his uncle's lucrative connections, he'd been able to procure one of the most luxurious houses in Houston to conduct his illegal business. The owner and his family were out of the country for business and personal travel for the next six months, ensuring Rashad's total seclusion for the duration of his mission.

Though the subdivision had plenty of houses, that specific house was situated on one of the largest lots, putting the nearest neighbor over a half acre away on either side. Inside the eight-thousand-square-foot, three-story estate, outsiders would be hard-pressed to see what he was up to regardless. The formal dining room located to the right of the expansive kitchen served as his creative space. The spacious dining table with enough seats for twelve people gave him plenty of room to spread out all his materials in a makeshift production line.

His resolve and conviction increased with each one he completed. When he had put the finishing touches on the completed product, he'd carefully move it to the sideboard buffet with the others. Alone, each ingredient was relatively harmless as long as it was handled as instructed. But mixed together, the combination became an instantly volatile and highly combustible powder.

He'd carefully planned the design himself to keep the crystallized powder secure until he was ready for it to detonate. Because it could self-detonate from the slightest friction, he insulated the outer containers with packing foam to reduce the movement of the glass cylinders. On his remote command, small devices inside each case would vibrate, creating one of the most brilliant explosions through a massive shock wave of energy.

The doorbell rang just as he placed the last one on the table. The sounds pealed throughout the house, echoing off the cathedral ceilings and carrying through the air like the most pleasant of wind chimes. Rashad glanced at his watch, and one side of his mouth quirked upward. "Right on time."

The delivery driver held the large box as Rashad signed his fake name on the delivery confirmation device. "Here you go," he said as he handed Rashad the cardboard box. "Guess I'll see you again in a day or two, huh?"

"Yeah, probably. I've ordered several things for my daughter's upcoming birthday party. It's a surprise, and we're going all out for it."

"Sounds like she'll love it. Have a good one."

"You, too," Rashad replied before closing the door. He kept up pretenses as a friendly, everyday guy next door to help to avoid blowing his cover. Not overly chatty, he gave just enough information about his fake family to keep anyone from suspecting him should anything happen to draw attention before he was ready.

He placed the box on the kitchen table and began removing the contents. One by one, he unwrapped the empty glass tubes from their protective coverings and ensured the black rubber plungers completely sealed each one before moving them to the dining room table. Once everything was in place, he began the process of filling each glass tube, carefully placing the plunger in the end, and securing it onto the custom-made trigger all over again.

His team would need an abundance of these devices to carry out their plans. Each one was small enough to carry at least ten in a standard backpack. Some would be carried in lunch coolers, others in briefcases. Obscurity was the name of the game, so the old-school suitcase-sized bombs with conspicuous wires sticking out would never work. Blending in, creating no ripples, and leaving no lasting impressions were the only surefire means of mission success.

"I wonder, Rebel, if you've considered this in all the plans you've made to find me. Has your friend Noah any idea what I'm capable of doing? I do hope you're both there to witness everything. But should you both get caught inside the grand celebration, I can live with the disappointment. However, you can't."

Rashad laughed maniacally to himself, picturing their faces as Rebel and Noah realized they were in the wrong place at the wrong time. When they realized the genius contraptions he'd built would lead to their demise and his plan would be carried out despite their pathetic attempts to stop him. It would be poetic, really, if Rashad were the type of man who believed in that kind of justice. In this case, he believed the result would be driven by divine intervention, so he would gladly accept whatever outcome lay in wait for them.

His vibrating cell phone pulled him from his inner thoughts and from the task of filling the glass vials with his concoction. He glanced at the screen before answering, instantly recognizing the name of one of the members of his team.

"Faruq, what news do you have for me, brother?" Rashad answered.

"We have teams going out tonight to locate the girl. She hasn't shown back up at the hospital, and time is running out. We need her to help complete our mission as planned."

"How do you plan to execute this idea?"

"Three teams of two men will go house to house in the neighborhood where you tracked her. We'll wait for the cover of night and look through as many windows as we can. At least we'll be able to start narrowing it down through the process of elimination so we can focus on the most likely houses."

"That's a good idea, Faruq. Tell the men to be especially careful of dogs. Any excessive barking will draw too much attention and endanger our overall mission."

"I will be sure to tell them. How are the other supplies coming along? Do you need any help with them?"

"No, they're coming along very nicely. All will be ready on schedule. I've ordered supplies in small quantities to avoid any flags of suspicious activity. I receive only enough to keep me busy for a couple of days, and then a new shipment arrives. I've timed it perfectly, though, and accounted for any delays with delivery schedules."

"It's an honor to be part of this mission with you, brother. I'll be back in touch once the men have scoured the neighborhood for the nurse."

"When they find her, have them take pictures of her and send them to me. I'll need them soon for the next step."

He disconnected and continued assembling the explosive devices. Rashad spent the rest of the day carefully measuring, cautiously constructing, and delicately moving the completed products. With each one, he pictured exactly where it would be placed and how the aftermath of the explosion would appear. That made him happy and gave him purpose, pushing him to complete what would otherwise be mundane, repetitive tasks. Each completed device was more beautiful and brilliant than the last. Each one represented a piece of the jigsaw puzzle and brought him closer to seeing the full picture in all its fiery magnificence.

"Why are you in disguise, Silas?" Joe finally asked. "You don't need a disguise to look creepy."

When the laughter died down, Silas explained. "I have to stay in disguise in case we run into anyone from Rashad's cell. I was undercover with them, but I never got close to him. His lower level thugs would recognize me, though. This persona is Charlie Murphy, if you need to use my name."

Once parked, the five burly men exited the vehicle and sauntered into yet another run-down, roach-infested building that should've long since been condemned. The halls were littered with garbage, dirty syringes, and empty baggies with faint white streaks as the only remnants of what was once inside. The men moved past the strung out inhabitants with red circles around their eyes so thick they almost glowed in the dimly lit space. The whites of their eyes were so bloodshot, it appeared they hadn't slept in weeks.

Silas stopped walking halfway down the hall and banged on the door with his hefty fist. He shook his head when the people inside began shuffling and whispering. He cut his eyes to Joe and said, "Paper-thin walls here too." Joe rolled his eyes in response, completely understanding his meaning.

The door creaked open, and a young teenage boy stood in the doorway. "Whatchu want?" The boy jerked his chin up defiantly as he asked, but his eyes betrayed the confidence his act projected.

"What do I want?" Silas replied casually, injecting a thick Southern accent to add to his disguise. "I want the man of the house to step out from behind that door, put his pansy-ass .22 down, and quit putting his kid in danger. He has about two seconds before I jam this door into his head and knock him the fuck out. That's what I want."

A resigned sigh fell from behind the door, and Reuben stepped out into the open. "Charlie, shit, dude. You been gone a long time, man. I thought you was dead."

Silas walked into the apartment, forcing the boy to move out of the way with his commanding presence alone. The other four men followed behind him, easily taking up all the space in the small room, especially once the door was closed. Reuben looked warily at each man, apprehension quickly overcoming his features.

"What's the word, Reuben?" Silas asked pointedly.

"Word 'bout what, man?"

"Don't play dumb with me. You know how much that pisses me

off." Silas slid his Bowie knife out of the sheath and casually flipped it around in his hand.

"You talking about the dudes from the Middle East?"

Silas sheathed his knife, crossed his arms over his thick chest, and nodded.

"Yo, look here, man. I don't want none of that action. I sent their asses on down the road."

"What'd they want, Reuben?"

"They wanted military-grade shit, Charlie. Like breaking into an army base and stealing weapons and shit. You know I'm not into that, man. Yo, man, my cousin is in the military. That's like betraying my family and shit. That ain't me."

"And you know there's no way in hell you could pull that off."

"Yeah, well, I ain't no superhero, dude. I can't fly over the fences and dodge bullets and shit."

"Do you realize you end every sentence with 'and shit' or 'man'?"

"It's just the way I talk, man," Reuben replied nervously. "What else you need?"

"Have you seen them again since then?"

"I haven't. But look here, they found my boy Gustavo and wanted him to get some over-the-counter shit for them."

"Like what?"

"Paint thinner and shit, man. Those extra-large buckets of bleach like they got at the big-ass wholesale stores. Rectangular plastic or glass containers. Stuff you can walk into any store and buy right off the shelves, man. Freaked Gustavo out so bad he told them to get the fuck out of our neighborhood and don't come back."

"It freaked him out to buy legal items instead of selling them illegal ones?" Rebel clarified.

"Hell yeah, man. If some dude won't go into the store to buy his own legal shit, something is really wrong with that shit. He's up to something really bad, and he'll pin that shit on someone else while he skips town. No way is that gonna be me or my boy Gus."

"Anything else we should know?"

"Yeah, man. Me and Gus, we got ourselves real jobs now. Next month, I'm moving my family out of this shitty place. I'm making good money now, and we're moving to those better apartments off of Challenger."

"That's good to hear, Reuben. Gus, too?"

"Yeah, man. We ride to work together. Save money on gas and shit."

"I'm happy for you, Reuben. I may be back in touch soon. Don't hide behind the door with an unloaded .22 again. That's a good way to get shot."

Reuben stared at him in disbelief. "How'd you know it was unloaded?"

Silas gave Reuben a lopsided grin and moved to the door. "It's what I do, Reuben."

Back inside the car, Silas mulled over the information Reuben had shared with them. "We need to make one more stop before we go to HQ."

"Gustavo's?" Joe asked.

"No. There's an undercover agent in town working on another case, but he may have heard something that'll help us."

After a thirty-minute drive, doubling back and circling block after block, Silas finally pulled into a community park. Everyone got out of the car and instinctively scouted the area.

"Wait here. I'll be back." Silas walked off toward a small patch of trees that gave a semblance of cover.

The other men casually walked off in different directions to keep an eye out for anything suspicious while Silas conducted his clandestine spy business. Noah approached Rebel on one of his trips around the perimeter.

"Heather will be moved back to your house when we're on the way to HQ. We're coordinating the time so she'll arrive when you do."

"Shadow's back?"

"Yeah. He's at the hotel now, and he's begging us to leave ASAP because Liz has created a love nest for the two of them."

Rebel couldn't contain his laughter, especially with his imagination running wild with what ideas Liz had for Shadow. "I'm really torn, Reap. Part of me says we need to take as much time as possible to get there so Liz has plenty of time to spend with her man. But a bigger part of me really wants to spend time with my wife."

"Decisions, decisions," Noah chuckled.

"There's nothing that could make me actually want to delay seeing Heather, but I want to make Shadow squirm so badly."

"I did hear Liz yelling something about running him a nice, hot bubble bath," Noah offered and quirked one eyebrow.

"For the sake of national security and the lives of all the civilians, we must do a thorough investigation. Talk to everyone in the city if necessary."

"Thought that may help you make up your mind."

A few minutes later, Silas walked out of the woods and straight to the car. The others joined him, retaking their original seats and waiting until they were out of the park before speaking. All eyes scanned the area as they left, ever vigilant of who and what was in their peripheral vision.

"There are a few guys a little too interested in us," Noah remarked.

"Undercover Vice," Silas replied. "They haven't quite mastered the art yet, have they?"

"Not quite. For the average thug, they're good enough. For a professional, they're too obvious."

"Maybe we should start a new company and train them in the ways of the invisible?" Silas suggested.

"Not a bad idea."

"All right, let's hear it. What'd your spook friend have to say?" Rebel asked.

"I never said he was a spook." Silas cut his eyes to the rearview mirror. "But whatever's about to go down is huge. We can't screw this one up, boys. The chatter on the ground is Rashad has a large-scale attack planned and his cell is recruiting heavily."

"Large-scale, as in what? Are we talking nuclear, chemical, what?" Bull asked.

"They're still trying to figure it out. They've intercepted coded messages and signals that they're trying to decipher."

"Get them. I'm trained to analyze them," Rebel replied. "Maybe I can crack the puzzle."

"I'll see what I can do. The things he's asking for don't align with anything nuclear. I wouldn't discount the possibility of a chemical or biological attack, though."

Noah's cell started ringing, and a smile covered his face. "It's Shadow. Wonder if Liz has him in that bubble bath yet." He smirked before answering. "Yeah, man, what's up?"

The silence in the car became deafening just before the tension notched up tenfold. The laughter immediately dissipated, each man attuned to the others' moods and mannerisms, acting and reacting as a single unit.

"I'm putting you on speaker. Say that again, Shadow."

"Another letter was delivered to the nurses' station, and we had it brought to a nearby restaurant by courier. I met him and just got back into the room to read the letter. This one is addressed to Steve.

> *"You've fought a good fight. You've lived a good life.*
> *But nothing good can stay.*
> *Now close your eyes, and say goodbye.*
> *I'll help you pass away.*

"Brad checked the hospital security system, and it was definitely Rashad. He was wearing a uniform that looked like maintenance, but it doesn't have the hospital logo on it. It's just close enough to blend in and not be questioned by most people. I've put one of our men on Steve's room and another undercover in the hospital."

"You know what this means, right?" Rebel asked.

"What?" Bull replied.

"First letter was to Heather. Second letter is to Steve. Brianna and Chaise are next. Maybe even Sara. He's going through our families to get to us," Rebel replied. "He's already signed his own death warrant. Now he's making it personal, and he's pissing me off."

"You mean we finally get to see Rebel get mad?" Shadow jeered. "This should be good. We'll even have front-row seats to this show."

"Should we move your dad?" Joe asked.

"We can't just yet. He's too sick as it is, and the medications for his clinical trials are there. We'll have to alert the local FBI and law enforcement so they can help with hospital security. If he's after our dad, he could take out half the hospital to get to him," Silas answered.

"Hey, Reap. Brad's program just finished running, and he's all excited about some information he uncovered. Says it's very important, and we need to get over there as soon as possible so he can translate his geek speak to regular English," Shadow interjected.

"We're on our way over there now. Get Heather and meet us at HQ. Park inside the garage, then Rebel can get her back to their house later when it's dark," Noah replied. "We'll be there within twenty minutes."

"Copy that. We're leaving now."

13

CHAPTER THIRTEEN

The large, two-story house on the street behind Rebel and Heather's house served as the headquarters for the team. By the time Noah and the others arrived, Roman, Alex, and Blake had finished their patrol of the neighborhood. With the miniature cameras in place to capture every possible angle around Rebel's house, they were confident any attempts made by Rashad's cell would be seen and quickly thwarted.

Brad had arranged to have furniture delivered by a team of agents who appeared to be everyday movers. The large truck sat parked by the curb for half a day while he pretended to oversee the correct placement of boxes and belongings. To anyone watching, he was simply a new neighbor waiting for the rest of his family to join him in their new home. Undercover crews arrived in nondescript construction company trucks with what appeared to be replacement sheets of drywall and a new door. A quick and simple repair job that would be quickly forgotten after a passing glance from anyone in the vicinity.

Inside those moving boxes, hidden underneath what appeared to be normal household items, was the most high-tech, military-grade equipment available. With each item Brad unpacked, he created an impressive control room in a virtually impenetrable fortress in the expansive entertainment room. The interior walls were lined with bullet-resistant panels, the wooden door was replaced with a steel door and frame, and computer monitors with a continuous display of the entire street covered the L-shaped workstation in the corner.

A large table sat in the middle of the room for the team to scour the original construction blueprints of the subdivision layout. New secure cell phones were laid out for each member of the team. The cells came complete with signal-jamming capabilities and direct chat features over constantly changing radio frequencies to prevent detection in the event of cell signal disruption. The collection of spy-worthy gear and tactical fighting equipment was enough for a small army.

Brad laughed to himself as he thought about how fitting that analogy was. Rashad may have declared his own war first, but Brad knew the Steele team would be the small army that finished it.

"What'd you find, Brad?" Noah asked as he entered the room with his entourage.

The team assembled around the table with Roman, Alex, and Blake, casually picking up their assigned gadgets and settling in for the briefing of Brad's discovery.

Brad opened his mouth to speak and immediately stopped himself when Silas stepped into his line of sight. His eyes narrowed and his brows furrowed upon taking in his appearance. "Reap, did you pick up a hitchhiking, homeless pimp on your way back?"

"Very funny, Bradford. My little brother wouldn't stop by the hotel to let me change first, so I get to be Charlie for a while longer."

"It's for your own protection. You never know when we'll run into one of Rashad's men, or if they'll see you first out somewhere. You have to stay in constant disguise," Noah retorted.

"Yeah, I know that. I have been a spy for a long time, you know. But I don't have to be *Charlie* all the time."

"Stop whining. It's not attractive when badass drug dealers whine," Noah chuckled. "Can we get back to the reason why we're here?"

"You're all here to see me," Shadow announced as he entered the room. "No small bills, please."

Heather walked to Rebel and took the seat next to him. Several of the men exchanged uncertain glances, knowing every bit of information they worked with was classified. With a determined expression, Heather reached over and laced her fingers with Rebel's in a silent declaration of her intentions.

Brad looked to Noah for direction, unsure of how to proceed in mixed company. Noah's lips quirked upward slightly on one side. "Go ahead, Brad. Heather is well aware if she hears something above top secret, we'll have to kill her."

"There are worse things than death, Reap. We could put her on Liz duty," Shadow suggested. "By the time Liz is finished with her, Heather's mind will be so jumbled, she won't know her colors from the alphabet."

"You boys think you're so funny. The truth is you're all afraid of me, and you know better than to try to kick me out of here." Heather rolled her eyes exaggeratedly, but the smile on her face belied her tone.

"I knew Liz reminded me of someone," Shadow flashed his full-on smile.

"Go ahead, Brad," Noah instructed when he quit laughing. "Before a fight breaks out in here."

"I'm still working to piece some of it together, but it's important enough you need to hear it now. I'm actually counting on your collective experience to help connect the dots. First piece is analysis of the chatter we've intercepted. Rebel, your assistance has been requested to help decipher some of these files. The messages have increased—drastically and suddenly—but they're unintelligible gibberish."

"I'll take them," Rebel replied.

"Next up, I searched for orders of anything that could be used to make bombs since that's our boy's specialty. Then I searched for any unusual items that wouldn't normally be delivered to a civilian or to a residential area. Cross-referencing the two files, I've narrowed the search area down to a few specific locations.

"A couple of them are less likely to be his hideout because of the locations and way too much public access. I wouldn't put anything past him, but I'm just not getting the feels from those areas. The one you should check out first is a gated subdivision in a high-end neighborhood. Very pricey, more than the average home, and the houses have ample room between them. This particular house has more yard than most, so it would make sense for his privacy," Brad explained.

"Was he stupid enough to have large shipments sent at once? That doesn't sound like our guy," Bull replied.

"No, these have been spaced out over a period of time. There were some shipments a few weeks ago, then they stopped, and now they've started up again. They're being shipped to that address every few days. With the access we have to government surveillance and intelligence systems, I was able to match these up in a matter of seconds. He's definitely not as tech-savvy as his brother was. Turan would've bought all this on the deep web," Brad explained. "The other addresses haven't had consistent shipments and haven't all been the same items."

"Could still be members of his cell. He could be sending parts to different people, thinking it wouldn't trip any sensors," Noah replied.

"We'll check the other addresses just to be sure. He could've been moving around, too," Shadow added.

"Reap, another letter has been delivered to the hospital. The guy watching over your dad is bringing it up. His shift just ended," Blake informed them.

Blake met him at the door and delivered the letter straight to Reaper. He was silent as he read it, but the vein popping out on his neck gave away his intense anger.

"What the hell?" Reaper demanded

"What does the little pussy have to say this time?" Bull asked.

"Our boy is quite the poet. Now he's after Brianna. Listen to this shit.

Your golden hair, your skin so fair.
Your travel abroad, your deathly fraud.

So quick your wit, so sharp your mind.
All these traits soon will make
An impressive tenth wife."

"Man, I wish he'd bring it on already. He must think his stupid little letters are getting to us, scaring us. He's really just annoying me," Bull replied.

"The problem with terrorist cells is they could go days without being seen when they're under orders to stay invisible. Stocked with enough provisions to last weeks, they could very well be inside one of the houses with the shades drawn tight and not be seen," Shadow replied.

For the following week, the men of Steele Security worked the leads they'd been given. Checking each house took time and around-the-clock monitoring. To avoid stretching their resources too thin, they each took shifts watching one house for a full forty-eight hours before moving on to the next one. They planned to keep this schedule up until someone made a move.

A call from headquarters brought all the men back to the house behind Rebel's home. Each man hoped for some kind of action that didn't involve sitting in a car, staring at an apparently empty house. The delivery of the cryptic poem had been the only physical evidence the cell was still around, and all the men were anxious to put an end to the case as soon as possible.

"Reap," Roman addressed him as soon as the men started filing into the surveillance room. "We have visitors."

All eyes swung to the monitors broadcasting the images from the surveillance cameras. Six figures moved through the darkness, exaggerated in their attempt to be stealthy in their crouched positions. Brad accessed the cameras remotely and activated the infrared night-vision setting. With their faces clearly shown, Brad captured the images and began running the facial recognition software.

"They're looking for Heather," Rebel announced as he entered the room with her in tow. "Let's help them out."

"Forcing their hand?" Silas asked.

"Something like that. I don't like feeling as if they're in control. We can let them think they are while we track them. If they're busy watching her, that car is unmanned, and we can get a tracking device on it," Rebel explained.

"Good plan. These guys are on the same step on the terrorist ladder I was when I was undercover with them. They're not his most skilled players," Silas added.

"Let's go catch some bad guys, babe." Rebel smiled at Heather. "By the way, there'd better not be cameras or bugs inside our house, Brad."

"I don't have a death wish, Rebel," Brad replied with a straight face.

"It wouldn't be me who got to you first, Brad." Rebel replied with a smirk and tugged on Heather's hand.

Following his lead, she rose and they scurried out the back door and across the lawns toward their own back door. Once inside, they strategically opened specific window coverings to limit the view of the inner details of their home. With the TV on and a shared bowl of popcorn, they snuggled closely together on the couch and waited for the terrorist recon team to work their way down the street to find them.

"When these idiots move on, you're all mine," Rebel whispered in Heather's ear. "We've been apart for far too long while I've been on this case. It's almost over, and I'll be so glad when it is."

"What do you have in mind?" she purred.

"I have every inch of your body in mind. I'm thinking about your intoxicating scent when you can't wait another second for me. I can't wait to hear the sounds you make when I put my mouth on you or my hands or my tongue. I want to feel your body underneath mine or on top of mine or both."

His mouth was close to her ear, his breath fanned out across her cheek, heating her to the core. With his arm around her and their bodies close together, it took all of her resolve to stay in place and wait them out.

"Can you hurry up and get rid of these guys?" Heather asked on a heavy breath.

"The guys walking around the neighborhood tonight? They'll be gone soon enough, and I'll have the rest of the night to remind you why you miss me so much when we're apart."

"Braxton Reed, you know exactly what you're doing to me."

"I'm just talking to you right now," he replied before placing a chaste kiss on her neck. "But soon, I'll do much more than just talk. I'll touch you. Kiss you. Lick you. Taste you. I'm a starving man, and you're the only one who can satisfy this hunger."

"Brax," she sighed.

"When I first take you upstairs, I'm going to fuck you without apology. Hard. Fast. Raw. Rough. Just when you think you can't take it a second longer, you'll beg me for more. Every time you think you can't come one more time, I'll prove you wrong. By the time I'm finished with the first round, you'll be as spent as a rag doll."

"Oh, my God." Her hooded eyes and her heaving chest left no doubt how much he affected her.

"Then I'll make love to you. I'll worship your body the way it's meant to be. Slow and steady, I'll prove beyond a shadow of a doubt your body was made to respond only to me. Every time I push inside you, I'll go deeper and your body will clench around me. Holding on to me, begging me to make you come again, until I take mercy on you and let you scream my name one last time before you pass out from exhaustion."

"Give me your gun. I'm going to shoot these guys and get it over with."

He chuckled and shook his head, knowing she was just as likely to shoot them as not. "As much as I'd like to do that myself, we have to let them lead us back to the rest of their cell."

"Brad has leads on where Rashad may be. Let the others go to those houses and find him."

"And if he's not at any of them? And if there are more members of his cell that can finish whatever he has planned?"

"I hate when you're right."

"It only happens once in a while in an argument with you. Let me have this one."

"Fine. I'll let you have it." The challenging gleam in her eye was a complete turn-on for Rebel. She lowered her voice to a seductive whisper and placed her lips against his ear. "I'll let you take me upstairs. Before you fuck me hard and rough, like you know I love it, I'll take you in my mouth and work you over until your knees buckle underneath you. By the time I'm done with you, you'll be gritting your teeth to hold on to any shred of self-control you can manage to muster."

"Fucking hell," Rebel muttered. "Look what you've done." He drew her hand to his crotch and placed it on his hardened cock.

"If you could see what you've done to me, we'd give those guys a real show when they peek through our window," she replied as she stroked him through his jeans.

He captured her mouth with his and held her face with his hands. He forced his tongue inside, taking total ownership of her without waiting for permission. When her muscles relaxed and her innate guard fell, he felt her melt into his embrace. Just when he started to lift her to straddle his lap, his cell phone began to ring.

Without asking, Heather knew who it was and why he was calling. "Your friends are severely cramping my style, Brax."

"Well, if you didn't have a madman stalking you and sending me pictures of you..." He let his teasing insinuation trail off before he answered his phone. She punched his arm as he connected. "Ow! Hello?"

"Ow, hello?" Noah laughed.

"Heather just punched me. I need hazard pay for this job, man," Rebel joked.

"Man, don't you know better than to harass a woman who has a black belt in Brazilian jiu-jitsu? She'll kick your ass and make you submit."

"Don't go dragging my sex life into this. That's not your business."

When the laughter on the other end of the line died down, Noah was finally able to brief Rebel on the latest. "They're two houses down from yours, looking in windows before quickly moving on. They're definitely looking for her. Roman and Alex are ready to tail the car, and we have GPS tracking on it. There's no way they're getting away from us tonight, but I doubt they lead us to Rashad just yet."

"We're ready and waiting. In fact, we're getting a little impatient. Can we just turn on all the outside lights and walk around in the yard? They're slow as fuck."

"Rebel, it's been several weeks since Brianna had the baby, so I know exactly how you feel. But let's not tip them off that we know they're out there, okay? We're watching the outside of your house in case they come back in the middle of the night, so you'll both be off duty. Make the most of it then."

"Expect the favor returned as soon as you're ready, man. Just say the word."

"Taking you up on that, brother. They're moving in your direction now. Look pretty for their cameras."

With that, Noah disconnected, and Rebel hid his secure phone under his leg. When the two dark figures moved into the view of the window, Rebel and Heather both almost laughed out loud.

"It would be funny if it wasn't so damn aggravating," Heather harrumphed. "Let's just go outside, kick their asses, and be done with them already."

"You know I would if it would help stop this. We're on them, babe. Don't worry. Let them take a few pictures of us to prove to their boss they're on top of things, and we'll take them all down at the same time. You'll get to kick the whole group's ass at once."

"Promises, promises. The two stooges are gone. Take me upstairs now. You have promises you're going to make good on tonight."

"Your pleasure," he quipped. "And mine."

14

CHAPTER FOURTEEN

Rebel walked to the window and closed the blinds before turning his heated stare to his wife. After all the years they'd been together, nothing had ever diminished or sated his desire for her. Every touch and taste of her only made him want her more. Even if they didn't already know each other well enough to interpret every expression and every touch, there was no mistaking the desire that burned like a white-hot flame in their eyes when their gazes met.

With a determined stride, he lifted her in his arms. She locked her arms around his neck and her legs around his waist, and their mouths clashed in desperate need. He took the stairs two at a time on his way to the master bedroom. When he kicked the door closed behind him, he immediately turned and pressed her back against it. With one hand supporting her weight, he used the other to remove her shirt. His fingers deftly unhooked the front clasp of her bra, and she let it slide off her arms.

"Brax," she pleaded.

With a growl, his kiss became even more demanding and possessive as he all but devoured her. So consumed with the feel of his mouth on hers, she didn't realize he'd moved her to the bed until she felt her jeans being unbuttoned. Like a predator stalking its prey, he moved with purpose when he crawled up her body.

"You're killing me, Brax," she moaned. "I'm dying a slow, amazing death."

"No, baby, you're not dying an amazing death yet. I'm only getting started with you."

He licked his lips as he raised his head and smirked knowingly at her. "You look so content and relaxed. You're even glowing. I'd say you need this treatment daily."

"At least daily," she agreed.

With a matched tempo, they moved together until their bodies were slick with sweat, their breathing was labored, and their energy was spent. Their mouths connected in a kiss, tongues caressed and danced, and fingers dug into skin when they finally reached the height of their pleasure and fell over the edge together.

With one smooth motion, he rotated them both as one body to avoid crushing her under his weight. Spent from sheer exhaustion, she rested her head on his chest and his arms encircled her, holding her tightly to him, savoring the moment. Within minutes, they were both fast asleep, their bodies still entwined, their hearts beating against the other's chest. It was hours later when Rebel stirred, trying to gingerly move Heather to a more comfortable sleeping position.

"I've missed you so much, Brax," she whispered in the darkness.

"I've missed you too. For the record, I never *want* to leave you, my love. I've never wanted that, and I will never want it."

"I hate it, Brax. I hate being apart from you, and I hate that we've missed out on so much time we could've spent together all these years. I've always been supportive because it's important to you. But it kills me every time I have to watch you leave. And every time, I wonder how much longer we can stay together while we're so far apart."

Though he'd thought along the same lines himself at one point or another, hearing her say the words out loud was like a knife to his heart. The quiver in her voice when she spoke was his only clue that she was crying. "Why didn't you ever tell me you felt this strongly about it?"

"I can't make you choose between your life with me and your life without me, Brax. We agreed to this arrangement a long time ago, so it's not fair for me to expect you to give up everything you've worked for. If I'm not willing to give up my life here, I can't ask you to give up your life in Miami. Somehow, we need to make our lives into a life, though."

"You asked me if I'd give it all up for you, and I told you I would in a heartbeat. You know me well enough by now to know those aren't just idle words to placate you. I honestly mean it. It sounds like you've let this build up for a while without saying anything and you're reaching the end of your rope. I'm not going to lose you, Heather."

"I want a baby, Braxton. I want us to have a family." She held her breath after she'd spoken the words while she waited for his reply.

After several long heartbeats of silence, he finally spoke. "Are you sure? I'm strong, but I'm not strong enough to go through that again."

That. He didn't have to elaborate. She knew exactly what he meant. "Brax, Dalton died from SIDS. It wasn't anything we did or didn't do. As terrible as it was, and as much as it hurt, it wasn't our fault. Of course, I'll be a nervous wreck for the first year after having a baby just because I'll be hyperaware of everything. But after going to nursing school and to counseling, I've learned a lot about what happened to us. We didn't do anything wrong."

"I know," he conceded. "My rational mind knows that, anyway."

"Promise me you'll think about it. We're not getting any younger, you know."

"You know I will."

After a restless night, Rebel and Heather left their house to head to the hotel for a meeting with the others. Brad, Roman, Alex, and Blake were still conducting surveillance of the properties, while the rest of the team worked leads they'd managed to put together from multiple sources. Rebel had enjoyed his assignment the most—his job was to guard his wife's body from every angle, at all hours of the day and night.

"We have a tail." Heather rolled her eyes. "Will they ever give up? They're terrible at this."

Rebel laughed. "Be glad they are. We don't want to lead them to Brianna and Amelia. They've already threatened Brianna's life as it is."

"Let's turn the tables on them. Lose them, but don't lose them, and we can follow them back to where they're staying."

"We already know where they're staying, babe, from the GPS tracker tailing them the other night. But they're not the guys we need to bust just yet. Although, this is a different car, and they could very well be staying somewhere else."

"They could lead us to the ones we need to nab first. You never know."

"You're going stir-crazy," Rebel replied, suddenly understanding.

"Yes, I am. I can't stare at the same four walls for much longer. This is the last week I have off of work, and then I need to get back to it. Two weeks off is a long time in the life of an oncology nurse. I haven't even gotten to see Steve Steele."

"Okay. We'll have some fun with your inept stalkers first, and when we get to the hotel, I'll suggest we go see Steve later this evening. I know Noah and Brianna have talked to him every day, so he's still doing okay. I'm sure he'd love to see everyone in person, though. Silas will have to go in disguise again."

"We can all go in disguise. It'll be fun."

"Yeah, you're definitely getting cabin fever all right." Rebel grinned and laid his hand on her leg. With a light squeeze, he continued. "Let's see what they've got, shall we?"

"It's about time we get to do something other than hiding out inside the house. I love you, babe, but I'm used to being on the move. I've missed training at my Brazilian jiu-jitsu academy. My rolling partners will think I've dropped out," she complained.

"No, they won't. They know you're obsessed with training, sparring, rolling, and otherwise taking them to the mat to make them tap out."

"Yes, that is very true," she agreed with a nod. "Let's make *these* guys tap out now."

As the light turned yellow, Rebel gunned the engine and sped through the intersection. After making a last-second left turn, he immediately turned right and parked in a street-level parking lot. The car that tailed them got caught behind other cars at the red light. From Rebel's vantage point, he watched the two men through his binoculars. The driver banged his fist on the steering wheel, anger seared on his face, and the passenger blatantly yelled in frustration.

"I think Dude Two is trying to get Dude One to drive on the wrong side of the road," Rebel chuckled. "These two are definitely not in the upper echelon of competent terrorists. In fact, I'm not convinced they're not meant to be a distraction."

"What if they are, Brax? I didn't even think of that."

"It doesn't matter if they are, babe. We need to vet it either way. Any little bit of information we can glean is better than no information at all."

"Here they come." Heather couldn't contain the excitement in her voice when she pointed toward the gunmetal gray compact car that darted around the other vehicles immediately when the light changed.

Rebel waited patiently as they passed by without a sideways glance in his direction. Allowing a few cars in between, he pulled out of the parking lot and casually followed them. Their erratic driving pattern of speeding to the next cross street, slowing to a crawl, then speeding up again until they reached the next intersection would soon attract the attention of the local police. "They're panicking, babe. They can't find us."

Cool and calm, Rebel continued following them, hidden in plain sight within the increasingly angry pack of drivers who were unlucky enough to be trapped behind the chaos. When they finally gave up searching for Rebel, they made a quick U-turn and sped off in the opposite direction. Rebel made the same maneuver at the next light to keep distance between them and not draw their attention to the cars behind them. As he suspected, they seemed oblivious to the casual tail following them.

They followed the nondescript car to a part of town where the residents turned a blind eye and a deaf ear to anything that went on around them. Any questions created problems, and every family had enough problems of their own without inviting trouble from strangers. As long as they didn't see, didn't hear, and didn't know, they couldn't be held accountable for anyone else's actions. When the terrorists pulled into the driveway of their run-down, ramshackle house, no one even glanced in their direction.

Rebel and Heather parked one street over, a block away from their targets, and kept a vigilant watch on the house. "This isn't one of the addresses Brad found," Heather pointed out.

"No, it's not. This is new intel."

"Is this what your job is like every day?"

"Some variation of it, yeah. Some days are more exciting than doing a simple tail and sitting through a boring stakeout. Today is a good day, though, because you're with me."

"This is actually fun. I love this cloak-and-dagger shit."

"It's not so much fun when the bullets start flying, babe."

"You can teach me what to do, Brax. You know all the tricks of the trade."

He cut his eyes to her and slowly raised his eyebrows. "You want me to teach my wife, the love of my life, about participating in a live ammunition shootout?"

"Yes."

"I know that look, Heather. You're not going to let this go, are you?"

"Nope."

"All right. But you have to promise me something first."

"Okay," she replied, drawing the word out with a dubious tone. "What?"

"You absolutely will not engage in anything remotely related to a shootout until you've completed the full training for it."

"I'll make that promise, as long as you promise to actually deliver the full training program within a reasonable amount of time that'll be determined by me at a later date," she countered.

"You can't determine the length of the training when you're the trainee. I'll know when you're ready."

"And I know you, and you'll keep me as a trainee for the rest of my life. You have to guarantee I'll move past trainee status within one year." Heather crossed her arms over her chest and gave him the most obstinate expression she could muster.

"When you meet the same proficiencies we require of anyone who joins our firm, you move past trainee status. If it takes you longer than a year, that's not my fault," Rebel negotiated.

"Are these proficiencies already in writing?"

"Yes."

"Deal."

"I know I'm going to regret this."

"Let's go peek in their windows," she suggested.

"In broad daylight? Have you not watched any spy movies?"

"Come on. It'll be fun. It's boring just sitting in the car, doing nothing but staring at the front door."

"This is part of the job, babe. This is also what you're signing up for. We can't give away our position and let them move somewhere else we don't know about. Speaking of, I'll send Brad the address now." With a few clicks on his phone, he sent the information to Brad so he could start gathering information and set up full-time surveillance.

Within minutes, an older car pulled up alongside them and rolled down the passenger window. Rebel looked the two guys over carefully and smiled. "Hello, Special Agents with the FBI. Where's your Crown Vic to alert the whole neighborhood you're with the Feds?"

"We're dressed down and in a car that fits the neighborhood. What more do you want?" The agent in the passenger seat huffed and rolled his eyes.

"You need to slouch down in the seat. Your back is straight as a rod. The people around here don't sit like that, especially when they're waiting for someone to show up to do business. Mess your hair up a little more. Narrow your eyes, but not like you're squinting from the sun. More like you're daring anyone to look in your general direction. The clothes and the car do not make the undercover man, your attitude does," Rebel explained. "I don't want you boys killed on my watch."

"Appreciate the concern," the driver deadpanned.

"And don't speak so formal. That's another dead giveaway that'll get you killed."

"We're here to take over surveillance for you. I'm Stahl, and this is Baer," the driver replied.

"'Preciate it," Rebel replied pointedly as he cranked the engine. "Yell if you need anything."

On the way back to the hotel, Reaper called Rebel's cell phone. "Hey, Reap. We're on our way."

The silence caught Heather's attention, and she knew something was wrong from the expression on his face.

"I'm putting you on speaker. Can you repeat that for Heather?"

"Sure. We received another letter from Rashad today. This one is for my mother.

> *With Steve soon gone, my task will be done.*
> *From you, what I want, I'll take.*
> *From your nightmare, you'll never wake.*
> *To a new land, you'll travel.*
> *And before long, your son will unravel."*

"That sounds like a threat to take your mom away, but also an indirect threat to you, Reap. He's going after your whole family," Rebel replied. "We'll be there in fifteen."

CHAPTER FIFTEEN

"Eyes on primary target," Shadow whispered into his comm. "Positive ID on Rashad. Shoot to kill approved?"

"Negative," Reaper replied. "Orders straight from the top. Latest intel says chatter is going wild. We've located the only known head of the cell, but he's not the top dog. We need him to find who he's taking orders from.

"Seriously?" Shadow answered, his voice thick with disappointment. "But I just got a new gun. It hasn't killed anyone yet."

Hushed chuckles reverberated through the comms. "Don't let that asshole get away with that, Reap," Rebel replied. "Primary threatened my wife first. My gun gets the pleasure."

"You win. I sure as fuck ain't getting married just to shoot someone," Shadow retorted.

"Man, if you got married, you'd be the one getting shot," Rebel countered.

Louder, uncontrollable snickers rolled through their earpieces as the men tried to contain their laughter at Shadow's expense. "I honestly can't argue with that," Shadow chuckled. "Primary on the move toward the west entrance."

"Delivery truck moving in your direction," Bull replied.

"Primary disabled the alarm system. If the delivery truck stops here, I'm gaining entry while he's distracted," Shadow whispered. "I have the alarm code if needed. Simple system, easy to bypass if I have to."

"Copy that," Reaper confirmed.

The delivery truck stopped at the curb, and the driver walked across the grass to deliver another large box of supplies. Rashad stood on the front porch with the door standing open behind him. He smiled and made idle chitchat with the driver while he signed for the package on the handheld device.

"Get the name he just used," Reaper commanded. "We're cross-checking everything."

"Copy that," Brad replied. "Rashad is signing the same name as the owner of the house. Sloppy, sloppy, sloppy. The owner has business ties back to his uncle, the ambassador."

"He doesn't know he's being sloppy. His cockiness will be his downfall," Bull responded. "It's the letters—he thinks we're distracted by them."

"And everyone he works with is spread out across the whole city. No one lives within ten miles of the others. That's for a reason," Silas advised. "Don't be fooled by his aloofness. Whatever they're planning, they have contingency plans."

"Agreed," Reaper replied. "So we take them all at once. Rebel, have you finished with those encrypted files?"

"Negative. I've partly decoded one, but they change the key frequently."

"I'm in," Shadow interjected. "Finding a comfy spot in the corner."

"I hope you took a piss before you went inside," Bull joked.

"Well. I didn't have to go, but now that you've mentioned it..."

"Delivery truck leaving," Bull noted. "Primary inside."

"He went downstairs," Shadow whispered. "There's a basement. Starting the jammer and going radio silent for a few. If there are any interior cameras, they'll be inoperable now." He retrieved a small signal jammer from his pocket and turned it on.

Shadow waited several minutes until he was sure Rashad was staying in the basement before leaving his hiding place. He moved silently through the expansive home, placing concealed cameras in various locations to provide his team with a perfect view of the interior. As small as miniature buttons, they came complete with strong adhesive on the back so they could be affixed to furniture, picture frames, or most anything else. When he'd covered all the areas he could, Shadow moved back to the door he'd entered through and crept back outside.

Shadow turned the signal jamming device off and waited for Brad to pick up the tiny spy cameras. "He forgot to turn the alarm back on," Shadow whispered when he was back in his place.

"All cameras are transmitting now," Brad notified the team. "Man, I love our new tech. Can you guys stay on active duty so we can keep everything they gave us to use?"

"You can always enlist," Bull deadpanned. "Then you can keep whatever you want."

"We need to get back into that house and see what's in the basement. I'd bet all of Brad's tech on finding more than what we need down there. I'll take first watch. If he leaves under the cover of darkness, I'm going down there," Reaper decided.

"Why don't you let me take first watch, Reap?" Shadow asked. "You need to go see your dad while he's awake. If our boy leaves, I have a few cameras left I can use in the basement."

"Ten-four. Brad, alert me immediately if Shadow enters the house again," Reaper replied.

The men left in different directions, covering their tracks and staying alert for any indication they'd been spotted. When they were each positive it was safe, they made their way back to the hotel. As soon as they walked through the door, Brianna, Chaise, and Heather were waiting impatiently for their safe return.

"Noah," Brianna sighed with relief and rushed into his arms. "It's about time."

"I was perfectly safe. Nowhere near harm, princess," he assured her.

"I think I'm getting too old for this," she laughed. "It isn't exciting anymore."

"See, Noah said there was no danger. Why couldn't I go with you?" Heather pulled her head back to look Rebel in the eye. "You said it would be dangerous."

"It would be dangerous for you to go. You'd try to storm the keep." He smiled before kissing her. "You were safer here than you would've been with me."

"Silas, come give me a hug and a big kiss," Liz asserted. "You look like you need someone to come home to."

While sputtering and coughing on the drink of water he'd swallowed just as Liz spoke, he pounded on his chest with his fist to clear his airway. "Um, well, I'd love to give you a hug, Liz." Silas wrapped his arm around her shoulders, lightly squeezed her, and kissed her on the top of the head, but his gaze swept toward Emily's amused smile.

"Where's Shadow?" Liz asked.

"He's still on the job."

"He was supposed to teach me some spy tricks this evening," Liz huffed. She looked up at Silas with wonder. "Hey, you're CIA, too. You know how to do the spy makeup tricks. I'll let you show me all your secrets." She waggled her eyebrows at him and swayed her hips a little more forcefully as she walked away. "Let's go to your room, Silas. Joe claimed he was too busy guarding all of us to teach me anything while you fellows were gone. It's time—right now."

Noah slid his hand over his mouth, trying to wipe the smile from his face, but he couldn't hide it. "You'd better get going, big brother. She doesn't like to be kept waiting. She's liable to help herself to your stuff."

"Silas," Liz called out. "What is this in here? Do you wear the thongs? I didn't know they made them for men, too. Woo, these are downright sexy."

Silas glanced around the room, catching all the snickers and stares, and was so horrified he was unable to respond.

"Oh, wait," she yelled. "It would've been sexy, but this patch of fabric is tiny. You know, I've seen commercials about these pills that enlarge your penis. You should look into those. They might help you get a girl. It didn't say how much the pills makes it grow, but even a little is better than nothing. Especially in your case."

"Liz, get out of my disguises. That's an eye patch, not a thong!" Silas yelled as he stormed into the bedroom.

"No need to be ashamed now, young man. We'll call it an eye patch if that makes you feel better."

"If anyone is going to the hospital with Bri and me, let's plan on leaving in the next fifteen minutes or so. We need to go see Dad while we can," Noah told the group.

"I'm going," Heather replied. "I need to check on my patients."

"That means I'm going, too." Rebel smiled.

"We're all going, Reap," Bull interjected. "We're family, no matter what."

Minutes later, the group reassembled in the common meeting area to go to the hospital together. When Chaise walked into Brianna's suite, she stopped short and her mouth dropped open. "Umm, how did you get into this room?"

"I can get into any room, sweetheart." The disheveled man sat casually on the couch, unconcerned with his intrusion, and held one bushy eyebrow in a defiant arc. His clothes were well-worn and varying shades of brown. So much so, he almost blended in with the couch beneath him. His short brown hair lay flat on his head, and his light five-o'clock shadow effectively hid any identifying characteristics. "What do you think you can do about it?"

"She doesn't have to do anything about it," Bull said as he stepped around Chaise, shielding her with his massive body. "That's what she has me for. You have about two seconds to start talking before you tragically fall from this luxury high-rise hotel floor."

"You can try."

Bull moved toward the man with his threatening stance and determined demeanor but was stopped by a large hand gripping his shoulder. "It's okay, Bull," Silas assured him. "Don't let him rile you."

When Bull turned and looked at Silas, he automatically stepped back and did a double take. Silas's normally black hair was sandy blond and curly. Even his eyebrows matched his lighter hair. The scruff that covered his jawline wasn't there just an hour before. His chocolate brown eyes were now a nondescript shade of green. "You have Silas's voice, but you don't look one bit like Silas."

"Well, I wouldn't *sound* like Silas if Liz hadn't stolen my voice synthesizer." Silas nodded toward the man sitting on the couch.

"Liz?" Chaise asked incredulously. "Is that you?"

"It's me, sweet pea. Silas made me up into one bad dude, didn't he?"

"So good that it's really freaking me out. How? What? I don't even know where to start with my questions," Chaise replied.

"Oh, no. Not you, too," Silas replied. "I've been tortured enough by Liz over my mad spy skills. No more trainees."

"Don't you worry, sweet girl. If you want to know anything, you just ask me. I'll get it out of Silas one way or another," Liz assured her.

Chaise laughed, knowing Liz would do just that if asked. "What's your clandestine name?"

"Chris Evans. No relation to the superhunk."

Silas shook his head and rolled his eyes at Liz. "You're supposed to pick an easily forgettable name."

"And you are?" Chaise asked Silas.

"Neil Brown."

"Boring," Liz retorted.

"How did you change your voice to a man's voice?" Chaise asked Liz.

"I could tell you, but then I'd have to kill you." Liz winked. "I've always wanted to say that. It's this little chip on my neck, hidden under a thin piece of latex that looks like skin. A little adhesive, a bit of blending, and voila—I'm a man."

"Let's go, guys," Noah announced as he, Brianna, and Amelia emerged from the bedroom. "Rebel and Heather are meeting us at the hospital, then they'll go back to their house tonight."

"Okay," Rebel announced.

Heather turned her attention to him as he drove and waited for him to finish his thought. After several heartbeats, she realized he had apparently already finished. "Okay? Okay, what?"

"Okay, I'm ready to have a baby. I'm ready to start a family. I'm ready to spend every day with you. As soon as this case is wrapped up and I'm off active duty again, we'll start actively trying to get pregnant. In the meantime, we'll keep practicing until we're perfect.

"I'll give my notice to Reaper as soon as possible so he can start looking to replace me. I don't want to do it just yet and distract him from the case, though. Roman is doing really well. Maybe Reap will take a chance and promote him into my position. I'll move back here, and we'll figure out the rest together."

"You're really going to quit the job you love, leave your best friends, and move back here?"

"I love you more." He shrugged. "There's never been any question about that."

"And you're sure you want to have a baby?"

"I'm sure. I watch Reaper and Bri with Amelia, and I know they're happier than they've ever been. They both wear their hearts on their sleeves, and there'll never be a day Reaper doesn't worry about them, but they'll never regret having her. You're right, we've missed enough time together living out our own lives. We put our marriage second whether we meant to or not."

"I never intentionally meant to put you or our marriage second, Brax," Heather replied in a pained whisper. Her eyes held a faraway gaze, lost in thought and retrospection.

"My best psycho-babble guess is we've lived our lives this way out of fear. Fear of a repeat. Fear that everyone was right when they told us we'd never make it. Fear that too much time together would bring all the memories flooding back to the surface and we wouldn't be able to deal with the pain. The truth is I've never been able to deal with the pain and the memories, but it's worse without you by my side.

"So before we do this—before we fully commit to it—I need you to be completely honest with me. Do I remind you of him? Of Dalton? Do you see him when you look at me?"

Heather turned in her seat to fully face him. "When I look at you, I see the one person I love most in the world. I see the boy I grew up with, the man I love, and the only one I'd ever want to be the father of my children. Of course, I think of Dalton when I look at you, but only because I would've wanted him to grow up to be just like you. The truth is, I'll see all of our children in you, and I wouldn't want to change that for anything."

"You have no idea how much I need you. You've always stood by me, loved me, believed in me, no matter what happened. You've walked through hell just to be beside me. No matter what the future holds, nothing can ever make me leave your side." Rebel squeezed her hand in his, emphasizing his sincerity.

"I feel guilty about you leaving Steele Security, your friends. I know they'll support you, too, but I also know how they've depended on you to have their backs. Will they secretly blame me for breaking up their little family?"

The concern in her eyes and her voice was sincere. The men had been through life-and-death missions together, formed bonds others couldn't comprehend, and trusted each other implicitly. The oaths they took weren't pledged lightly, and the code of honor directing their promises ran deep in their veins. Would they view her as the person who disrupted their carefully constructed world?

"My love and commitment to you have never been kept secret from them, Heather. They'll all support whatever decision we make because they're our friends and they love us. We know what's best for our life together, and that's all they want. It's not like we won't ever see them again," Rebel assured her.

"Brax, I'm so excited about this I can hardly wait. Can't we just go shoot Rashad and close the case right now?"

Rebel threw his head back in laughter. "I thought your martial arts training taught you to be patient, watch your opponent for weaknesses, and then use them against him to take him down."

"It did teach me all of that, absolutely. And Rashad's weakness is a bullet to the head. I'd like to use that weakness to take him down."

"You're a little too much like me, babe," he laughed. "It's kind of scary."

"I haven't been this excited to start a new chapter in my life in a long time. I never realized it, but looking forward to this makes it seem like the rest of my life has been put on hold, just waiting for this moment. I'm only trying to help it along."

"You have no idea how much I appreciate the gesture, but we really need to get them all at once. A bullet to Rashad's head would only give someone else a spot to move into."

Rebel parked in the hospital parking garage, and hand in hand, they walked inside. Heather's step had a new spring in it, her uncontainable delight bubbling over, while Rebel appeared invincible and proud to have the love of his life at his side. Heather's coworkers stopped their activities and watched her with questioning expressions.

"You look suspiciously happy today," Becca commented as she approached Heather. "Did you finally snap and leave all sanity behind?"

"Something like that." She beamed. "My husband is going to move in with me permanently very soon."

"You are one brave man," Becca teased. "Just going out to eat with her is scary enough. I can't imagine living with her all the time."

"Don't listen to her, babe. She has begged and begged to move in with me, but I won't let her. She's just jealous of you," Heather commented to Rebel. Turning back to Becca, she continued. "How are my patients? Have you been mean to them while I've been away?"

"Of course. That's my job, isn't it?" she joked. "You know I'm not mean to them. They love me. Steve's been asking about you, though. Since Sara has been staying here with him over the past week, he doesn't get enough firsthand information about your well-being. You should probably go see him first."

"That's exactly where I'm headed. Have you seen any strange men hanging around the last few days? Anyone you haven't seen before suddenly show up?"

"No. The big, scary guys parked outside Steve's room have been pretty effective at keeping the creepers away."

"Great, thanks. We're going to visit Steve now. I'll talk to you later."

As Heather and Rebel walked away, Heather looked up at him and whispered, "That's odd, isn't it? He sent a letter threatening Steve's life, then doesn't show up here again. Do you think he's waiting for Steve to be discharged?"

"No, I don't. I think the letters are only mean to distract us, divide up our resources, and give his cell more breathing room. He knows we have to err on the side of caution. In fact, I think he's banking on it."

Heather knocked on Steve's door and slowly pushed it open when she heard Sara call out. "How's my favorite patient in the whole world doing this evening?"

"Better now that my favorite nurse in the whole world finally showed back up," Steve replied weakly. "Are you finished being a slacker now?"

"Nowhere near finished. In fact, I'm getting a little too used to being off work. Think they'd pay me to stay away?"

By keeping up her normal, witty banter with him, she was able to hide her concern for his increasingly gray skin, gaunt appearance, and lackluster eyes. The nearly lethal cocktail of experimental chemotherapy drugs was taking a hard toll on his already compromised health. The treatment always affected people differently, but all of the more aggressive schedules eventually resulted in the same outcome.

"No way I'd let that happen," Steve smiled. "They know I'm the boss around here."

"I guess we need to get you well as soon as possible so I can kick you out of here, then," Heather teased. "Besides, it seems unfair to pick on you while you're a patient. It's just too easy."

"Don't you worry, little girl. I'm going to beat this. One way or another."

After a quick kiss to his cheek and a promise to visit him again soon, Rebel and Heather went room to room, checking in on her patients and visiting with her coworkers. Most asked when she'd return to work, but she had to keep her answers vague because of the potential threat to national security Rashad and his group posed. As long as he remained on the loose, she knew she had to limit her time around others so they didn't also become a target.

16

CHAPTER SIXTEEN

"This group couldn't be inconspicuous if we tried," Liz commented aloud as they walked down the hospital corridor toward Steve's room. "Look at you men. All buff, sexy, and dominant in every cell of your body. Not a single one of you blends in like I do. Face it, I was born to be a spy."

"Liz," Silas chastised her with the tone of his voice. "We're not trying to blend in. We're out in the open, in plain sight. If we didn't want to be seen, you wouldn't ever know we were there."

Turning to Noah, Silas asked, "How the hell did I become her new best friend?"

"Shadow took first watch."

"Bastard," Silas muttered under his breath.

"I heard that," Liz remarked. "You'll pay for that later."

"Sorry," he replied begrudgingly, only because he knew Liz would make good on her threat otherwise.

When they reached Steve's door, Noah turned and looked at the horde waiting behind him. "Maybe we should take turns going in and not crash in all at once?"

"You and Brianna go ahead," Chaise suggested. "Let him hold

Amelia while he has some energy. By the time he gets through all of us, he'll be worn-out."

Noah kissed her cheek. "Good thinking, little sister. Bri and I will be out in a few minutes, though I have a feeling we'll have to leave Amelia with Mom."

"I'm going to roam around the halls and see if I can find my son. He may still be here making rounds," Liz announced. "I want to see how long it takes him to recognize me in this getup."

"Don't wander off too far," Noah replied. "Unless you take Silas with you."

"Ppffftttt," Liz retorted. "He'd give me away in a heartbeat. I'll be fine."

Noah, Bull, and Silas all exchanged glances as Liz sauntered away, working her best masculine walk as much as she could. She had to admit, to herself if not to Silas, her disguise was just bland enough to make her nearly invisible in the crowded hallways. No distinguishing features, nothing that was particularly interesting, and nothing that anyone would remember once they'd passed her and moved on their way. The conversations she was able to eavesdrop on amazed her and made her want it even more.

She continued her leisurely stroll, glancing around for her son the doctor when she remembered her original purpose. People everywhere shared the most personal information because they didn't realize anyone else was around. It was all far too interesting for her to ignore or resist. After a few twists and turns through the connecting hallways, she found herself in a more deserted area of the hospital. Unwavering in her quest, she continued her exploration with a relaxed casualness until a familiar face stopped her cold.

He wore a navy blue uniform that could've easily been mistaken for a maintenance crew worker. His ball cap sat low on his forehead, shielding the majority of his face, coupled with the fact that he kept his eyes on the floor as he walked. But the glimpse she got was all she needed. The similarity to Turan, the man who'd tried to kill her, was unmistakable. She had no doubt the man walking slightly ahead of her was his brother, Rashad.

The very man of the hour.

She slowed her pace, taking advantage of the advanced age her disguise suggested she was to avoid arousing his suspicion while she followed him. When he turned, opened a door, and disappeared into a room, she quickened her pace to read the plaque on the door. *Medical Gas Storage Room. Caution: Oxidizing Gas(es) Stored Within. No Smoking. No open flames.*

A chill ran down her spine, causing her whole body to shiver from the ominous undertone of the commonplace placard. A sign anyone else would pass by without a second thought suddenly became a genuine cause for panic when an explosives expert was added to the mix. Liz slipped into a janitorial closet a few doors down and on the opposite side of the hall. She left the door slightly cracked to watch for Rashad so she could try to figure out what he had planned.

When the door to the medical gases storage room opened, Rashad pushed a large metal cart loaded with oxygen tanks, the factory seal still visible on the gauges to indicate they were completely full cylinders. The tanks weren't secured in any discernible fashion and rocked unsteadily as he rolled the cart through the doorway. When he turned to lock the door behind him, one of the cylinders rolled off the bottom rack, making a loud clanging noise when it hit the floor.

Seizing her chance, Liz slipped out of the closet and strode up behind an anxious Rashad. She calmly picked up the wayward tank and handed it to him. "Seems like they'd make these carts to hold the tanks vertically so they couldn't roll off and hit your foot."

After all the years her son was in college, medical school, internship, and residency before joining his current practice, Liz knew a thing or two about hospital protocol. Like how the medical gas storage room was supposed to be locked so only personnel could access it, and the tanks were supposed to be transported in a specific vertical storage cart. Her nonchalant statement was meant to be a test of how educated Rashad was on hospital protocols.

"I should invent one and make a lot of money, huh?" Rashad

replied, no hint of recognition in his eye when he briefly made eye contact. Her disguise was holding true. "It would make my job easier, anyway."

"Yeah, and at least a computer couldn't replace the work you do. All these high-tech gadgets the young people use today," *Chris Evans* tsked. "Everyone's too dependent on computers these days. Don't you agree?"

"You're right. Everything is electronic now."

Liz could tell Rashad only replied with quick, noncommittal replies to be polite while avoiding prolonging the conversation. She also knew his social skills were no match for her own.

"You look like you're fairly young, part of the Millennials who grew up with a laptop in one hand and a cell phone in the other. Think you could come to my wife's hospital room and fix our laptop for us?"

"I'm afraid I wouldn't be much help. My brother was the tech-savvy one in the family, but I never cared much for computers."

"Let me guess. You were more into the outdoorsy, physical stuff?"

"Something like that." Rashad nodded, then glanced longingly down the corridor. Away from the intruder and the conversation he wanted no part in.

"Just as well. Those techies are usually pansies. It was just a few months back when one of those wimpy boys tried to kill an old lady. You remember that? It made national news. They were somewhere in Colorado, though. Not around here. He wasn't even man enough to kill a helpless old lady. Not that I'm condoning killing old ladies, mind you. I just mean a young man should have more gumption than an old lady has."

Liz watched with masked amusement as Rashad worked his jaw, biting back his anger. He was desperate to retaliate, but he knew he couldn't without giving himself away. She opened her mouth to continue her veiled assault on Rashad's family when her cell phone began ringing. Rashad seized the opportunity to escape from his chatty captor. With a single nod goodbye to her, he quickened his stride and pushed the cart of tanks down the hall.

"Chris Evans," Liz answered.

"Liz. Where are you?" Noah asked. "We've been worried about you."

"I've just been talking to Rashad."

"You what?" Noah shouted.

"He's here in the hospital, but he's not here for us." Liz relayed her location and the entire interaction to Noah while he, Bull, and Silas made their way in her direction. When they reached her, she pointed down the hall. "He went that way, but I couldn't follow him without arousing his suspicion."

"I'll take it," Silas replied. "He'll recognize anyone else. Have Roman and Blake get the ladies out of here before Rashad sees them. Make sure Rebel and Heather are gone, too."

"They are," Bull replied. "Rebel sent me a text a few minutes ago saying they were going back to their house in case we needed them for anything."

"Liz, call your son and see if there's any way we can get Dad set up in the hotel with around-the-clock nursing care. If he can be moved, we need to do it—for his safety and everyone else's. Rashad is getting ready to make his move if he's stealing oxygen tanks," Silas directed.

"I don't understand what oxygen tanks have to do with making a move soon. But I'll call Daryl right away," Liz agreed.

"We really need Rebel to finish deciphering those encrypted files. This piece of the puzzle may shed some light on how to decode the parts he's having trouble with. I'll call him on my way back and fill him in. I'll meet you back at HQ in two hours." Silas stopped and met Noah's gaze pointedly. "Watch your six, little brother."

"Copy that. You do the same."

Noah watched his brother's back until Silas was out of his line of sight. The sinking feeling settled like a lead weight in the pit of his stomach. "Let's go," he said solemnly. "It's going to be a long night."

On their way back to Steve's room, Liz and Bull were each on their phones, making arrangements to keep their loved ones protected. Noah's phone rang, and that bad feeling he'd had suddenly turned grave.

"Let's hear it, Shadow," Noah answered.

"Reap, it's bad, man. Bad, bad. The residue indicates he's been concocting a mixture of acetone, acid, and industrial-grade hydrogen peroxide. From the amount of supplies Brad has tracked and the types of containers he ordered, his group will have very deadly and portable bombs," Shadow explained. "We need to make a move of some kind, man, or we'll look completely incompetent when everything goes down."

"Acetone, acid, and industrial-strength hydrogen peroxide? TATP. He just stole a large cart full of oxygen tanks from the hospital."

"My guess is that's where he found the high-test hydrogen peroxide, too. There aren't many other places that would need industrial-strength peroxide. The oxygen supply is self-explanatory."

"Silas is meeting us back at HQ in two hours. We're heading over there now to create our battle plan. He thinks he'll have enough intel to help Rebel piece together the last of the cipher code on those encrypted files. We can at least start contacting the cooperating agencies and arrange twenty-four-seven surveillance on all the locations we've identified," Noah replied.

"I'll be waiting for you there in twenty," Shadow replied and disconnected.

"Daryl is on his way here to make the arrangements for Steve. He'll be moved tonight, and two home health nurses will stay with them in one of the suites on our floor at all times. Your dad will be well taken care of, Noah," Liz assured him. "As much as Heather loves him, I wouldn't be surprised if she didn't insist on helping too."

"Thank you, Liz, and thank Daryl for me." He turned to the men and continued. "We need to move now. He's using TATP, so whatever he's planning will happen in the next few days, if that long."

"Hello, Braxton. It's been a while since I last saw you. How have you been?" Emmett asked as he stood to shake hands.

"I've been good, sir. Just very busy with work over the last few months."

The relationship between the two men was better than when Rebel and Heather first married, but not by much. Each man tolerated the other for the sake of family, but the mutual animosity simmered just under the surface. Their contention often made their standing country club dinner reservations awkward at times.

"Too busy to come home to see your wife?"

Rebel inhaled a deep breath and kept his eyes trained on Emmett's. "I can assure you the only reason I haven't been home with my wife in a while is because the case I've been on is crucial. And top secret. But I'm confident it'll wrap up soon."

"Dad," Heather interjected sternly. "I talk to my husband every single day, multiple times a day, even. Not once have I ever felt like the case came before me, nor have I ever felt the need to make him feel guilty for doing this country a great service."

"Braxton, I'm sorry—that's not what I meant, though I see how it could be easily misinterpreted. I know how important Heather is to you. I was only saying you must've been really busy if you couldn't get home to see her," Emmett clarified.

"No apology necessary," Rebel replied coolly.

"We have wonderful news," Heather stated emphatically, quickly changing the subject.

"Let's hear it," Kay encouraged her daughter.

"Braxton is leaving Steele Security after this case is wrapped up and moving back here permanently."

"Oh, Braxton, that is great news. Heather is obviously ecstatic, but I'm sure your parents are as well," Kay replied sincerely.

"I actually haven't even had a chance to tell them yet. Moving back is something I've considered for quite a while, but now I know it's time." He reached across and took Heather's hand in his before he continued. "My wife is more important to me than anything."

"I'm really so very happy for you both," Kay replied. "Have you started exploring other employment opportunities? Or will you start your own company here?"

Rebel chuckled. "We honestly haven't gotten that far in our discussions yet. This case is demanding my full attention at the moment, so I'm avoiding anything that divides my focus."

Emmett pressed his lips together into a tight line and glanced around the restaurant. He cleared his throat and looked at Rebel. "It just so happens the head of my security department is retiring soon. I need someone dependable, knowledgeable, and trustworthy to take over. In all honesty, I can't think of anyone who better fits that description than you. I won't put you on the spot for an answer right now, but think it over and let me know in a couple of days or so."

"I'll do that. Thank you, sir."

"Kay and I are leaving next week, and we'll be gone for several weeks. We're acquiring another company, and as the president and CEO, I have to be there for the final regulatory compliance review. Plus, it's just better for the overall morale of the employees who are being acquired. The whole mergers and acquisition process leaves them all feeling very vulnerable."

"If there's anything I can do to help while you're away, don't hesitate to say the word," Rebel replied. "I'm happy to do whatever you need me to."

"Just take care of my little girl, Brax. Make her happy. That's all a father can really ask of his son-in-law," Emmett replied with a genuine smile. One that confirmed he already knew Rebel wouldn't disappoint him.

Conversations during dinner flowed easier between the two men than ever before. Guards were lowered. Walls were torn down. Beginning bonds were formed, however fragile. But it was enough to allow hope to take root, along with a renewed sense of excitement for what the future would hold for their extended families.

Back in the car on the way home, Rebel glanced over at Heather, noting the natural glow on her face that only came from true happiness. "I've been waiting all damn day to get you home alone."

"Oh, yeah?" She grinned as she cut her eyes sideways toward him.

"Definitely. It's been a long day, and it's going to be an even longer night. I have you all to myself, and I plan to turn you every way but loose."

"I love when you talk dirty to me," she purred.

"Yeah, I know you do. When I tell you everything I want to do to you. When I tell you how I'm going to take you. When I pick you up and carry you over my shoulder to the bedroom to have my way with you."

"You need to hurry up and get me home."

"We're going to start practicing to have that baby. Practice makes perfect, you know."

"You're going to make my ovaries explode from just talking about it."

Rebel reared his head back in laughter. "We can't have that. I'm going to take care of you as soon as I get you home."

The second they walked into the house, hands groped and bodies collided in desperate need of the other. Rebel was never happier to made good on a promise.

CHAPTER SEVENTEEN

"You've been staring at that computer screen for hours. You're going to go blind," Heather complained.

Rebel chuckled but didn't look up. "I spent a lot of time deciphering hidden code during my time in the Army. I'm immune to blindness now."

"Are you also immune to a good, swift kick in the pants? Because that's what you'll get if you keep ignoring me."

With a smile plastered across his face, Rebel looked up from his assignment to please his wife. "Yes, my love? How can I serve you today?"

"That's better. You may continue now."

"You just wanted to see if you could make me look up, didn't you?"

"Yep. I won."

He shook his head good-naturedly. "Babe, there will never be a time you won't win when it comes to you getting my attention."

"I know," she replied as she straddled his lap, forcing him to move his laptop to the side. "I'm just so bored, Brax. I've been cooped up in this house forever."

"It's been two days, babe. Two days is not forever. And you've hardly been cooped up. We've been to the hotel to see everyone there and to HQ to meet with the guys at least a couple of times."

"HQ doesn't count. And it sure as hell feels like forever. I'm going to go to Mom's and visit with her for a while today."

"Heather, you know what's going on, what we're up against. Let's not go through this again."

"Brax, there are people out there living their lives. Carrying on with their daily activities because they have no idea something terrible is coming. I want to be one of those people. We've pretty well established he isn't actually after me. The letters and pictures were to distract you."

"No. The letters about the others were to distract us. He would kill you to hurt me because I'm the one who killed his father. Don't give him the opportunity to do that to me, Heather. There are a lot of things I can live without, but you're not one of them."

"I promise I won't take any unnecessary chances. I will go straight there and straight home. You said now that you have more concrete evidence that he's making a move soon, there are more agencies involved and more eyes on him and his crew. He's busy preparing for his grand finale fireworks show. He's not concerned with me," she argued.

"I'll take you over there. You and Kay can chill in the pool while I work on these. That'll at least give me some peace of mind and a change of scenery."

"That works for me. I'll grab both our bathing suits, in case you decide to take a break and join us. I'll be ready to go in just a few minutes."

She leaned in and planted a kiss on his lips while she rubbed her fingers through his beard. His strong arms encircled her, pulling her chest flush with his. "You are my reason for living, Heather. Your love has kept me sane through so many hard times over the years. I only want to keep you safe and with me."

"I know, babe. I am going stir-crazy, but I honestly need to discuss something important with my parents. She's home today, but I'll have to catch Daddy another time before they leave for the acquisition."

He smacked her behind playfully. "Go get ready to leave, then. One of us has work to do." She laughed along with him, loving their playful banter and the natural give-and-take they shared.

On the drive to her parents' house, Rebel was extra-vigilant about watching every car, every person crossing at the intersections, and every other thing around them when they were stopped at a red light. The serious mood inside the vehicle was so unlike Rebel's usually calm persona, Heather started to second-guess her insistence on taking the short trip. Once they pulled into the open space of her parents' three-car garage, she was finally able to relax and breathe easier.

Kay met them at the door as they walked in from the garage. She pulled Heather into her arms and kissed her cheek. "How's my girl?"

"Glad to be released from my prison cell," she joked.

"Your home is hardly a prison cell." Kay shook her head and playfully rolled her eyes.

"Shhh—don't tell Brax. That's the only reason the warden let me out for the day."

"I can hear you," Rebel replied dryly from beside her.

"Ready to swim?" she asked, smiling.

"You two go ahead. I'm making progress on this file with the information Silas shared, and I need to try to wrap it up today if at all possible," Rebel replied.

"You can use Emmett's office, Braxton. It should have everything you need, but let me know if I can get you anything," Kay offered.

"Thanks, Kay. You ladies have fun."

Rebel left them to their mother-daughter time and made his way through the expansive home toward Emmett's study. Once seated in the plush, high-backed leather office chair, Rebel once again focused on piecing together the jagged edges of the puzzle, hoping the information he uncovered would put an end to the case once and for all. Multiple files of encrypted data had to be pieced together and interpreted without missing a key element that could change the entire meaning of the text.

After several hours of cross-referencing, double-checking, and verifying the key, he'd deciphered the hidden instructions for the extremist group. He read the message several times before the full meaning of it hit him.

Mother of Satan at Portno. Greater than eleven. Cut off fuel. Cripple the lanes. Stop the flow. Babylon falls when we slay the great harlot. Allahu Akbar!

He grabbed his secure phone and hit send. "Reaper, I discovered the hidden message." He read the message to Noah and waited for the words to sink in.

"Mother of Satan...the nickname for TATP," Noah replied. "What is Portno?"

"Port of New Orleans. The only deep-water port where foreign oil is brought into the United States."

"That could explain the 'cut off fuel' reference. And the 'greater than eleven' could mean they intend to rival the damage inflicted from the attacks on September 11. Or they want more to cause more fatalities," Noah replied. "Good work, Rebel. I knew you'd figure it out. I'll call Homeland Security and all the other agencies involved. They can send teams down there to help intercept and take them out."

"Deciphering it doesn't mean I've figured out everything he means. There's no doubt they know exactly what to do now. Does anyone have eyes on Rashad?"

"Joe has been tailing Rashad since the day Silas followed him out of the hospital. He packed up all his belongings and left the house in the gated community. He's at one of the other run-down shacks now," Noah replied. "Silas and Shadow had a talk with the director at the CIA to help clear Joe's name. I'm sure he was on the receiving end of a good tongue-lashing, and I know they'll still investigate him, but they've put him under Shadow's command for now."

"Joe had better not be hiding anything. Shadow is like a human lie detector and a revealer of secrets. He'll know every dirty little secret Joe has in no time," Rebel chuckled. "You know, if Rashad changed houses, that means he must've finished making his part of the bombs."

"That's my guess. He left in the middle of the night, and Joe said Rashad drove *very* carefully."

"Yeah, I bet he did. Those bombs are highly unstable and can go off prematurely from the slightest jarring. This could literally be going down at any time. Are we going to New Orleans?"

"We didn't do all this work to sit on the sidelines, did we?" Noah laughed. "They'll probably try to keep us out so they can take credit for it. But you know we don't do this for the fame and glory anyway."

Rebel raised his eyes to the window, watching Heather laugh and have fun with her mother in the heated pool. "No, that's not why we do it at all."

Rebel's gaze lingered on Heather, watching her every move, considering how his life would be without her, and pushing away the foreboding thoughts that the worst was yet to come. Knowing his wife like he did, he had no doubt she'd insist on going to New Orleans with him rather than staying in Houston, a safe distance away from the action. The problem was, he didn't know if he could leave her behind when the time came.

"You look happier than I've seen you in years." Kay smiled at her daughter with a wisp of sadness in her eyes. "Does your handsome husband have anything to do with that?"

"Maybe," she replied coyly. "I've missed him even more than I realized. It feels so good to have him home for an extended time instead of just a long weekend here and there."

"When this case is over, he'll be home every night. I'm sure working at the office and the oil fields will be a lot different than what he does now. Definitely not as exciting, but not as dangerous either. At least then he'll move back to Houston and be at home with you." Kay smiled warmly.

"That's actually what I wanted to talk to you about today. I haven't told Brax yet because I want to surprise him."

"What? You haven't told him what?" Kay leaned forward, her brow furrowed, and her eyes narrowed. "Are you pregnant?"

"No, I'm not pregnant. Don't get all excited." Heather put her hands up in front of her, palms out, indicating for her mother to calm down. "I've decided to do what I should've done a long time ago. I'm moving to Miami to be with Brax."

"But what about the job with your father? You two being here with us and his parents?"

The pleading tone of her mother's voice broke her heart, but she'd made up her mind. Her heart, her life, and her home would be with Brax.

"I can't let Brax move here and give up everything he's built in Miami. He's doing it for me, leaving his friends and the company he helped build behind. He'd never even complain about it, but part of him would always be missing."

"But your job..." Kay stammered. "You're a nurse here."

"I can be a nurse anywhere. I can transfer my nursing license, and we'll make a new life together. It'll be okay, Mom. You and Dad can come visit us anytime—we'll expect you to be there often. You'd do the same for Dad."

The tears glistened in Kay's eyes before she wiped them away. "I'm honestly shocked it took you this long to decide to move. Since the day you two met, your whole world has revolved around him. You two were meant to be together, and I guess it's way past time for you to actually live together."

Heather wrapped her arms around her mother's neck and pulled her close. "I love you, Mom. I'll miss you."

"I'll miss you, so much. When are you going to tell your dad?" Kay pulled back from their embrace. "Since he's started working on this acquisition, he stays at the office very late every day and even on weekends."

"I'll go to his office today to talk to him in person and make him give me a few minutes. I need to tell him before you go to Oklahoma for the several weeks to complete the deal."

Heather and Rebel left after having lunch with Kay on the veranda. During the ride back to their house, she approached the subject she knew would most certainly start a fight.

"Babe, I'm going to see Dad at work this afternoon. Do you want to go with me?"

"I can't go today, sweetheart. Rashad is making more moves, and we're on him. He has something big planned, no doubt. I'd rather you didn't go without me. Now isn't the time to mess around. The chatter in the intel community is deafening—even more so than usual."

"Have you deciphered the code yet?"

"Yes, but we haven't figured out all of its meaning yet. I can't help but think we missed a big part of the message. It could've been sent through a different method and the cells put the two together."

"What does it say?"

"It talks about crippling Babylon and watching the downfall of the great harlot. In both cases, they're referring to the US. One part appears to pinpoint New Orleans."

"Then he could be using Houston as his safe place and hit another city with his brainwashed sheep."

"I don't think so. Rashad is the type who would want to see it happen. He'll be a safe distance from the action, but he made the bombs here for a reason. We're not the only ones watching him. Every agency with any type of initials—and a few that don't even exist on paper—are monitoring him and his network."

"So you'll know when he makes a move. With so much attention on him and his guys, you'll stop him before it's too late. I really need to talk to Dad today, and this afternoon is the only time I'll have to do it."

"I can arrest you, ya know? Put you in shackles in a safe house, chained to the bed."

"You could, yes. But you'd have to unshackle me at some point. And when you do, your ass would be mine."

"Why now, Heather? Why can't it wait until this is over?" Rebel sighed, knowing he was about to lose this argument. As headstrong as he was, his wife was even worse when she set her sights on a goal.

"He's been really busy with this acquisition deal. He's working late and on weekends to finalize all the paperwork. In a couple of days, he'll leave for Tulsa, and he's staying there for the next several weeks as they complete the takeover. Mom's going with him, but I've already talked to her. This is really important to me, Brax. I wouldn't ask otherwise." She placed her hand on his arm, sealing their connection and stressing how important her request was.

Rebel parked in their driveway and stared at her for a long minute, warring in his mind and heart about letting her go alone. His heart wouldn't let him deny her anything she wanted, anything she asked of him. His mind knew the dangers were too real that Rashad would make good on his threats.

"Come on, Brax. Dad's offices are in one of the most heavily guarded areas and even well outside of Houston city limits. I have a hard time getting through security, and I'm the CEO's daughter."

"Fine. But you're taking one of the guys with you."

"He stays in the car. He's not coming into the office with me."

"Heather."

"Braxton."

He glared at her, intentionally giving her his meanest expression he usually reserved for criminals under interrogation. His intimidating glower caused her to break out into a fit of laughter.

"Be reasonable."

"I am, Brax. I've been vetted, and the security there knows me. I can get in and out much faster alone than if I took one of your men in with me. I could argue that I'm already unnecessarily taking a much needed set of eyes and ears out of the equation as it is. He wouldn't be allowed to keep his handy ear comms in—security would have a field day with that," she argued.

"I don't know why you picked nursing school. You'd be one hell of a politician—spinning the facts to meet your needs. Okay. Your escort waits outside. You keep your cell phone on you at all times. If there's one suspicious thing, you get out and call me first. For the record, I don't approve of this. But if I don't set it up, you'll just sneak off on your own.

"It's scary how well you know me." Heather beamed, happy she'd won that war of wills.

A couple of hours later, Roman and Heather drove together to the Port of Houston, home of the largest oil refinery in the United States. The waterways in the port were constantly busy with vessels entering and leaving with imported and exported goods. Large container ships looked more like floating cities with one large container stacked on top of the other like skyscrapers.

After clearing port security, they drove to the corporate offices where Emmett spent his days. The guard at the entrance to the parking lot eyed Roman suspiciously as he double-checked the visitor list for the day.

"I'm sorry, Ms. Reed, but I don't see you on the list for today. Is Mr. Greer expecting you?"

"No, but I need to see him. Please call and get approval," she replied.

"And your guest?"

"He'll wait in the car."

The guard looked even more suspicious and more uncomfortable with that answer. "Then I'll need to check your driver's licenses first." He nodded toward Roman. The guard walked back to his station to check Roman's identification and to contact Emmett for permission to allow Heather up to the executive wing. After several minutes, the guard finally stepped back to the vehicle window and returned their licenses.

18

CHAPTER EIGHTEEN

"You're cleared to go in now. Use the visitor parking spaces at the front of the building. Ms. Reed, your father said to come on up to his office. He's cleared his schedule for you." The guard smiled warmly.

"Mr. Ramsey," he addressed Roman. "I'm sorry I didn't recognize you at first. You're well-known in the sniper and sharpshooting world. It's an honor to meet you."

Roman nodded in appreciation. "Good to meet you, Bell," he replied, looking at the name tag bearing the guard's last name. "Army?"

"Yes, sir. Ranger." He directed them to the parking area and waved as they drove away.

"I recognize that look." Heather grinned slyly.

"What?"

"You think he'd make a good addition to the team. You want to recruit him."

"Don't you have a meeting to go to?" Roman asked sardonically, one side of his mouth lifting in a half grin.

Heather laughed as she opened the car door. "I won't be too long. I'm sorry to make you wait out here, but it's best I do this alone."

"No problem. I've had worse details."

She took a deep breath as she pulled the giant glass door toward her. The meeting with her dad would be hard for them both, but she'd decided on the best course of action for her life. Her priorities had changed over the years, and she'd finally realized the focus on what was most important to her had shifted.

The ride up to the twelfth floor was agonizingly slow. She had way too much time to second-guess the speech she had rehearsed to perfection. Steeling her spine, she walked into the large executive office wing, and her father's secretary escorted her directly into his office. "You have a visitor, Mr. Greer," Betty announced.

"Come in, sweetheart. It's so good to see you. I've missed you." He rose and pulled her into his arms, hugging her close to him and kissing the side of her head. "Have a seat. Your mom said you went by to see her earlier. I've been so busy with work I haven't been home much lately."

"Yes, I know you have. That's why I came here. I know the two of you are leaving for a while to finalize this deal. This is the only way I'll get to see you before you leave."

"So, what do you have to tell me?" he asked, leveling her with his fatherly expression. "You don't just show up at my office for a chat."

"We need to talk about a couple of decisions I've made before you take off for Oklahoma. I've spent years being proud of my independence and ability to handle everything on my own. But the truth is, I've missed a lot of time with Brax over those years, and I don't want to miss one minute more.

"He's been the love of my life since the day I met him, and he will be until the day I die. We're talking about starting a family soon. Well, actually, I brought it up and told him I'm ready, and he's agreed he is, too. So, that's the good news—you'll hopefully have a grandbaby soon."

Emmett turned his chair to the side and remained uncharacteristically silent for longer than Heather felt comfortable waiting for his response.

"Say something, Daddy."

He turned his head and locked his gaze with hers. The tears shimmering in his eyes made her heart skip a beat, and the air seized in her lungs. He cleared his throat and prepared to respond.

"You've lost a lot of years and opportunities to make the best memories of your life because of me."

"Because of you?" The shock in her voice relayed her confusion.

"Yes. It's my fault—all of it. I'm the reason why Braxton left town. He joined the Army and stayed away on assignments because of me. I was so mad at him for ruining your life, all your plans for the future. You were so young when you got pregnant."

"He was the same exact age I was, Dad. We were both young and just trying to find our way."

"I know. I'm not saying I was right, sweetheart. I was slightly distraught because you were pregnant during your senior year of high school, you got married too young, and you were going to miss out on the whole college experience.

"Then Dalton died, and I was mad for all new reasons. The pain I had to watch you suffer through was almost unbearable to me. I still don't know how you were able to withstand it. I blamed him for putting you in that predicament in the first place.

"It seems he never told you about our run-in just before he left, which shouldn't surprise me because it speaks volumes about what a good man Braxton is."

He paused and inhaled deeply before forcefully releasing his breath, dreading the conversation ahead of him. "You were such a mess, sweetheart, and it killed me to see you that way. The doctor had prescribed a sedative for you, and I stood in the doorway watching you for several minutes. You were finally sleeping soundly after days of going through living hell.

"My anger reached a boiling point, and I lashed out at Braxton. When I told him it was all his fault you were going through this in the first place, he thought I was blaming him for letting Dalton die. As if he didn't do his job as a husband and father. I didn't correct him, especially when I realized it meant he was leaving. I thought that would mean a chance for you to be happy again."

"When did you ever see me unhappy with Braxton?"

He froze in place and openly gaped at her as her words sank in. The verbal slap in the face stung worse than he realized it would, though he couldn't deny he deserved it.

"I've never seen Brax make you unhappy. I've seen you get mad at him, but never to the point where you wanted to walk away."

"And I never will. You've always underestimated our bond. We started out as best friends and knew everything about each other before starting our relationship. Even now, after being apart like we have been, I couldn't imagine not having him in my life every day. Which brings me to the other reason why I'm here today, the bad news, so to speak. I've decided I'm moving to Miami to be with Braxton."

"What? Why? We already talked about him moving back here. He has a good job waiting for him right here."

"Yes, I know we did. And I appreciate you offering him a job as head of security here, but I know my husband. He'd do it for me and never hold it against me, but he wouldn't be as happy with it as he is with Steele Security. I can't do this to him or let him do it for us. I can work as a nurse in Miami as easily as I can here in Houston.

"It's time for me to be with my husband every single day I can. When we start our family, I expect you and Mom to visit us often. I'm sure his parents will too. I miss having him all the time, and I refuse to lose one more minute of being with him."

Emmett steepled his hands over his face, his forehead rested on his fingertips, and his eyes were squeezed shut. His chest rose and fell rapidly in time with his flaring nostrils. When he'd composed himself enough to speak, he cut his eyes to Heather and dropped his hands in his lap.

"All I want is for my baby girl to be happy. I want to talk to Brax again. To apologize for what I've done to you both. To tell him I'm so very proud of him, what he has accomplished, and how he's always taken care of you. I couldn't ask for a better son-in-law, and if he'd let me call him 'son,' I'd be honored."

Heather rose and flew around the large executive desk, and

Emmett stood to embrace her. Father and daughter clung to each other, letting years of strife and disagreement melt away into oblivion. The healing and bonding between the two of them was long overdue, as was the release of unspoken resentments that had festered over the years.

"You have no idea how much this means to me. Thank you, Daddy," she said softly.

"I love you, Heather. And I love Brax like he's my own son. It's time I told him. Thank you for not giving up on your stubborn, hard-headed dad."

"Never. Brax loves you too. He's told me many times how he wants your approval and wants a good relationship with you. You'll just have to come to Miami to see us frequently."

Emmett pulled away, kissed her forehead, and gave her a sad smile. "You'll get sick of seeing us, we'll be there so often."

"We'll buy a house with a separate apartment so you can come as often and stay as long as you want."

Without warning or preamble, an intense rumbling emanated from all around them and shook the entire building, knocking pictures from the walls and office supplies off the desk. The windows rattled and broke into shards. Sharp pieces flew into the room, forcing them both to duck and shield their heads with their arms. Wave after wave, the noise grew louder and mixed with the sounds of people running and screaming in terror. The power blinked a few times before it completely shut off. In a matter of milliseconds, the world around Heather and Emmett ceased to make sense.

"What the hell is going on? Is this an earthquake?" Emmett bellowed and rushed to open his office door. The twelve-story building was in complete chaos. On the top floor, employees ran past his office frantically, tears streaming down their cheeks. Panic-stricken faces were contorted in pain as blood dripped down their temples, arms, and legs.

"Run, Emmett!" His chief operating officer, Russ, yelled. Emmett watched, dazed and confused, as his friend limped by. Russ rushed as quickly as his injured leg would allow, blood trickling down the side of his face and dripping from his chin.

The building was unexpectedly rocked by another blast. The force of the second explosion shook it even harder, knocking several people off-balance, and they fell to the floor. Emmett and Heather watched in horror as some were trampled underfoot by the terrified mass of people. As if in a surreal dream, Emmett stood rooted to the floor while he looked down the hall toward the direction where the blast originated. In his confounded state, his brain could barely process what his eyes saw.

What had once been a luxury office complex was now reduced to mostly rubble, devoid of any form or resemblance of what it once was. The wall at the far end of the hall that held the bank of floor-to-ceiling windows, giving a full view of the refinery operations behind the building, was completely gone. The majority of the back half of the building was missing, the floors and walls that once framed it lay in piles of wreckage and debris many stories below.

The refinery stations which had stood tall and proud had been replaced with enormous balls of orange flames. Everything outside was on fire as far as his eyes could see. The large vats that once held the refined oil were reduced to heaps of twisted metal and gnarled debris. Sirens screamed from every direction, alarms rang, and voices shouted, but their words were indecipherable.

In what remained of the office building, injured and dead bodies littered the floors below his, visible from where Emmett remained cemented in his spot. In the chaos and wreckage, nothing made sense to his logical and analytical mind. Operating with complete bedlam and turmoil surrounding him was not his strong suit.

It was like a war zone.

His mind screamed, *What the fuck is happening?*

"Dad!" Heather yelled and shook him hard. "We have to move. Now! Those blasts are timed—spaced apart intentionally. Everyone is running in one direction, and the blasts are quickly following. He's trapping everyone in one place."

"Who? Who's trapping everyone?"

"The terrorist! I'll explain it all later. We have to find another way out. Right now!"

"This way—down the back steps. They're a direct connection to the executive wing from the first floor, so there won't be many people in this stairwell."

Emmett led her to a locked door and dug his keys out of his pocket to open it. He swung the door open wide and locked the swing arm in place to keep the door propped open. "This way, everyone! Follow me!"

Emmett and Heather led the way down the stairwell, running and taking multiple steps at a time.

Twelve floors, Heather thought. *We'll never make it out in time.*

At that moment, another explosion tore through what was left of the building. More powerful than the last, the aftershock of the blast knocked their legs out from under them, split the concrete stairs in two, and separated the outer wall of the building from the stairwell. Rising to her knees, trying to steady her shaking legs, Heather peered over the edge of the broken concrete. The rebar jutted out, twisted unnaturally from the force of the blast. The platform shifted precariously underneath her, revealing more of the scenery outside and the ground below. Quickly counting back, Heather realized they'd only made it down to the eighth floor, at most.

Still at least eighty feet high, she thought. *We'd never survive a jump from this height.*

"What do we do?" a frightened woman behind Heather screamed. "Oh my God, we're all going to die! I'll never see my kids again!"

"If we die, it won't be from a lack of trying to get out," Heather yelled in response, forcing the woman to stop her hysterics long enough to make eye contact. "We can't go back up. We'll keep going down as far as we can. Then we'll jump. A broken leg is better than being buried in the rubble of this building."

"Okay," the woman sniffled. "Okay, let's go."

Emmett and Heather jumped to their feet and again led the descent down the shaky and fragile steps as fast as they could move. Heather glanced up every few seconds, watching the sway of the tons of concrete above their heads. She prayed they would reach a floor close enough to the ground so they could jump before the materials holding the now-frail building together finally gave way.

The frightened woman's cry continued to ring in her ears with every step she took. She thought about never seeing Brax again, of dying in a tomb of steel and concrete, of never fully realizing her dream of having a family with the man she loved. Those thoughts made her want to shut down, to allow the fear simply to take over so she wouldn't have to deal with the overwhelming possibility of it all for one more second.

It was the thought of letting Rashad win by using her to hurt Braxton that pushed her on. She could hear her husband's voice in her head, urging her to come to him, commanding her to never surrender, and demanding she keep going even when she didn't think she could take one more step. It was his love that gave her the strength she needed to fight off the anxiety and fear trying to incapacitate her.

With the next blast, the outer wall crumbled to the ground below. The stairwell became completely exposed to the outside elements, and the stairs began breaking beneath their feet.

"Heather, we have to jump now, or we'll be buried by the floors above us," Emmett shouted over the roar of the disintegrating building.

"Okay, let's do it, then," Heather agreed, scared out of her mind. She glanced over the edge and estimated they were somewhere around the third or fourth floor.

Thirty to forty feet to fall, she thought. *Thirty feet is the outer limit for surviving a free fall. Half the people live. But half of them die.*

"I'll lower you over the edge so you don't have as far to drop. Then I'll be right behind you," he assured her, as if he were reading her mind.

"Together," she insisted.

"No. My arms are longer, and that gives us both a better advantage." He spoke as he guided her to the edge.

She sat with her legs dangling over the side and tried to mentally prepare herself for the terrifying move she had to make. Emmett took her hands in his as he knelt behind her. She slid over the edge, and he stretched out on his stomach, lowering her as far as he could over the jagged side. Men behind him grabbed his legs, allowing him to slide the upper half of his body over the edge to get her closer to the ground.

Tears flowed from his eyes as he forced himself to turn loose of his baby girl. His daughter he'd held as soon as she was born. The little girl he'd taught to ride a bike, drive a stick shift, and enrolled in martial arts so she could always take care of herself. The little girl he'd watched grow into a beautiful, caring, independent woman.

The daughter he'd given away to another man, never truly trusting Braxton would love and care for her in the same way a father would love and care for his daughter. He'd never healed the wounds he'd inflicted on Braxton, and by extension, on her.

The daughter he'd never witnessed enjoying raising a child of her own. The joys and heartaches he could've experienced with her passed before his eyes. There were so many firsts and seconds, celebrations and disappointments, everything that makes up a life, that he'd missed out on before, and in his current predicament, knew he'd miss in the future.

So many things he'd do differently.

Her fingers slipped through his, and he watched as she landed on the ground below. She kept her knees slightly bent and rolled with the momentum of the fall, coming to a stop on her side. He watched with bated breath as she remained motionless for several seconds. Fear, horror, and grief tore through him. Fear that he'd insisted on her jumping too soon gripped him. Horror because he'd just dropped his daughter to her death rather than to safety. And grief, so much grief because the thought of life without her took away his desire to survive himself.

19

CHAPTEN NINETEEN

A slight movement in her arm had his heart pumping in triple time. "Heather!"

She gingerly pushed up to a sitting position and looked up at him. From her blank expression and fumbling movements, she was obviously dazed from her jarring landing. But she was alive, and that was all that mattered to Emmett.

"Heather, are you okay?"

"I'm okay," she replied, her voice quivering. "Get out of there, Daddy! Jump!"

Her vacant expression faded away, and comprehension of the situation took its place. In that moment, she wished her wits hadn't returned because she was able to fully grasp the devastation laid out before her. The instability of the building petrified her, but all the frantic and pleading eyes of the people stranded in the stairwell ripped her heart out. She was shocked even part of the building was still standing. What was left would come down with the next puff of wind.

And her dad was still inside.

The shrill shriek of the panicked woman's cry abruptly filled the air and echoed off the rubble. "Tell my babies I love them. And I'm sorry I couldn't be there for them while they grow up."

Heather watched as Emmett glanced over his shoulder toward the lady, then back at the men who still held his legs. The scene played out in slow motion in Heather's mind as they each nodded before Emmett turned his gaze back to her.

When their eyes met, she knew.

"No, Daddy!" She pushed up to stand, and the pain shot through her leg. Ignoring the intense agony, she limped closer to the building, stumbling over debris, but she kept her eyes locked on his. "No! I need you. You said you'd be right behind me."

"I love you, Heather. With all of my heart. I'm so very proud of you. I want you and Brax to have a wonderful life together. Tell your mother I love her, and I'll be waiting for her. Tell Brax I love him like the son I never had.

"Now, I have to help these people get home to their loved ones. I have to give them a fighting chance, precious."

With tears flowing unchecked down her cheeks, her vision blurred and a sob racked her body. "I love you, Daddy. Please come home with me. We need you."

Emmett took the frightened lady's hands and lowered her as far over the side as he could before he released her. One person after the other stepped up, and he dropped them to the ground below. All the while, Heather begged him to save himself, too. The slight sway of the building's remains did not bode well for the number of people still trapped, waiting for their turn to be lowered to safety.

Because they were unwilling to wait any longer or were afraid to fall from that height, many people decided to continue down the steps behind Emmett. When the first few made their move, several more fell in line behind them. The sudden movement of that many people on an already unstable structure quickly became a recipe for disaster.

Heather limped forward to shout at the people rushing down the stairs. "Go back! The stairwell is blocked. You can't go down any farther. You'll be trapped!"

The portion of the building still standing erect began to sway visibly from side to side. Slightly at first, then with more force and momentum. Heather gasped, her hand covered her mouth, and her eyes flew open wide when she realized the rocking wouldn't stop until the building had completely collapsed.

Panicked screams emanated from every floor when the final blow was dealt. A loud explosion, different from the others, filled the air just before a huge ball of fire rolled through the tattered remains of the carnage on the upper floors, consuming everything in its path.

"Dad—jump!" she pleaded.

Emmett slid over the side, gripping the concrete with his fingers and stretching his body to lessen the height of his drop.

"Just let go!" she urged. "Let go!"

"Heather!"

A voice from behind her called, and she turned to see Roman's panic-stricken face. When his expression morphed into terror before her eyes, she turned back toward the building in time to see it collapsing from the top down.

Toward her.

WHILE WAITING IN THE CAR, Roman heard the first blast, and his senses immediately went on high alert. The explosion could've come from a multitude of places with a variety of reasons behind it at a major oil refinery, but his gut told him this wasn't an industrial accident. Something was very wrong, and he had a very bad feeling about the outcome.

He jumped out of the car and ran in the direction of the noise. The entire area behind the office building looked like a demolition zone. Fires had erupted in multiple places at the refinery, unbridled flames shot straight up into the air and quickly jumped to the next highly flammable source. Some of the employees rushed to help the wounded, while others tried to stop the infernos that were raging out of control.

The next blast was just as powerful as the first but originated from the office building. The explosions were intentional and purposeful—that much was clear. His heart hammered in his chest as he ran toward the danger. He knew Heather and her father were still somewhere inside the building, but he didn't know where exactly. The possible locations were too numerous—in Emmett's office, searching for a safe place, attempting to get out, or worse, buried under the rubble in the blast zone.

"Brad," he barked into his cell. "I need an exact location on Heather. Then alert Rebel and get everyone down here to the port."

Brad checked the coordinates on the GPS tracker in Heather's cell and told Roman where to find her. "What happened, Roman? And what is all that noise?"

As he ran to find her, he filled Brad in on the situation, giving him all the details he could to help the team be as prepared as possible when they arrived. When he reached the area where he expected to find Heather, most of the building lay in crumbled ruins on the ground. The amount of devastation was staggering, and the task of finding her in it seemed all but impossible. Her screams registered before he could come to terms with the scene unfolding in front of him.

"Heather!"

Startled, she quickly turned her attention over her shoulder in his direction. The first set of explosions were all powerful bursts of energy, designed to cause as much structural damage as possible. The final discharge that devastated what remained of the structure had completely different elements and intentions. The ball of fire that ripped through the upper floors, which Heather and Emmett had just vacated, originated from an intense heat source designed to obliterate anything that remained after the primary blasts.

The reinforced concrete floors began to crumble, conceding to the high-temperature accelerant after all the punishment that had already been inflicted. When the top floor collapsed onto the one below, Roman knew no one else would get out alive. He ran as hard and fast as he could toward Heather, hoping beyond hope he would make it in time to rescue her. His eyes traveled up to the many people who were still inside the stairwell when its tethers broke loose, and it tipped outward past the point of no return. With no reliable load-bearing source left, the crushing weight created a domino effect of destruction until the remains were completely unrecognizable.

Roman skidded to a halt at the edge of the debris, ignoring the cuts and bruises he'd suffered from the shards that had flown from the demolished building. His chest heaved like he'd just finished a marathon at a sprinter's pace. His heart thumped against his rib cage, ready to explode out of his chest at any moment. He bent at the waist with his hands on this thighs, gulping air. But overexertion wasn't the cause of his hypoxic state.

He had failed.

He'd failed Heather.

He'd failed Rebel.

He didn't reach her in time.

She was buried under the remnants of the razed building.

"THEY DID WHAT?" Rebel demanded, moving into his threatening stance. "How can they do that?"

"They took us off the case, with the exception of sending Blake, Alex, and Joe to New Orleans to work with our DEA liaison. Don't think I haven't argued this with everything I have," Noah replied. "I even talked directly with the president since we're taking our orders from him on this case. His advisors said it would be best to let the dual CIA-FBI Task Force take over the operations since we're coming down to the wire. Delta Force is still officially unofficial as far as the rest of the world is concerned. When Rashad is taken down, there will be so much media coverage all over it, the president is concerned we'll get caught in the cross fire of camera flashes."

"That's complete bullshit. Our team has done most of the work and found all the best leads. We should be there to take him out," Bull argued. "Fucking hypocrites."

"I agree. But we can't ignore orders to stay away from New Orleans and from any of the cell's rental houses when that order comes directly from our president," Noah replied. "You know as well as I do what'll happen to us if we disobey. I'm all for breaking the rules, but I don't want to wake up in a six-foot-by-nine-foot dark room for the rest of my life."

"Fuck them. Do you have any idea how long I worked on that damn encrypted code?" Rebel shook his head in disgust and dropped down in his chair. "If I'd known this, I would've gone with Heather to see her father at work."

"Why would she go to his office to see him instead of his house?"

"His company is buying another oil company in Oklahoma. Emmett and Kay are leaving in a couple of days to spend the next several weeks up there, finalizing the deal and making the new employees feel more secure in their jobs. Heather said she needed to talk to him about something before he leaves, and going to his office is the only way she can get time with him."

Noah narrowed his eyes, drew his brows together, and moved quickly to rifle through the case file in the middle of the table. When he found the information, he released a haggard breath. "Is the name of that company Vessel Petroleum?"

Rebel's face fell, and his pulse quickened. He knew this couldn't be good. "Yes. Why do you ask?"

"Remember when Rashad's brother, Turan, transferred that money from an oil company to all those Homeland Security employees? It was Vessel Petroleum's account he used."

"Where'd you get that information?" Bull asked.

"A copy of the confidential case file Shadow somehow managed to get his hands on."

"You think Turan was trying to get Rashad to look into that company because of Emmett's relation to me? Why wouldn't he just tell Rashad outright?" Rebel asked.

"Maybe Rashad wouldn't listen to him. Turan pulled a lot of pranks that brought too much attention to him, whereas Rashad prefers the cover of anonymity. But Rashad didn't bother with you until after Turan disappeared, so maybe he's taken over his brother's vendetta now," Noah deduced.

"The mere fact it's the same company Emmett is preparing to take over changes everything. Portno is definitely Port of New Orleans, but what if they're planning to hit both ports at once? Taking out the Port of Houston would do just as much damage to the country's economic stability as taking out the one in New Orleans. But taking out both ports would completely cripple us.

"No imported oil coming in, no exported goods going out. On top of that, our largest oil refinery is in Houston's port. Without that production, the smaller refineries wouldn't be able to keep up with the demand, and we'd run out of fuel across the country. Can you imagine the level of chaos that would cause? Is that what they meant by 'greater than eleven'?"

"The only thing that seems certain at this point is the task force leaders have jumped the gun by taking the whole team to New Orleans. You know how I feel about coincidences," Noah replied.

"No such thing."

Shadow marched into the room, determination in his every step and masked trepidation in his expression. "Let's go. Now. We have to move."

"What's wrong?" Noah asked.

The hairs on Rebel's arms stood at attention when Shadow's eyes swung to meet his. The acid churned in his stomach, making the original sinking feeling mutate into a black hole intent on draining the life from him. He jumped to his feet, ready to move into action, and drew up to his full height. "Tell me."

"Roman just called Brad. Ringgold Refineries has just been hit, and the damage is extensive. He's calling us all in," Shadow replied stoically.

"Heather?" Rebel held his breath and waited for Shadow to answer his one-word question. The only word that held any meaning to him. The one word that could change his entire life.

"Brad used the GPS tracker on her phone to tell Roman exactly where she was about two minutes ago. Brad said there was a lot of noise in the background, and Roman said multiple bombs had been detonated. The building and refinery are presumed to be a total loss. But since Brad was able to locate her, that tells me her phone was still operable, and that's a good sign. That's all I know at this point," Shadow explained. "Can you handle going to the scene?"

"Try to stop me." Rebel quickly grabbed his gear, focusing on each task to keep his sanity in check. When he'd finished gearing up, he called over his shoulder as he rushed out the door. "I'm leaving. If you ladies are riding with me, you'd better have your asses in the truck."

With the team loaded and ready to roll, Rebel slid behind the wheel and took off like a bullet toward the port. The normal travel time from their location averaged just over thirty minutes. Rebel made the trip in less than fifteen minutes with speeds in excess of 120 miles per hour and weaving effortlessly from lane to lane through the traffic.

Nothing could've prepared him for what he saw when his truck skidded to a halt in the parking lot. He threw it into park, jumped out, and sprinted to the location Brad had given them. The devastation extended as far as he could see. Where the once regal office building had stood was now little more than a pile of rocks, twisted metal, and unidentifiable scraps.

His eyes scanned the area, frantically searching for Heather, when the sight of a man on his knees caught his attention. He was furiously moving the rocks and debris, attempting to tunnel through the carnage. The earth ceased to spin, a vacuum sealed around Rebel and squeezed the oxygen from his lungs, and his heart stopped beating in his chest.

The man hastily digging through the mounds of crumbled concrete was Roman.

"Heather!" Rebel yelled. "Hang on, baby. I'll get you out of there. Just hang on."

In the blink of an eye, Rebel was at Roman's side, moving the large pieces of concrete as if they weighed no more than a pebble. When hands on either side of him grabbed his arms and stopped his progress, he finally looked up.

"Rebel, you have to slow down. You don't want the weight to shift and cause more to fall on her," Shadow reasoned. "Methodical and calculated moves are what you need to focus on right now."

"You're right." He sat back, wiped the sweat from his brow, and tried to calm his racing heart and mind.

"This is a giant puzzle, and we have to move it one strategic piece at a time. I'm calling in the search and rescue dogs. Bull, get the professional search and rescue team out here with their equipment. They have cameras and heat-sensing equipment so we don't waste time digging in the wrong area. We're going to need all the help we can get," Noah directed.

"I'll get security in place. We don't need news helicopters and crews swarming the place, broadcasting the damage so the radicals can celebrate anything. This all has to stay under wraps for as long as possible," Shadow added.

He made a few quick phone calls and, within minutes, the entire area was cordoned off by members of the National Guard. Military and police helicopters patrolled a wide perimeter to prevent civilian aircraft from entering the airspace. Off-duty National Guard members showed up in force to assist with the search and rescue operation.

While all the plans and preparations were being made by the professionals, Rebel maintained his focus on finding his wife by moving one piece at a time. One of the dog handlers approached Rebel and spoke in a calm and reassuring manner.

"Hey, I'm Tim, and this pretty little lady is Robin. Would you mind if we help you search?"

Rebel turned to look at Tim, but he found himself face-to-face with Robin instead. Her expressive milk chocolate eyes pleaded with him to let her do her job. As if the black Labrador felt his pain, she slowly extended her snout and lovingly licked his face.

"I'd love to have some help. Thanks, Tim," he replied as he scratched behind the dog's ear. "And thank you, Robin. I really needed that."

20

CHAPTER TWENTY

Rashad watched all the commotion from inside the port while keeping a safe distance away from the blasts. A fiendish smile crawled across his face at the thought of seeing his mission come to fruition. The infidels had interfered with his country, his beliefs, and his family for long enough. His intentions were to prove how vulnerable the arrogant people really were, while bringing them to their knees. Part one of the current plan was well underway and coming together as expected.

He'd been warned against lingering in the port after he'd detonated the bombs, but he'd decided to take his chances. For his father, his brother, and his cause, he was obligated to see it through to the end. To him, it meant the difference in dying an honorable and worthy death, and dying a shameful and irrelevant death. A job only half completed would be dishonorable and prevent him from collecting his heavenly rewards.

The excitement that had been lacking in his life all the years he had been in the US built inside him with each explosion. With every piece of debris, shrapnel, and projectile flying from the refinery site, his elation increased from knowing he'd been instrumental in ensuring its complete destruction. Secondary explosions from the spreading fire in the fields were like a sign from Allah, praising him for his work and awarding him with a double portion for his good deeds.

The pride he felt when the first bomb detonated in the office quickly grew to a crescendo of arrogance and superiority. The final bomb in the office building culminated in the climax of his egotism. "I will be immortal now, transcending all time. Songs will be written and sung about me for the rest of time."

He'd rigged the final bomb with special care and a singular purpose in mind. The first set of bombs caused widespread devastation, but C-4 made a more impactful statement, in his opinion. The enormous, heat-generating blast was easily activated with his remote detonator and would've created an impressive explosion on its own, but the flowing oxygen from the tanks he'd procured from the hospital helped create an even more powerful force. Watching the giant ball of fire roll through several floors at the top of the building was the greatest vision he'd ever beheld. Every news outlet in the world would carry footage of his creation, memorializing his name and his innovation forever.

His cell phone began to ring just as the building made its final descent. "Yes."

"You should be well on your way to New Orleans by now. What is your current location?"

Rashad had visions of killing the man calling all the shots and giving the orders on their mission. He obeyed because he'd been ordered by his cleric to follow every command. His cleric—his teacher—was wise and was the most knowledgeable man in Islamic law he knew. For those reasons, he'd followed the rules and allowed the interloper to meddle in matters he had no business in.

Of course, he'd followed all orders with the exception of leaving the port immediately after the first explosion.

"I'm in the truck, still in the Port of Houston, making sure everything goes off without a hitch."

The silence on the other end of the line contradicted the outrage and condemnation simmering just under the surface.

"Get out of there right now," he replied through gritted teeth.

"The blasts in the second site haven't been triggered yet. Something could be wrong, and I may need to improvise. I can't do that from five hours away."

"You know as well as I do those bombs will detonate with or without you. As soon as they move the first crate, they'll all blow. Hell, even if the cargo ship slightly rocks from a wave, that's all it needs. Move your ass before you ruin this for both of us."

"As you wish," Rashad replied coolly, waiting for the day of his revenge.

"You're too damn late," he growled. "The fucking National Guard has been mobilized. They're shutting down everything and everyone in and out of the port right now. Find somewhere to park that fucking truck, get out of it, and then stay the hell out of sight." He then hung up before Rashad could respond.

"Yours is coming, my friend. Very soon, you will no longer be protected," Rashad hissed to his silent phone.

He fired up the diesel engine of the eighteen-wheeler and pulled out of his current parking spot overlooking the devastation he'd created. Several other trucks had been rerouted away from the crime scene, so he took the opportunity to fall in line with them. When they pulled into an enormous parking lot lined with one truck after the other, he smirked to himself at the brilliance of his simple hiding spot.

After he gathered his belongings that could potentially identify him from the cab of the truck, he took off on foot toward the waterway. Rashad knew from his research shutting down the port was no small feat, nor was the decision to prevent any ships from entering or leaving the area. With the enormous ships now stationary and the exits blocked by military personnel, he only had to find a seat and wait for the real fireworks to begin.

"Silas Steele, CIA," he introduced himself and extended his hand.

"Kevin Robbins, Port Authority Officer. Good to meet you."

"I need your help, Kevin. I'm afraid this isn't over, and something just isn't adding up for me. Can you help me out?"

"Of course. What do you need?"

"Pull up the security tapes from just before the first explosion," Silas directed. "Start with the refinery plant area first."

"You got it."

The multiple flat screens that covered the wall displayed varying images around the port. Kevin keyed in the coordinates of the refinery field and brought up every recording that captured any angle of it in the camera's range of view. Together, they reviewed each frame in the few minutes prior to the initial blast. Silas memorized where every person, vehicle, and piece of equipment was located, filing it away for easy comparison when something different jumped out at him.

An eighteen-wheeler tanker truck pulled up beside one of the large vats, and a crew of men moved toward it, gathering connectors and large hoses to begin the transfer of refined petroleum. The driver's door opened, and a pair of legs swung out into view. The driver handed the ground crewman his orders and stepped out of the big rig. Ground crew members had begun to make the connection from the vat to the truck when the blast filled the screen.

The instantly mangled truck became a deadly projectile, the damaged equipment and free-flowing gasoline became all the accelerant the fire needed to rage out of control instantaneously. Everyone in a fifty-yard vicinity of the blast was killed, and many more well past that range were severely injured.

Silas paused the recording and stared at the screen in disbelief. He noted the exact time of the blast from the recording. "Kevin, can you pull up the office building security tapes and start just a few seconds before this time?"

"Sure," he replied, clearly shaken from the graphic scene he'd just watched. When the digital recording reached the time Silas requested, Kevin put the image on the bigger screen in the middle of the wall. He had a hunch why Silas had requested that recording. "Here it is."

With his gaze carefully watching both the building and the time, Silas waited for what he knew in his gut was about to happen. At precisely the same time as the truck exploded, one end of the office building disappeared in an enormous blast of energy. Both bombs were on the same detonator, and the person holding that trigger had to be nearby. He quickly stopped the recording, unwilling to watch any further at that point because it simply hit too close to home.

"Kevin, can you trace the truck back to when it first entered the port? See if it stopped anywhere else, let anyone out, dropped anything off. Let's get a good look at the driver, possibly tie him to others who conspired in this attack. We need to take them all down."

"I'll gladly help with that. Let me know if you need an alibi."

Kevin and Silas watched the truck in rewind as it wound through the streets of the enormous industrial area. It only stopped when required. No one got in or out. Nothing was removed or put inside it. When they reached the port gates, the camera angle switched to the one on the guard's station, giving them a close-up view of the driver.

"Son of a bitch." Silas had hoped he was wrong when he saw the driver on the recording get out of the truck just before the blast. The mannerisms were the same, but he'd hoped he was wrong regardless.

"You know him?"

"Yeah. I know him. He was actually a pretty good kid. Just recently got a job here and was looking forward to being able to move to a better place soon. His name was Reuben Silva." Silas rubbed his forehead and exhaled forcefully. He'd just watched one of his confidential informants get blown up, the image forever burned into his memory.

"Hey, he said his friend Gustavo got a job here at the same time. If they're being used as pawns, his vehicle could be rigged too. Can you link into his truck's GPS and see where he is?"

"Absolutely. What's his last name?"

"Montes."

With a few clicks on his computer, he had signed in to the truck monitoring system the port maintained. "His truck is currently parked in the shipping yard cargo area. We had to use it as an overflow area for trucks because of the attack—nothing moving in or out right now."

"Get on the radio and get everyone out of that lot right now. Don't send any men into it, but contact anyone who's in there and tell them to get out. They need to leave their trucks behind. I'm on my way over to check out that truck. Jot down the license plate and description of his truck for me."

"I'll do ya one better than that. I'll print a live shot picture so you can see exactly where it is and everything surrounding it, too. Take the security Jeep parked outside." Kevin tossed the keys to Silas.

"You're a good man, Kevin."

With the picture in hand, Silas jogged out to the Jeep and squealed the tires when he pulled out of the parking lot.

"Noah," Silas yelled into his phone. "There may be another truck with a bomb in the port. I'm on my way over to check it out."

"What truck?"

Silas gave Noah a condensed version of what he'd just learned and where he was headed. "I'll be in touch soon. Or you'll hear a big bang. Either way, I'll let you know what I find."

When he reached the overflow lot, people were rushing away from the area in droves. He had no doubt the word was quickly spread regarding the possibility of another bomb. He skidded to a stop just behind the eighteen-wheeler assigned to Gustavo and cautiously approached it. He squatted low to the ground and frequently checked underneath the trailer for explosive devices. He moved along the side of the truck to the cab and slowly opened the driver's door.

He climbed up on the step and peered inside, carefully checking every possible hiding place, before moving toward the sleeping quarters. When he pulled the curtain back, Gustavo's lifeless face stared back at him.

"Shit!" Jerking his phone from his pocket, he called the Port Authority office.

"Robbins."

"Kevin—I need your help again. Can you find when this truck pulled into the overflow lot? Can you see when someone get out of it? And if so, can you get me a picture?"

"Based on where it's parked, I can check some of the trucks around it and see when they came in. That'll help narrow down a time when he pulled into that lot. Give me a sec, and I'll call you back."

While he waited for Kevin's return call, Silas walked to the back of the truck and very cautiously checked the locks before opening it. He knew with every move, he could set off another explosion, killing himself and others in the process. But if he didn't check and it hid a bomb on a timer, the results would be just as devastating. When he was confident he could safely get in the trailer, he swung the metal doors open as far as they would go, letting the failing sunlight illuminate the inside. Then he took a step back as his breath hitched in his chest.

His cell pinged and vibrated simultaneously with a text from a local number, startling him and making him jump. When he opened it, he found pictures from Kevin showing Rashad as he climbed out of the truck and left the parking lot on foot.

"Fucking hell!" he roared and hit Noah's number again. "He's here, Noah. He's still in the port. There's another truck with bombs in the trailer. I'm going in to disarm them now. There are multiple bombs connected to one timer, rigged to all go off at once. He parked it and left on foot. Gus is dead in the cab."

"You need help disarming it? I can be there in thirty seconds."

"It's a simple trigger, bro. This isn't one of his more sophisticated ones. I got this. Keep looking for Heather. Get everyone else looking for Rashad. He'll try to walk out of here after dark. I'm forwarding you a text with pictures of him getting out of the truck. Share it with everyone."

"On it. And Silas? Be careful."

"Always."

Moving slower than he'd ever moved in his life, Silas climbed into the trailer and inched toward the bomb. "These damn bomb lovers, they always make something tricky in them. They have to outsmart everyone else. Not this time, dickhead. Not this time."

After several harrowing minutes inside, he was able to breathe again when the timer stopped and the wires were disconnected from the explosives. When he climbed out of the trailer, he alerted the National Guard commander, and the explosives technicians took charge of the disposal.

It was well after dark by the time he returned to the search and rescue site. Bull was taking a break and guzzling a bottle of cold water when Silas walked up.

"Nothing on Heather yet?"

"No, not yet. There's just so much construction material to dig through. They have the dogs out there trying to lock on to a scent, but they haven't hit one so far. They're checking crevices with the heat-sensing equipment, but so far they can't get deep enough to lock on to a heat signature. Rebel has talked to Kay a few times, keeping her in the loop since they won't let anyone into the port area.

"The good news is the majority of the people who have been cleared to leave have opted to stay and help search the grounds. After you found that other truck with explosives, a growing concern there are more out there started moving through the workers. They're checking their normal work areas. If they find anything in the least bit out of the ordinary, the ordnance disposal unit will go in and check it out."

"They're allowing civilians to get involved?"

Bull shrugged. "It's a big port, and no one knows what's supposed to be in their area like the people actually doing the work. It's a matter of national security now, and every patriotic Texan wants to help. An armed National Guard member is stationed close to every major area in case anyone sees Rashad lurking in the shadows. We'd flush him out if we were out there, but Heather is our top priority, especially since *officially* we're off the case."

"She'd be our priority anyway."

Rebel, Roman, Tim, and Robin were still hard at work trying to find Heather, working in the general area Roman last saw her before the stairwell collapsed, when Silas joined them. Noah and Shadow were on the outer edge, working inward toward Rebel, so he slid his hands into a pair of gloves, joined Bull on the opposite side, and started moving the chunks of debris out of the search area.

"Good job with locating that other truck, Silas," Rebel interrupted the silence. "Listen, guys, I've been thinking a lot about the encrypted message I decoded, trying to keep my mind on something other than...just trying to stay focused while I keep digging through the rubble. The CIA analysts think 'cripple the lanes' means shutting down our interstates by cutting off our oil and gas supply. But I think their interpretation is completely wrong, and they're looking in the wrong place."

Silas glanced over at Rebel's bare hands, bleeding and raw from working nonstop over the past several hours. "What do you think it means?"

"It's pretty obvious now, isn't it? They're not just taking out our current *access* to oil and gas. They want to take out the actual *shipping* lanes—not the *driving* lanes. We'd have nothing at all coming in or out if they shut down the ports indefinitely because of a catastrophic attack. Noah and I talked about this bit earlier, before we got the call, but we didn't get to finish. The more I think about it, the more I'm convinced I'm right. Which means..."

"It means if there are more explosives, they're on the cargo ships floating in the waterway right now," Shadow replied, realization setting in. "They could have them set to explode at the same time, here and in New Orleans."

"That's why he's here," Silas muttered to himself.

"Why who's here?" Rebel asked, cutting his deadly gaze up to Silas. "Rashad is still in the port?"

"He was as of a couple of hours ago. He was caught on camera walking toward the general direction of the waterway. I thought he'd try to escape on foot after the cover of darkness, but now I think you're right."

"He may get out of the port tonight, but he will never escape from me. That I can guarantee."

21

CHAPTER TWENTY-ONE

Bill paced back and forth, growing angrier by the second. Rashad had always followed orders, had always performed the tasks expected of him. Until now. Until it mattered the most. Until their fucking necks were on the line and any failures would fall on Bill's shoulders.

"That little prick is pulling this shit on purpose," Bill spat out. "He's double-crossing me. Just like I knew his stupid ass would do. I should've listened to my gut on this one."

Bill shook his head and continued pacing, torn between calling Rashad again and just disappearing to let his partner take the fall alone. Everyone thought he was dead anyway. Only a couple of people knew he was still very much alive, that he wasn't the one who walked into the house minutes before it exploded that day. He'd taken advantage of an eager new recruit who was anxious to prove his exceptional disguise skills. One of two people who knew about it was Rashad himself, but that didn't bother Bill. No one would believe the word of a wanted terrorist who insisted a dead CIA agent was actually still alive—and dirty to boot.

As badly as he wanted to walk away, he also wanted what was promised to him. Rashad accepted this mission for honor, glory, and furthering their cause. The reason Bill joined them was much simpler—it had dollar signs tied to it. He was promised a life he'd like to become accustomed to rather than his life of barely scraping by. He wasn't naïve enough to think they wouldn't betray him if the opportunity presented itself.

He had the same plan himself.

But greed won over self-preservation, and he called Rashad again against his better judgment. "Status?"

"Something is wrong. The second location hasn't detonated, and it is way past time. I've been waiting for the opportunity to get onboard and check it out for myself. Have you heard from our brothers in New Orleans yet?"

"Yes, everyone is in place, and they're waiting for the final word from us. But the whole place is crawling with agents. They're methodically checking everything in the port. It's only a matter of time before they start boarding ships and checking crates. So far, they haven't interrupted our plans, but we're dangerously close to pulling the plug and walking away."

"No. We can't walk away now. There is still work to be done. The only way you get paid is when the New Orleans port is inoperable and the oil tankers are on fire. Then you can take your money and move to another country with your new name."

"You have twenty minutes to handle your part. If that means you have to sit in that tanker and blow yourself sky high, then so be it. If I don't see evidence of it in nineteen minutes and thirty seconds, you're on your own."

Bill disconnected, decided he'd take matters into his own hands, and packed a backpack with the materials he'd need to pull off his improvised changes. The original plan had called for the two separate attacks to occur simultaneously. The division in resources would cause chaos in the law enforcement agencies and FEMA response times. Whatever hiccup had caused the delay in Houston didn't mean they couldn't proceed with their plans for the port in New Orleans, though.

He reasoned the alternating attacks could wreak just as much havoc as dual, synchronized ones would. They wouldn't know where to expect the next hit. Every major government installation would be on high alert, and therefore, would hold on to their staff for defense rather than sending them to the Gulf for support. In his mind, doing something was infinitely better than doing nothing at all. And something needed to be done in order for him to be paid for his services.

Considerable extra security had been put in place at the Port of New Orleans. When Bill approached the entrance, he was stopped by soldiers in full combat gear. With a hand on his sidearm, one soldier approached the driver's side window while another circled the car with a bomb-sniffing dog. A third soldier stood off to the side, maintaining his intense glare and diligent observation.

"What brings you to the port tonight, sir?"

Bill held up his fake orders from the CIA director for inspection. "Just doing my job."

The soldier eyed his paperwork speculatively. "You're getting in a little late, aren't you?"

"Late by what standards? Do you think all of the investigation into the threats on the port is done inside here? Some of us have been out pounding the pavement to get tips and leads." Bill's displeased tone conveyed his annoyance with the soldier's questioning.

Satisfied with his response and acknowledgment of a clean car, the soldiers allowed Bill to pass through the roadblock. The truth was, Bill had long been unhappy with keeping secrets, not having the finer things in life, and envying the jet-setter mentality of the lowlife thugs he'd met with over the years. When he was approached to be the informant rather than the officer, with considerable benefits as perks, he jumped at the chance for a brand-new life. That was the precise reason why he was in the one place he shouldn't be—an area crawling with federal officers who were all bound and determined to foil a planned terrorist attack.

Once parked, he retrieved the items from his backpack and concealed his identity with the few essentials he had at his disposal. When he climbed out of his car, the tiny hairs on the back of his neck stood straight up and demanded his attention. A chill ran down his spine, and his pulse kicked up a notch. The only time he'd had that reaction in the past was when he was being watched.

Walking around his car nonchalantly, he used the time to stealthily examine his surroundings. Nothing appeared out of place to his observant eyes. No moving shadows. No lurking figures. But he was certain someone, somewhere, was watching him nonetheless. He walked toward the water, stepping into the shadow of the surrounding buildings for cover, and looked over his shoulder repeatedly for anyone tailing him.

He pulled his phone from his pocket and punched in the number for his local contact. After a couple of rings, the line connected, but he was met with silence. Bill understood the other man wasn't in a position where he could respond, prompting Bill to quietly issue his directive.

"Initiate the plan for the primary target. I'm implementing the contingency plan."

"Understood."

Bill disconnected and continued on his way to the cruise ship docks. The secondary target would destroy the few cruise ships docked in port overnight. The hint at civilian targets, and the few inevitable civilian deaths, would only serve to heighten the threat risk in other ports. Another safeguard he'd decided to employ to help ensure no additional troops were sent to his location.

He accessed the first cruise ship from the dock-level employee entrance. With all the commotion in the port, his presence onboard was barely noticed. No doubt other federal agents and port officers had made their rounds, checking anywhere and everywhere a device would be hidden to cause the most damage. The crew members onboard were busy preparing for their next voyage and had no time or interest to question him about his intentions.

"Your sacrifices will not be in vain," he mumbled to himself. "You're helping me retire to a life of luxury." He set the timer to give himself enough time to complete his tasks and get away from the last ship before the first one blew.

It was all coming together, one tactical piece at a time.

"He's on the move. Stay on him," Nick Tucker whispered into his comms.

"Got him," Blake replied. "He's not getting away."

"He's headed my way now," Alex replied. "On him."

"Picking up the trail now," Joe whispered.

"I'm coming up on the opposite side," Tucker replied and took off in a silent sprint.

The four-man covert team consistently rotated positions, keeping tabs on Bill's exact location as he stole through the night. With the four men watching from their hidden points when Bill entered the cruise ship, Tucker and Blake elected to take point while Joe and Alex stayed outside to cover the exits.

The organized chaos onboard the ship while the crew prepared for their next sailing was nearly as busy as the troops and agents scouring the port for weapons of destruction. The hustle and bustle helped Tucker and Blake to blend in and gave them large pallets of inventory for the perfect cover. With each bomb Bill set, Tucker and Blake immediately moved in behind him to disarm it.

"That's the last one on this ship," Tucker advised. "He's headed back out."

A couple of minutes later, Bill walked across the ramp, no longer even bothering to try to be invisible. "He's going into the next ship down," Joe alerted. "Alex and I will take this one."

"Roger that. We'll be waiting for him outside," Blake replied.

When he emerged from the second ship, Bill tossed his backpack into the water and picked up his pace in the direction of his car. Tucker chuckled lightly into his comm, making the others laugh along with him.

"Good luck with your car, buddy." Joe's tone dripped with contempt for his former partner. "See how you like being set up."

"He'll get his, Brown." Tucker's confidence was reassuring. He wasn't a man who was easily rattled—or lightly fucked with. "Soon."

In much the same manner they tailed him to the cruise docks, they coordinated tracking him to his next location. When he rounded the last building corner before returning to where his car should have been, all four men waited with smiles plastered on their faces. His cartoonish skid to a halt when he realized his car was gone elicited hushed laughs and insulting epithets from the group.

"Someone moved his cheese and left a rat trap instead. That's just rude," Alex quipped.

"Taking bets on what he does next. I say it's the typical head in the hands move," Blake hedged.

Bill ran his fingers through his hair, angrily grabbing handfuls before shaking his fists in the air. "Oh! Good call, man. He's dying to shout at the top of his lungs right now," Joe chuckled.

"He'll have that feeling again soon, but for completely different reasons." The malice in Tucker's voice was palpable.

"What are you going to do with him?" Blake asked.

Tucker glanced down at his watch. "Reaper's team is currently being advised they are back on the case, but their orders to locate and apprehend the suspects have changed."

"Changed to what?" Blake asked for clarification.

"Apprehend is no longer in their orders. It's now locate and eradicate. I think Rebel would appreciate eradicating this traitor himself, right after I help the team locate him," Tucker explained.

"Why did their orders change all of a sudden? What happened?"

"One of the tankers in Houston just blew a couple of minutes ago. They're already scrambling agents to the site. Reaper warned them this would happen, and now they're concerned it'll only get worse. My boss just now alerted me about the call to eradicate."

"He was my partner. He framed me. Maybe I should go ahead and take him out," Joe replied.

"I get that, Brown. But he helped bury Rebel's wife in Houston. That gives him first dibs in my book."

"On the move again," Blake interrupted. "Toward the oil tankers."

"He'll be looking for his new partners. We should let him help us find the rest of them."

"Good thinking, Alex. Everyone, move out. Don't lose him, no matter what." Tucker emphasized each of his last three words.

Moving effortlessly through the night, the four men followed Bill with precision and ease.

Tucker patched into the FBI command center. ""He's on the phone. Trace that call. Who's he talking to?"

"Got it. It's one of them." The FBI analyst located the exact coordinates in the port where the cell phone was located and relayed the information to the team. "Bring them in."

"Copy that," Tucker replied. "Blake, Alex—apprehend that cowardly terrorist. Joe, you're with me on Bill. Move out."

They split up, each team clear on the intentions of their mission. Bill took the long way around the port, doubling back and skirting around buildings in his attempts to lose a tail and avoid detection, adding too many precious minutes to his journey. When he finally reached his destination, a rendezvous point with the comrade he'd recently spoken to in the hull of an oil tanker, he once again found he'd reached his destination too late.

His partner in crime was gone, as were the crucial items he needed to carry out his part of the plan. Joe knew the very second the dread overcame him as understanding dawned.

"Your gut told you, didn't it? That old feeling of knowing when you're being watched. Being followed. You felt it and ignored it, thought you could get away before it was too late." Joe spoke calmly as he approached Bill from behind. Bill stood motionless, with the exception of dropping his chin to his chest. "But there's no escaping now, Bill. It would be foolish even to try. But if that's what you're thinking, go ahead and try. I won't hesitate to shoot you in the head."

"Is that any way to treat your partner?" Bill replied.

"No, it's not," Joe conceded. "But that is how traitors are treated. You betrayed me, framed me for your treachery, and left me to take the fall in your place. For that alone, you deserve to be shot."

"But that decision isn't up to us," Tucker added. Bill turned to look at him, unaware another man was in the hull of the ship with them.

"Oh? Who is it up to?" Bill asked, mock amusement in his tone and his expression.

"Rebel. The man whose wife was buried in the explosion in Houston. The man who's still digging to find her, praying she's still alive under all those tons of concrete and steel. That's who decides your fate," Tucker replied.

The shock that registered on Bill's face could not be faked. "I...I didn't know his wife was in the building."

"That doesn't matter. You knew others were in it. But the fact that *she* was sealed your fate."

"What do you owe him anyway?"

"I served under Reaper while in the Army, then worked for Steele Security for a while before taking a private security job. Now I'm DEA and I owe them my allegiance, and they have it."

"Your time here is through, Bill," Joe concluded. "Your friends have started singing like canaries, giving up the locations where you told them to put the explosives. Pity you didn't use men who were true to the cause. Hired hands have no loyalty, especially when they're facing life in prison with no possibility of parole for forty years for treason."

"Let's go. There is one person who will be glad to see you."

The five-hour ride back to Houston was mostly silent. While Tucker normally didn't approve of cold-blooded murder, what Bill had done to his friend Rebel deserved to have justice served. The orders for eradication came from the president. With no higher office in the land, it was fitting that command apply to both of the main conspirators in the plot. He had no doubt Rebel and team would find Rashad as soon as they located Heather, and delivering Bill to him was the least he could do to help his friend.

By the time they reached the Port of Houston, Rebel had been searching for Heather in the remains of the twelve-story building for more than eighteen hours. Even with the briefing of what had occurred, Tucker couldn't comprehend what his eyes saw. Before he'd seen it firsthand, he held out some hope for Heather's safe return. But the complete demolition of the building before him left the most hopeless—and helpless—feeling he'd ever experienced.

In spite of that, the first thing he did after securing his prisoner was don a pair of gloves and join the search and rescue effort. No matter how bleak the situation appeared to him, he would work nonstop as long as Rebel and his other brothers remained out there. Day and night, for as long as it took.

Reaper approached Tucker and extended his hand. "Good to see you again, Tucker. It's been a while."

"I hate that it's under these circumstances. Have you told Rebel about your change in orders yet?"

Reaper shook his head from side to side. "It wouldn't matter to him. Rashad is already dead as soon as Rebel's finished here. The fact that his death is now sanctioned means nothing."

"I brought Rashad's partner with me to give Rebel first dibs on him."

"Who is it?"

"The dirty CIA agent who faked his death, Bill Smith."

"Fucking bastard," Reaper growled. "When did DEA Special Agents start handing over dirty CIA operatives for execution?"

Tucker shrugged one shoulder and lifted one side of his mouth in a lopsided grin. "Call it an early Christmas present."

22

CHAPTER TWENTY-TWO

During the second day, the feeling and sensations of pain in Rebel's hands were long since gone, but he kept moving chunks of concrete, gnarled metal, and destroyed remnants of office furniture in his quest to find Heather. The twisted feelings inside him had only increased with every minute that ticked by on the clock with no real progress being made. Tim, one of the search and rescue crew members, and Robin, his loyal black Lab, had worked diligently throughout the night in solidarity with Rebel.

"Robin has bonded with you, ya know?" Tim chatted with Rebel off and on during the night, lending his moral support in every way he knew how. "Every time I try to get her to take a break, she stares at you and whines until I bring her back out here."

"She's a good girl," Rebel replied, forcing a small smile and consciously keeping his irritation under wraps. "You've trained her well. It's actually very impressive to see the search and rescue dogs in action out here."

A few other dogs and handlers had located survivors buried under the demolished building. With each round of clapping and cheering, Rebel's hope for Heather being found alive waxed and waned. His conflicting feelings of being elated there were still survivors, and envy that it wasn't his wife they'd found, created a constant war in his heart. He'd never give up until he found her, but the state he would find her in was a constant burden on his mind and his spirits.

How far underneath the debris could she be buried?

Was there enough oxygen down there to keep her alive, or would it completely run out?

Had the crumbled concrete buried and suffocated her?

When he allowed these questions to fester inside him, the desire to find Rashad and tear him apart with his bare hands built to levels that would rival a hydrogen bomb explosion. That bled over into his interactions with everyone else. He'd tried to distance himself as much as possible because the stress of it all was tearing him apart. Tim and Robin had been a godsend in keeping him sane and level-headed for the time being, forcing him to be around at least one other person during a time he'd rather have been left alone. After she was found, he'd deal with Rashad in his own special way.

"Come on, girl. Let's get you some water," Tim called to Robin, but she ignored him. "Robin. Come."

Robin locked in place and started barking vigorously. Her excitement was almost uncontainable, causing her to jump back and forth on top of the debris. But she kept her snout pointed to a single crack between two large pieces of building material. Rebel stopped in mid-motion and stared at her for several seconds before his gaze swung to Tim. His eyes asked the question he couldn't bring himself to verbalize.

"She's got something! We need some help over here," Tim yelled.

Group members from every direction swarmed on the location Robin indicated. Reaper, Shadow, Bull, Roman, Joe, and Tucker surrounded Rebel. Everyone watched on pins and needles as a small camera on the end of a flexible tube was passed through the crack and into the darkness below. The tiny LED light illuminated the cave-like fissure, and the image was transmitted up to the screen held by the camera operator. Rebel started to move so he could see the screen, but Tim stopped him.

"Wait. There's a reason why the image isn't broadcast for everyone to see. Give him a few seconds to determine what we're dealing with down there."

In his mind, Rebel knew Tim was correct. She may still be alive, but the image of her current condition would forever be burned into his memory if he dared to look at the screen. In the event she didn't survive, Tim was only trying to save him from a lifetime of the haunting scene. Rebel nodded once, agreeing to wait for their signal it was safe to look.

Tim cupped Rebel's shoulder and squeezed. "I know I'm asking a lot of you."

"You have no idea how hard it is for me not to grab that camera from his hands and do it myself. My whole life is down there, and I don't know if she's alive or dead."

"I need you to also consider there's a possibility Robin found another victim. It's hard not to get your hopes up, but there were a lot of people in this building," Tim added.

"It's Heather," Rebel replied. "I feel her. I know it's her."

Tim nodded his head, but his dubious expression conveyed his honest thoughts. Unable to wait any longer, Rebel darted behind the camera operator and watched the live streaming images over his shoulder. What appeared to be a twisted metal cage came into view and the camera operator halted to fine-tune the resolution.

"What is that?" He talked to himself absently as he worked the equipment, moving the camera around for a different angle.

"It's the framework for the stairs. The concrete is gone, but that's the mangled steel frame the steps were built on," Rebel replied. "Zoom in right there."

When the camera zoomed in tighter, they both saw an arm move inside the cage. "There! Did you see that?" Rebel wanted to dive headfirst into the opening and bring the search and rescue mission to an end. He wanted his wife back at his side.

The camera operator adjusted the resolution again now that he had a specific target to identify. The camera panned out, giving a wider view, and Rebel's heart surged in his chest. There, buried beneath the piles of ruin and wreckage, lay the love of his life. Boulder-sized chunks of building remains surrounded her, but the thick steel frame of the stairwell had essentially cocooned her, creating a bent and contorted cage that supported the weight of the remains directly above it.

"Call the structural engineers and get them over here immediately!" The group leader instantly took control of the scene. "Everyone in the section immediately around us, carefully move to the sides. Be careful where and how you step. We don't want any shifting if we can avoid it."

Another volunteer sent a small speaker down the shaft to her and unclipped the headset from his utility belt. He extended his hand toward Rebel and passed the headset to him. "Talk to her. Let her know what we're doing and that she's not alone."

Rebel hooked it over his ear, and the volunteer gave him the go-ahead nod when he'd turned it on. For the first time in what felt like forever, he was at a loss for words of what to say to his wife. He had no idea how to reassure her. He had no way of knowing how long it would take to safely get her out of the dungeon she was buried in. He had no clue what he was supposed to say.

Her back was propped up against one side of her protective cage. The camera focused on her face, displaying the streaks of dried blood, cuts, scrapes, and bruises lying under layers of concrete dust. Her hair was matted to her head in places, wild and untamed in others. Though she kept her eyes closed, they fluttered every few seconds as she attempted to open them.

In that moment, Rebel realized he'd never seen anyone or anything more beautiful in his entire life.

"Hey, baby. I have to admit, this hiding spot was a pretty brilliant idea for our ongoing game of hide-and-seek. You've really set the bar high with this one. But as you can see, I found you. Surely by now, you know me better than to think I'd let something as trivial as a few hundred tons of steel and concrete stand in my way."

He bit back the emotions that threatened to overtake him when he saw a small smile play on her lips.

"We're using a small camera to see you and a one-way speaker to talk to you. All you have to do is nod or something to give me a sign. I'll keep talking and keep you company. You know me—I won't leave here until you're safe in my arms again. In fact, I'm never leaving you again. Not for Miami, not for the government, nothing can keep us apart again. Now that I have you in my sights, you'll be out of there as soon as possible. We have all kinds of people up here plotting and planning, brilliant minds who can figure this out in no time. I'm right here with you, Heather."

She slowly nodded to indicate she understood, her sluggish movements leaving no doubt of the trauma her body had sustained. She tried to open her eyes again but quickly shut them and winced in pain.

"Leave your eyes closed, sweetheart," Rebel coaxed her. "There's a lot of concrete dust, and it can scratch your eyes and make them hurt like hell. We'll get them rinsed good when we get you out of there. Do you remember what happened?"

She nodded, and her face fell as sadness overcame her.

"I know you're sad, and I know you're scared. But we'll get through this together, okay? You and me. Oh, and there's someone up here I can't wait for you to meet. She already loves you, and she hasn't even met you yet. She's been beside me all night, searching for you and refusing to rest until she found you. Her name is Robin, and she has the most beautiful brown eyes you'll ever see."

Heather arched one eyebrow, daring him to continue complimenting another woman to her.

Rebel laughed good-naturedly. "And she has the shiniest black hair. Come to think of it, her hair color does remind me of yours. Anyway, let me see if I can get her over here to say hello to you."

He looked up from the screen to find Tim there, smiling and waiting with Robin. Rebel knelt down beside her then Tim gave the command. "Speak to the lady, Robin."

"Rrr-ruff!" Robin barked.

Rebel ran his fingers over the screen, his heart bursting with love when Heather responded with a full smile. "Robin says hello, babe.

She's a gorgeous black Lab with a heart of gold. You'll love her, and I'm pretty sure you'll want to keep her."

Engineers and construction crews approached, poised to explain the plan they'd devised for extricating her. Apprehension unlike anything he'd ever experienced before gripped him tightly, squeezing him like a vise from the inside. He put the headset on mute before he addressed them.

"I just found her after almost two days of searching. Do not do anything that could take her away from me again." The threatening timbre of his voice left no room for misunderstanding.

"We'll take good care of her. Everything will be handled one step at a time to make sure all the supports are in place." The engineer attempted to assure him, but Rebel would only rest easy when she was finally rescued.

"Okay, baby," he said softly. "We're starting the process of getting you out of there. You'll hear a lot of noise. They're bringing in heavy equipment to move the larger pieces out of the way. You'll feel vibrations, which will almost certainly shake smaller pieces onto you. Keep your head covered just in case, but I'll be here watching their every move, every second."

She mouthed *I love you* in response, and tears began to trickle down her cheeks.

"I've loved you every single day since the day we first met. You're my best friend, my lover, and my wife, and you're the best person I know. You're beautiful and sexy and caring and giving and funny and strong and independent and supportive—and so much more.

"I'm not saying goodbye, my love. You're not leaving me. Want to know how I know that? Because I can feel you. I feel you inside me, beside me, all around me. Because you're the best part of me, the part I can't live without. The day I can't feel you anymore will be the day I die. But that's not today, Heather. We still have a life to live out together. So don't you dare give up and even think about leaving me."

Her tears continued to roll down her cheeks, but the trepidation that had covered her expression was replaced with the determination he recognized. She nodded and mouthed *okay*. When the extrication work began, she did as he'd instructed and covered her head with her arms. He didn't miss the grimace of pain that flashed across her face when she raised both arms, but she didn't let it stop her.

Piece by piece, they carefully moved the largest chunks of debris at the top of the pile away from the rescue site. With every movement, the engineers reevaluated the structure of what remained and identified what to clear next. Inevitably, a portion would break loose and free-fall into the space below, tumbling through the twisted metal that imprisoned her before hitting her. Her muffled cries of pain and fright drove Rebel mad. In the tight space where she was trapped by the metal, she had nowhere to move to dodge the shards. When they'd cleared a hole barely large enough for a person to fit through on the surface, he thrust the headset back to the volunteer and jumped feet-first into the opening before anyone could stop him.

"I'm here, baby. I'm with you."

He reached his arms through the steel bars that still caged her and covered her head with his muscular arms. The metal had been driven deep into the ground around her and still supported some of the wreckage that hadn't yet been moved. Though she didn't have much room to move, she slid toward him, flush with the metal, and wrapped her arms as far around him as she could reach through the metal bars. Her fingers were battered and sobs racked her body, but she held on to him with all the strength she had left.

"You shouldn't be here." Her voice barely came across as a rough whisper with her throat and mouth coated in the dust from the devastated building.

"This is exactly where I should be—it's where you are."

Through each meticulous step of the work, Rebel stayed at her side. His strong arms protected her from falling dangers. His words soothed her frazzled nerves. His presence gave her the strength she needed to hold on. In between activities, volunteers lowered several bottles of water down to them. In the first delivery, he used the bottles meant for his rehydration to wash the grit out of her eyes and clean the dust off her face. After clearing the dust from her mouth and throat, he nursed her wounds and made sure she was well hydrated.

Each time the equipment started up, he gathered her in his arms through the metal bars and used his body to shield hers.

The sun was setting again when they'd cleared enough away to safely cut the metal and get her out. A blowtorch was lowered to Rebel, and he hesitantly examined the cage that surrounded her. If the cut weakened the metal any further, the weight could shift and bury them both. But they'd been in the danger zone long enough, and the odds of something tragic happening increased. Their lives were in the hands of the structural engineers.

Rebel held his breath while he made the cuts at the precise locations in which he was instructed. When he'd cut enough away for Heather to squeeze through, he scooped her up in his arms and crushed her to him while she cried tears of joy and relief. The team above lowered harnesses down to them to pull them out to safety and freedom. He helped Heather into her harness before stepping into his own and pulling her back into his arms for safekeeping.

The thunderous roar of the crowd when they emerged from the certain death trap was humbling. Heather looked around her, blinking repeatedly from the pain and from the tears that blurred her vision, and was awed at the scene. The mass of people who'd voluntarily worked hours on end to find and free as many as possible was unbelievable.

"Brax," she choked out, unable to express anything else.

"I know, love. Believe me when I say every single one of them wanted to be here. To help in any way. And I'm so grateful for them."

Paramedics were waiting in the wings and rushed in as quickly as the workers unhooked their harnesses. At first, Heather tried to resist medical treatment.

"I'm a nurse," she rasped and waved the gurney away. "I'm okay."

"Nurses are almost as bad at being a patient as paramedics are," one of them joked but didn't move away.

"You're a wonderful nurse. You're not okay. You're injured, and you're a patient as of right now. Get on the gurney." Rebel crossed his arms over his wide chest and dared her to argue with him.

She climbed onto the gurney, careful to avoid further injury to her side and leg, and stretched out. One of the paramedics started an IV for her hydration while the other performed an initial medical assessment.

"Which hospital do you want to go to?" the one who performed the assessment asked her pointedly.

Resigned to the fact she genuinely did need medical attention, she nodded when Rebel gave the name of the hospital where she worked. The uncertainty swirling in her mind was the only reason she didn't want to leave for the hospital. She knew she needed treatment, but she wasn't ready to face the questions she couldn't bring herself to ask.

Has my dad been found?

Was he transported to the hospital?

How bad were his injuries?

When can I see him?

Is he still alive?

Loaded and ready to go, Rebel jumped into the back of the ambulance with her, staying at her side as he promised.

"Do you want us to meet you there? I don't want to intrude if the two of you need some time alone." Noah stood at the back of the ambulance, holding the edge of the door.

Heather raised her head and replied for them both. "You're our family. You don't have to ask."

Noah grinned and winked at her. "We'll be there, then. Rebel, I got a call, and we're back on for locate and eradicate. It's your call, but personally, I don't think you want to sit this one out."

Through their nonverbal conversation, Rebel read between the lines and instantly understood the difference in their assignment.

"This investigation belongs to me. There's no way in hell I'd miss it."

CHAPTER TWENTY-THREE

On the ride from the port to the hospital, Brax handed Heather his cell phone.

"Let your mom hear your voice so she knows you're okay. She's been worried sick, and they wouldn't let her in the port."

She dialed her number, and her heart ripped in two from the panic in Kay's voice when she answered.

"Brax? Is she okay?"

"I'm okay, Mom."

Completely choked with emotion, neither could speak after that simple exchange, so Rebel took the phone and finished the conversation.

"Kay, we're heading to Heather's hospital, where she knows the doctors and nurses. Meet us in the ER when you've calmed down and can safely drive. You don't have to rush, she's really okay. We'll see you soon."

Rebel leaned over and gently kissed Heather while lovingly stroking her matted hair. "It's okay, baby. You can cry all you need to. I'll be here to dry your tears and take care of you."

Kay was waiting in the emergency room when the ambulance arrived. Even though it had only been a couple of days since Heather had last seen her, she noted how the stress and worry appeared to have aged her mother by several years.

Kay rushed to her when she was wheeled in and looked her over. "Heather, are you okay? How badly are you hurt? What can I do?"

"Just my ribs and my leg hurt, Mom. I'm okay. Brax has been taking good care of me," she replied weakly.

"Thank God you were found. I don't know what I would do if..."

What Kay didn't say told Heather more than she wanted to know at the moment. Compartmentalizing the traumatic event was helping her stay sane. She wasn't prepared to know everything all at once. Whatever information Kay had about Emmett's condition couldn't be good news, and that fact nearly pushed her into a panic attack.

She was thoroughly evaluated, questioned, poked, prodded, X-rayed, treated, and medicated for the injuries she'd sustained. From the trauma and stress her body had sustained, the doctor decided to keep her for a twenty-three-hour observation and make a determination about admitting or discharging her at that time. She was moved to a large private room to give Brax enough room to stay with her.

When the doctor made his rounds the following morning, she convinced him she would convalesce much better at home than in the hospital. With assurances that Rebel, Kay, and the rest of their extended family would be there to help her, the doctor agreed to let her go home. Bull brought Heather's Land Rover to the hospital, and Rebel drove his wife home.

Later that evening, she was surrounded by her friends and family in the comfort of her own home.

"I'm fine, really. You don't have to put your lives on hold for me." Heather tried to reassure everyone she was fine, but Rebel could see through her carefully crafted façade.

After everyone left, she attempted to rest and relax, but it was fleeting. Every time she closed her eyes, she saw her father hanging from the broken steps. She saw the terrified eyes of the other victims looking to her for answers she didn't have. She saw the building collapse on her, trapping her under an enormous amount of solid concrete inside a metal cage.

She was certain she'd die in that cage. That it would become her tomb, and she'd suffer an agonizingly slow death she couldn't do anything about. She made the mistake once of turning on the television and watching the news. The list of the identified victim's names scrolled across the bottom of the screen; each one was harder to deal with than the previous. When the footage of the attack scene filled the screen, it triggered a full-on panic attack.

Over the following few days, sleep mostly escaped her because the visions turned into nightmares, and she'd wake, screaming and crying. When Kay showed up, her eyes red and nearly swollen shut from crying, Heather knew they'd found her father before her mother had spoken a word. They'd found his body several yards from where Heather had been trapped, but he hadn't been sheltered by the steel frame. He'd been buried underneath the concrete that had caved in on the stairs below him, where many other victims had been trapped despite her attempts to tell them to go back up.

As far as injuries sustained, she felt blessed to only have a broken ankle, hairline fractures in her ribs, and too many cuts, scrapes, and bruises to count.

It was the psychological injuries she wasn't confident would ever fully heal.

"Good morning, my love."

It was early morning, and they were still in the bed, facing each other. Rebel had been her lifesaver—both literally and figuratively. He'd gotten her out of that concrete tomb, and he'd been by her side through every episode of anxiety she'd endured since.

"Good morning, honey. You didn't sleep at all last night," she observed. "I can tell by your eyes."

"You don't need to be concerned about me. I'm the one who's worried about you. You didn't sleep much at all, and you were screaming and crying in your sleep."

She dropped her eyes to focus on his chest, trying to hide the fear that had a tight grip on her. "I'm sorry if I woke you. Just having bad dreams."

"Don't be sorry. When that happens, I wrap my arms around you and whisper in your ear. Your entire body relaxes against me, and you go back to sleep. I'm glad I'm here to help you."

"I'm glad you're here, too, Brax. They haven't caught Rashad yet, have they?"

She glanced up at his face and caught the flash of murderous rage before it was quickly masked again. "Not yet. Is that what's scaring you so badly? You think he'll come back after you?"

She nodded, and tears slipped from her eyes before she could stop them. "That, and I'm really not ready to attend my daddy's funeral today. How can I say goodbye?"

"You don't, sweetheart. Your love for him won't end today, and you don't have to say goodbye to it. His love for you didn't end with his death, he took it with him. You'll miss him. You'll wish he were here. But you never have to say goodbye."

"Is that how you dealt with it?"

"With losing Dalton? Yes. It took me a while, but I eventually realized that, and it helped me."

"Thank you. It does help to look at it that way."

"Back to Rashad. How much do you think about that? How often does he frighten you?"

"All the time," she admitted reluctantly.

Rebel stroked her face with his hand, wiping the tears from her eyes with the pad of his thumb. "You don't have to worry about him ever again. Very soon, he'll be no more than a memory. Memories can't come back to life and hurt you."

"Is he dead?" she whispered.

"Not yet." *But he will be.*

"You know where he is?"

"I know exactly where he is at all times."

"But you haven't taken him in yet?"

"I've been waiting until you were feeling a little better, a little more secure. When I go get him, I'll have some people come to keep you company while I'm out. It won't take long. But no one has moved on him because his ass is mine. Now that I know he's causing you most of this fear and anxiety, I'll close up this case very soon. Today, we'll pay our respects to your father."

EVERY PEW in the expansive church was full with friends, family, and employees who wanted to pay their respects to the man who was larger than life. Many who made it out of the building had asked if they could speak at his memorial, to share what he'd meant to them. Kay was so moved by the requests to honor her late husband she couldn't deny them.

One after the other approached the pulpit with their written speech in hand, but most never even referred to their notes. The graphic memories of how he'd sacrificed his own life to save theirs in the stairwell that day were forever etched onto their psyche. Notes would never do the actual event any justice.

When Heather rose and walked toward the pulpit, Rebel watched her in shocked amazement. She hadn't mentioned to him she would be one of the speakers at her father's funeral. The events had weighed on her heavily enough, and he was genuinely concerned reliving that day in front of everyone would be her breaking point. He sat on the edge of the pew, ready to spring into action and carry her out if that's what it took to save her.

He watched as she took a deep breath to calm her racing heart. She picked up a tissue and dabbed at the corners of her eyes, already fighting back the tears before she'd uttered the first word. She hid the slight tremor in her hand by gripping the sides of the podium. This was killing her, but she still faced it like a champion.

"Listening to all your stories of how my daddy saved you has been a blessing in disguise. I can't describe how very much I have dreaded this day, this service, and facing what it'll mean to my family when everything is said and done. But each of you has given me back a piece of my father to hold on to for the rest of my life, and for that, I thank you from the bottom of my heart.

"I'm not here to share the story of how he also saved my life, which he did. That's not something I can talk about just yet. But I do want to share with you a very different story about my father from that same day. You see, I went to his office to talk to him because he was rarely home while the acquisition process was underway. I love my dad very much, and I needed him to understand and support a decision I'd recently made."

Brax sat motionless and waited for her to continue, to share with him and the rest of the congregation why she went to his office on that day of all days.

"He had offered my husband a job so we could stay here in Houston and be together as a family. Brax accepted it so he could be with me. He agreed to leave behind a business he'd help build from scratch, a group of friends who are as close as family to him, and a life he was accustomed to in Miami—all for me. Because he loves me.

"That day, I told my father about two decisions I'd made and wanted to explain why they were so important to me. The first one I told him was Brax and I have decided to start a family soon. He was thrilled about that, about the prospects of being a doting grandfather and spoiling the baby even more than we could.

"The second decision was that I couldn't let Brax give up everything he'd worked so hard to build into a success just because I didn't want to give up what I was comfortable with here. It wasn't fair to my husband because I can be a nurse anywhere. So, instead of him moving here to work for my dad, I'd move to Miami and be a nurse there.

"What I thought would end up in a huge fight became the best conversation I've ever had with my father. We broke down walls that had been between us for years. We cried, we forgave, we healed, we loved. He asked me to pass on a couple of messages for him—from that conversation and then again after he saved me—because he knew he wouldn't make it out.

"Mom, he asked me to tell you he loves you and he'll be waiting for you.

"Brax, he asked me to tell you he loves you like the son he never had. In his office, he talked about some mistakes he'd made years ago, things he allowed you to believe but he never meant. He intended to ask for your forgiveness, and he said he'd be honored if you'd allow him to call you 'son.' He was proud of you and everything you've accomplished, and he was supportive of my decision to move to be with you.

"I'm sharing all of this personal information about my father with you to say this... He wasn't perfect. He made mistakes. He was stubborn and hard-headed at times. He was a hero. He saved my life. He saved many of your lives. All of these qualities and characteristics made him the man he was.

"We all have some variation of these qualities. So, in honor of my father, I simply ask this...in some way, it doesn't matter if it's big or small, be a hero to someone else who needs your help. You never know when one small thing you do makes a big difference in someone else's life."

After she took her seat next to Rebel again as the music played, he wrapped his arm around her and tucked her into his side, instinctively protecting and shielding her. He leaned over, his lips grazed her ear, and whispered to her. "I'm so proud of you for doing that. I know how hard that was for you to do. Are you sure you want to leave Houston, and move to Miami with me? Do you need time to think about it?"

She met his gaze with her tear-laden eyes. "I've thought about it for a long time now, my love. My mind was already made up before all this happened, but this has only reaffirmed to me I've made the right decision. You're everything to me, Brax, and with you is the only place I want to be."

When they left from the graveside service, Rebel noticed a familiar pair standing off to the side, patiently waiting for them to approach. He glanced over at Heather as she raised her hand to her face and wiped away the tears that continued to fall.

"Babe, I told you there was someone I wanted you to meet the night we got you out of that hole. She's here now, and I think you'd love her."

"Okay, Brax. Who is she?"

He led the way, holding her hand and giving her silent reassurances. "Heather, this is Robin. She worked with me, almost nonstop, until she locked on to your scent."

Heather leaned down in front of her and was instantly drawn into her expressive brown eyes. She fondly stroked Robin's shiny coat. "Thank you for finding me, Robin. You saved my life. You didn't even know me, but you kept working without being asked or forced to do it. I owe you everything, sweet girl."

Robin leaned into Heather, placing her head against Heather's chest. Heather lowered her head until her forehead rested on top of Robin's head, the two bonding and blocking out the rest of the world.

"Babe, this is Tim. He's Robin's handler, and he was out there helping, too. Tim and Robin were the key to my sanity out there."

Heather looked up at Tim. "I can't thank you enough, Tim. It's humbling and overwhelming when I think about how you and the others voluntarily put your own lives in danger to save complete strangers."

"We enjoy helping others. It gives us a sense of purpose, really. I have to tell you Robin has never bonded with anyone like she has the two of you. She has acted like she was in mourning for the last few days. Now that I see her with you, I know she was. She's claimed you as her family."

Rebel and Heather exchanged glances. "Are you saying you want us to take her?" Heather asked.

"If you'll love her, give her a good home, and treat her like family. She wouldn't have attached herself to you if she didn't sense you were good, honest people."

"I'd love to take her home with us, Tim. But I'd feel guilty taking your dog from you."

"She is a great dog and I love her, but she's not my only one. As sad as she's been lately, I really think she'd rather be with you."

"Then she's welcome to come home with us," Rebel replied. "I don't know how to repay you for this."

"You don't owe me anything. Give your love to Robin and we'll call it even."

The men shook hands then Heather stood and threw her arms around Tim's neck. "Thank you so much," she choked out. "Thank you."

Rebel collected Robin's things from Tim's vehicle and took his two ladies home to rest.

LATER THAT EVENING, Rebel and Heather were alone in their home, drained from the emotional toll the day had taken on them. Heather was stretched out on the couch with her head in Rebel's lap while he lovingly massaged her head. Robin had stretched out on the love seat, content and cozy in her new home. Within minutes, Heather was sound asleep, sleeping better than she had since the whole ordeal began. Her breaths were even and her muscles were relaxed. For once, she wasn't having nightmares, reliving being buried alive, existing in fear.

Her eyes fluttered and she opened them, looking up at Rebel. Her hand followed her gaze, cupping his face in her palm and running her fingers through the stubble of his beard. "I've missed you, Brax."

"I'm right here, baby. I haven't left."

She pushed up on one hand, only wincing slightly at the pain in her side. "No, that's not what I meant."

She covered his lips with hers, teased them apart with the tip of her tongue, and then claimed ownership of his mouth. She moved cautiously, minding her injuries, and straddled his lap.

"I mean like this," she purred. "This is how I've missed you."

His fingers threaded through her short black hair before gripping a handful and holding it tightly. He tilted her head to the side, exposing the sensitive area of her neck, before he voraciously feasted on her succulent skin.

"Yes," she hissed in ecstasy. "I love how that feels."

Their bodies slick with sweat, their hearts pounding against their chests, they made love for hours. Rediscovering one another. Reconnecting after a harrowing event. Reestablishing the connection that had carried them through so many happy and sad times throughout the years.

Their love was stronger than the blast that had rocked their world.

It was more powerful than the terrorist who had threatened their existence.

It was more consuming than the fear that had tried to tear them apart.

It was alive.

CHAPTER TWENTY-FOUR

Over the next few weeks, Rebel watched Heather become stronger and seemingly more like herself, until the sun went down and darkness covered the world like a heavy blanket shrouding the light. Her external wounds were healing, but the psychological injuries were still taking a toll on her.

He'd waited until he was certain she could manage without him continuously being at her side. Then he arranged for Brianna, Chaise, and Amelia to keep her company while he went out to finish his job. When Brianna suggested the whole family spend the day together to initiate a return to normalcy, Rebel heartily agreed.

"I'll be back as soon as I can. There are a couple of loose ends Tucker and I need to wrap up." He sealed his promise with a kiss while he lovingly stroked her cheek. "Introduce Robin to Amelia while I'm gone."

"All I want is for you to be careful and come back home to me. Say it. Promise me."

"I promise. I will be careful, and I will be back home with you before you even know I'm gone. Our house will be full of people, and they'll keep you very occupied. I have to go meet Tucker now, babe. I love you."

"I love you, Brax."

He opened the front door to leave and was greeted by a large group of their friends and family. "Look, babe. Some of our guests are already here to see you. I'll be quick."

"Oh, good! I'm glad they're here." Heather walked to the door to greet their friends, but Rebel felt her eyes boring into his back until he was out of sight.

REBEL DROVE to their rendezvous point, parked his truck, and walked in silence alongside Tucker over the last two blocks to their final destination. Rebel opened the front door, walked inside, and quickly assessed the scene. Tucker inclined his head toward Rebel and closed the door behind him on his way back out. Rebel moved around the small, dilapidated house, arranging the supplies and perfectly setting the stage.

"You're probably wondering what the fuck is happening right about now." Rebel paused when he realized Rashad was awake, and he looked down directly into Rashad's eyes. "I'll be glad to explain it to you. We don't have much time, though, so I'll have to talk while I work."

He walked to the freezer and removed the vials of TATP Rashad had already made. He carefully set them up in a row on the small end table beside where Rashad lay on the couch.

"You are about to blow yourself up with your own devices. Yeah, I know it's a little shocking since you can't move at all right now. But it'll make sense by the end of this story. Try to keep up with me.

"My wife is the best person I know. She's a nurse, as you well know since you followed her around the hospital and took pictures of her. She takes care of people who are very sick and fighting for their lives. As an oncology nurse, she's seen her fair share of tragedy over the years. But she keeps going back, she keeps trying to help, because there are always those patients who defy the odds and beat the cancer growing inside them. She's an amazing person."

Rebel rearranged the furniture in the small room as he talked, moving everything away from in front of the front window so there was nothing obstructing the view into the living room. When he was satisfied with the setup, he turned back to Rashad.

"You can't imagine the rage and fury I felt when I learned that my wife, the love of my life, the one person I can't live without, was buried alive in that explosion you created in the port. For nearly forty-eight hours straight, I did nothing but move rock, concrete, metal, and garbage, desperately looking for my wife.

"One thing you probably don't know about me is I've always been known for being very level-headed, always considering all sides of the equation before making a final decision, playing devil's advocate to get others to think differently.

"But not that night.

"That night, you changed me, Rashad. What you did to my wife flipped a switch in my brain, and the only thing that kept me focused during that forty-eight-hour journey through hell was meticulously planning every detail of how I'd kill you. And Rashad, I have a great plan.

"That plan brings us to today. You are a coward, plain and simple. You've been in hiding since the bombing, thinking you got away with it all. Thinking I didn't know exactly where you were and what you were doing every minute of every hour of every day. But I did. The only reason you've been alive the last few weeks is because my wife has needed me with her.

"Imagine my surprise when she told me she can't get past the fear of knowing you're still out here, roaming free, and could possibly hurt her again. She needs you to be dead to feel safe. I'm paraphrasing here for the sake of time. The bottom line is you'll be dead in just a couple of minutes because my wife comes first. Always.

"You may be wondering why you can't move a muscle, but you're fully aware of everything happening to you. As I mentioned, my wife is a nurse, and we've always shared every detail about our days, no matter how mundane it is. Turns out, something she mentioned a long time ago suddenly became very useful to me today.

"You can't see him because you can't turn your head, but your cohort Bill Smith is here with you. After my buddy Tucker knocked you over the head and brought you back here along with Bill, I gave each of you a shot. The medical name is long and very scientific sounding, succinylcholine, so most of the medical personnel just call it 'sux' for short. When you think about it, that's very fitting for this situation because it definitely sucks to be you right now.

"Anyway, 'sux' is a paralytic, but it allows you to remain alert and fully aware of everything happening to you and around you. I couldn't give you the full dosage because that would make your diaphragm stop working and you'd quit breathing. I don't want you to die too early. Remember I mentioned that you buried my wife in a tomb of concrete and metal? She was conscious during that whole ordeal, just like you'll both be when this house blows up with you in it.

"You're going to stay right here on this couch, and your little invention will be right here at your head. By the way, your head will be the first thing you lose when this blows, in case you haven't figured that out yet.

"Maybe you noticed I just moved some furniture around in here. That's because I need a clear line of sight to shoot these vials of TATP beside your head. When they explode, you'll be fully awake. You'll hear me leave the house. You'll hear the door latch behind me. You'll wait while the clock ticks, one excruciating second at a time. I'll take a stroll down the street to my vantage point, set the sights of my rifle on your bomb materials right here by your head, and I'll squeeze the trigger.

"When the force of my bullet connects with the temperamental nature of this compound you made, there will be nothing left of you or Bill or this house. For all intents and purposes, what little specs of DNA are left will indicate you blew up your own damn self while playing with the Mother of Satan. You'll be out of our lives forever. No ghosts. No shadows. No looking over our shoulders for psychos hell-bent on revenge.

"Speaking of psychos with a need for revenge. Yes, I shot and killed your father. But to be fair, I was rescuing hostages he'd taken from us. He shot at my friends and me first. I simply returned fire while trying to leave his house with the people who didn't belong there. Technically, he brought all that shit on himself.

"Like father, like son, I guess. I'll leave you to sort that out in the few seconds you have left alive. It's time for me to get home to my wife. Plus, that shot I gave you will start wearing off any time now. Can't have you moving around too much before the house blows to hell and back, can we?

"This is the part of the story where I'd normally tell you to bend over and kiss your ass goodbye, but you can't move. So feel free to just envision yourself doing it instead."

Rebel picked up his rifle, walked to the door, and didn't look back until he was in his spot a block away. He casually lifted his rifle to his shoulder, set his sights on the glass vials that held the volatile concoction, and squeezed the trigger with ease. The resulting explosion was so severe, it not only obliterated everything that had been in the old house, but it also knocked down the condemned houses surrounding it.

He smiled to himself. "Not a trace of evidence left."

Rebel exited through the back door and hopped into the waiting car.

"Feel better now?" Tucker asked.

"Much better. It's a beautiful morning, isn't it? Let's head back to my house now. Everyone is already there with Heather for our little get-together. We don't want to be late joining the party."

REBEL AND TUCKER pulled up to the house and found the driveway was completely full of cars.

"Shit. We're late. Everyone else beat us here."

"Will Heather ground you for it?" Tucker smirked, enjoying busting Rebel's balls.

Rebel cut his eyes sharply toward Tucker. "You know I just killed two men."

A broad, shit-eating grin crawled across Tucker's face. "Of course, I do. I helped."

"Now I know why Shadow enjoyed working with you on that case in Dallas so much. You two are so much alike."

They climbed out of the car and walked into the house, the sounds of laughter and chatter filling the air. When Rebel stepped into the living room, he immediately sought out Heather. Relief flooded him when he saw she was safe, sound, and laughing as she chatted with Liz and Becca. He walked around the room and greeted everyone individually. Becca approached him with outstretched arms and wrapped her arms around his neck.

"It's so good to see you again, Brax. I always know when you're home because Heather absolutely glows with love. Thank you so much for never giving up and saving my best friend." She wiped an errant tear from her eye when she pulled away.

"I said no crying today," Heather teasingly chastised her.

"Who's crying?" Becca challenged with a sly smile.

"Believe me, there was no way I would've left that site without my wife. Thank you for taking such good care of her in the ER. I'm surprised they didn't toss you out of there on your ear with all the demands you made." Rebel replied.

"They couldn't. I wasn't working–I was there as a visitor. Plus, they know me and they know they'd have to deal with me at some point later." Her devious smile and devilish laugh left no doubt Becca would've followed through on her veiled threat.

"If you two will excuse me, I need to speak with the boss for a minute."

After a kiss to Heather's cheek, he easily weaved through the many people celebrating Heather's recovery. When he reached Noah, he held his hand a second longer than normal when he shook hands. With a pointed look, he delivered a hidden mission update in his innocuous greeting. "It's a beautiful day for a celebration. There was a big gust of wind earlier, but it blew over in no time."

Comprehension lit in Noah's eyes. "Sometimes a nice breeze can make your whole day."

"It most certainly did that."

When Noah rejoined Brianna, Heather approached Rebel from behind and wrapped her arms around his waist. She pressed her face against his back and inhaled deeply, drawing in the scent that was uniquely his. With his hands on her arms, he lovingly caressed her while remaining cognizant of her healing wounds. He took her hand in his and tenderly pulled her around to stand in front of him, changing places by wrapping his arms around her waist protectively.

"You must have missed me this morning." He smiled against the side of her head and pressed his lips to her hair. "I missed you, too."

"I did miss you. Not that I haven't enjoyed our company, but it's always better when you're here with me."

"I'm here now. Just had to wrap up some loose ends this morning. How's your mom holding up?"

"Subtle change of subject, Brax. She alternates between a complete nervous breakdown and saying she's fine."

"And how are you holding up?"

"I alternate between a complete nervous breakdown and saying I'm fine."

He turned her in his arms to face him. "If it's too soon for everyone to be here, just say the word. They'll understand."

"No, it actually helps to have them here. Mom and I have been able to share stories about Dad with them. Talking about him helps because it makes me feel like he's still here with me. Like you said."

He lowered his head and softly kissed her lips. "If it's any consolation, you're completely safe now."

"You got him?"

"He'll never be seen or heard from again. I promise."

She threw her arms around his neck and murmured against his skin, her words in a breathy staccato. "Thank you. So much. I'm so relieved."

Rebel looked up to find Tucker watching them, his head cocked to the side and his eyebrow arched in silent questioning. "Fine. Tucker helped. A little."

Heather chuckled and turned to locate him. "Thank you for helping, Tucker. I really appreciate it."

"My pleasure." He winked and chuckled.

"Was he the secret contact you met in the park?" Rebel asked Silas.

"Yeah. Tucker had been following Bill since he faked his death and skipped out of Miami. We knew he'd eventually meet back up with Rashad," Silas confirmed. "We couldn't risk taking them out too soon, but unfortunately, our sources didn't have all the information about their plans."

"You warned us about that from the beginning, Silas. We don't blame either of you for what they did." Rebel knew the guilt of that night stayed with Silas, and he tried to reassure him no one on the team held him responsible.

Roman dropped his eyes to the floor, and he didn't seem to hold his shoulders as strong and proud as he normally did.

Heather noticed Roman's remorseful expression. "We don't blame you either, Roman. You tried to warn me, I remember that very vividly."

"That's right. Everyone in this room went above and beyond to help and support us during that time. We couldn't ask for a better family." Rebel made it a point to look each person in the eye, conveying the seriousness of his message.

"Speaking of family, I think Steve has an announcement he'd like to make now." Heather released Rebel and moved to stand next to Steve.

The aggressive chemotherapy treatments had taken a toll on his body, leaving his muscles weak and his energy level at a negative number based on a scale of one to ten. Ever the nurse, Heather reached down to steady and assist him when he began to stand up and address the crowd.

"Yes, I do, my favorite nurse in the world." Steve winked. "I've been a fighter all my life. I've worked hard, built a successful company, and took no prisoners. On the outside, everything in my life appeared to be the epitome of success. Houses, cars, money, nice things—on the surface, I had it all.

"It wasn't until many years later when I realized everything I'd worked for and spent my hard-earned money on was worthless without my family by my side. As hard as this is to say, finding out I had advanced cancer was a blessing in disguise because it brought my kids back to me. With them, I gained another son, another daughter, and now a granddaughter. If I could just get Silas married off, I'd have one more daughter. Hint, hint."

The room erupted in laughter, and all eyes swung to Silas.

"Yeah, don't hold your breath on that, old man." Silas laughed good-naturedly with his father.

"By extension, my new daughter brought Liz into the fold, who brought her son, my doctor, in. The cancer brought me here to Houston for treatment, where I met my favorite nurse in the world, only to find out her husband is one of my son's best friends. While I hate cancer and what it's done to my body, I wouldn't trade one thing I've lost during the last several months of treatment for all the wonderful things I've gained.

"I love you all. I want to thank you for standing by me, checking on me, taking care of me, and making sure I got the best care possible. I would've been dead long ago if it weren't for all of you. I would've missed my daughter's wedding, getting to hold my granddaughter, and so many important events in my family's lives."

Sara sat behind Steve, sniffling and attempting to control her emotions. He turned to take her hand and jerk his head to the side, indicating for her to join him. The room was silent as Sara stood next to her husband, hand in hand, waiting for Steve to continue. The air hung thick with apprehension as they tried to gauge what he would say next.

"We received some unexpected news recently we haven't had a chance to share with you because of everything that's occurred. We wanted to tell everyone at the same time because of how much you all mean to us. Dr. Stanton put me through the full gamut of blood work and body scans, and he said the experimental treatment has been a success. There's no sign of any cancer cells or tumors anywhere in my body."

Tears of happiness and relief flowed freely among the shouts and cheers of excitement.

"It's been a long, hard road. Many times, we weren't convinced he could withstand another round of treatment. But he refused to give up. He kept saying his kids needed him, so he had to try anything they threw at him." Sara spoke through her tears, sharing a tiny portion of the months of hell she'd witnessed firsthand. "With all the sadness that wicked man caused, we thought everyone could use some good news."

"That is truly wonderful news, and I'm so grateful you shared it with us today. Seeing something good emerge after all the evil of the last few days lifts my spirits and renews my faith," Kay replied. "I'm sure some will think I've made a rash decision, and maybe I have, but everything Steve said only reinforces to me it's the right one."

"What decision, Mom?"

"I'm moving to the Miami area to be close to my family. With Emmett gone, there's nothing holding me here now. Honestly, we'd talked about moving there in a couple of years when he retired. He wanted to see the merger through first to make sure everyone's jobs were preserved. My timetable has just changed. As soon as I can get odds and ends wrapped up here, I'll join you in sunny Florida."

"Mom, I'm so glad. I've been sick just thinking about leaving you." Heather hobbled in her boot over to Kay and wrapped her arms around her.

"Bryan and Jackie, no pressure or anything." Shadow playfully teased Rebel's parents. "It's not like everyone here is going back to Miami soon or anything."

"We may just surprise you one day. You never know," Bryan replied with a gleam of challenge in his eye.

"Joe and Emily, all eyes are on you now," Silas added. "Don't think you're immune from the peer pressure of this group."

"We are definitely going back to Miami," Emily confirmed. "I never wanted to leave in the first place."

"Since we're all sharing good news, Colton and I have some news to share." Chaise looked lovingly at her husband before turning back to her expanded family. "We're pregnant!"

After a boisterous round of congratulations for Chaise and intentionally harsh backslaps for Bull, the mood in the group was decidedly upbeat and hopeful for the future. Everyone gathered on the back porch where the men argued over grilling burgers and hot dogs and the women chatted about the excitement their futures held.

Throughout the day, Heather and Rebel passed unspoken messages to each other. Messages that conveyed how thankful one was to have the other. Messages of the deep-rooted need for the other they shared. Messages that said they knew tomorrow wasn't promised, so love would be given freely as if every day were their last day.

The wicked intentions of one man only served to strengthen their bonds of steel.

EPILOGUE

Two Years Later

"Yes!" Bull demanded in his most commanding voice.

"No," Chaise replied with her hand on her hip and a definitive dare in her gaze.

"Chaise, it's time."

"Colton, no it's not." She mimicked his take-charge stance and assertive tone.

"Baby." He quickly changed his tactic and his tone, showing his charming side that was reserved only for Chaise. "Cason needs a little sister."

"Cason is barely a year and a half old. He doesn't need a little sister yet."

"But Rebel and Heather are already talking about having another baby. We can't let them beat us."

"Colton, this is not a race."

"Brianna is due any day now," he continued his argument. With a bogus pout, Bull attempted to make her feel sorry for him.

"That look doesn't work on me."

"I know what works on you." Bull scooped her up in his arms, threw her over his shoulder, and marched toward their bedroom. "You love it when I'm a caveman."

"You know I love it," she replied seductively. "And I gladly invite you to try all you want, but it won't work since I'm still on the pill."

"Dammit, woman." He playfully popped the rounded globe of her ass cheek. "Where are they? I'm flushing them."

Chaise's laughter echoed off the walls as he carried her down the hall toward the bedroom. "What if I told you I've actually already quit taking them?"

Bull stopped in his tracks and lowered Chaise to her feet. His eyes narrowed in suspicion as he leveled her with his penetrating stare. "Are you fucking with me right now?"

"No, honey, I'm not. You've been after me for months to have another baby. I quit taking them about two months ago, so we should be good to seriously try now."

"First man to the finish wins," Bull replied confidently.

"Don't even think about finishing before I do." Chaise arched one brow in mock threat.

"You will 'finish' many times before I do. I *guaran-damn-tee* you that."

~

"Babe, can you put Kinsley down for her nap? I need to change Elias before I put him down."

"You mean they're both taking a nap at the same time, so I can spend some alone time with my wife? Come with me, my beautiful baby girl. It's nap time for my Kinsley." He lifted his daughter, held her against his chest, and her head automatically lowered to rest on his broad shoulder. "I get Mommy all to myself for the next hour."

"Don't jinx us, Brax. I don't think they've taken a nap at the same time more than once or twice in the last eighteen months since they were born."

"I'm already getting excited just thinking about it. Do you think we'll have twins again?"

Heather's jaw dropped open and she stared incredulously at Rebel. "Why would you even wish that on me again? Do you have any idea how hard it is to carry two of your babies at the same time?"

"I'll help."

After she quit laughing, she wiped the tears from her eyes and shook her head at him. "And how, exactly, do you propose to help with that?"

"Oh, you meant carrying them while you're pregnant." Each word was pronounced exaggeratedly, as if he had finally caught on to her meaning.

"Yeah, don't play dumb with me. What's this about? You've been obsessed with having another set of twins. As quickly as possible."

"I've just been thinking about it a lot lately. You know Brianna is due any day, so they'll have two kids. Bull and Chaise are talking about getting pregnant again, so they'll have two kids before long."

"And?" Heather's eyebrows disappeared under her bangs, she held her hands out, palms up, and narrowed her eyes.

"And," he hesitated. "I just think it's time we have another baby so we don't fall behind."

"Wait. Hold up a second. You want to have another baby, or two, right away, so our friends don't beat us in the 'how many kids do you have' category?"

He shrugged one shoulder but avoided direct eye contact. "I like having more kids than they have. Makes me feel proud. Plus, I love seeing you pregnant, my baby growing inside you, knowing we made that little person you're carrying. It turns me on."

"I guess we'd better get them down soon, then. While they're both sleepy. My husband just made my ovaries explode inside my body. I'll be surprised if we don't have triplets now."

"Don't tease me, woman." He followed her into the twins' bedroom and placed Kinsley in her crib while Heather put Elias in his.

"I wouldn't dare tease a big, bad, Delta Force operative. You're liable to handcuff me to bed and torture me in all kinds of devious ways."

"Definitely." He advanced on her, a predatory gleam in his eye and a determined gait in his swagger. "I'll show you all the ways I play dirty."

~

"You know, princess. I almost feel sorry for Bull and Rebel." Noah casually broached the subject as he massaged lotion on his wife's very pregnant belly.

"Why?" Brianna asked, her face scrunched in confusion.

"It's purely conjecture, really. A vicious rumor about me. But apparently, somehow I instigated a bet with them. Just a little wager between friends, as they say. My understanding is Shadow and Silas declined to participate."

"A bet, huh? And what was the alleged bet, exactly?" Brianna cut her eyes at Noah, titled her head to the side, and silently challenged him to confess.

"Somehow they got the idea that whoever has the most kids by the end of next year wins bragging rights for life."

Brianna threw her head back in laughter, picturing the three men arguing over who was the most virile. "Bull and Rebel both fell for that?"

"Hook. Line. And sinker. They're just too easy."

"Yeah, 'too easy' describes Bull and Rebel," Brianna replied sardonically. "Let me guess. Not one of them has any idea we're having twins in a couple of weeks, do they?"

"Nope. Not a clue." Noah smiled widely and leaned over to kiss Brianna's swollen belly. "You two little miracles will give me bragging rights for life."

Brianna ran her fingers through his hair, lovingly stroking his scalp and watching him talk animatedly with their unborn children. Noah looked up and locked eyes with her, love radiating from every ounce of him.

"Actually, I have to take that back. Brianna, you gave me bragging rights for life the day you agreed to be mine. Now with our girls,

Amelia, and soon-to-be Emery, and our soon-to-be son, Gray, my life is more than complete. It's absolutely perfect."

Can't get enough of the men of Steele Security? There's more in Wicked Shadows!

~

***Keep reading for a FREE sneak peek
of Wicked Shadows!***

WICKED SHADOWS SNEAK PEEK

WICKED SHADOWS

PROLOGUE

Twenty-One Years Prior

Elle Moore crouched low to the ground, darting from her hiding spot behind a shrub to a new position behind a tree. Her best friend and partner-in-crime, Beth Condra, followed her, staying close on her heels until she joined Elle behind the huge oak tree. Elle covered her lips with her index finger, indicating for her cohort to remain silent before she pointed toward the driveway they were casing.

"He's standing beside Jeff's car," Elle whispered and dropped to her knees on the ground. "Peek around the tree, but don't let them see you."

Beth slowly knelt, keeping her eyes locked on Elle's. "What if they see me? What should I do?"

"Just do it real slow." Elle emphasized the words with an emphatic pump of her arms, her fingers spread wide and her palms down.

"Okay." Beth put one hand on the ground to steady herself and peered around the tree, her movements painstakingly measured. "I see him. He's with Jeff. And he's not wearing a shirt!"

"What? Let me see!"

Elle jerked Beth back and quickly assumed her partner's vantage point. She was mesmerized by the black-haired, muscular young man with her brother. "Oh my gosh," she gasped. "Is he supposed to do that out here? He's almost naked. What if someone calls the cops on him?"

His athletic shorts sat low on his waist, revealing all of his upper body, from his broad shoulders to his narrow, muscular waist. Elle blatantly stared, completely enraptured by his presence, and wished there were a tree closer to the driveway so she could get a closer look at him, her hero.

"I don't know why we're even doing this. I mean, he's *old*, Elle. He's, like, in high school or something," Beth complained, suddenly bored with their mission. "Why don't you just go out with Scott? He likes you a lot. He keeps asking you to be his girlfriend."

Elle shook her head from side to side but kept her eyes trained on her singular focus. "Scott's all right, I guess. But no one else will ever compare to Devon Kane. I'm gonna marry him one day, Beth. You just wait. Besides, the house down the street is for sale. Maybe we can live there."

"Yeah, that's a good idea. Then you'll still be close to home," Beth agreed, with all of her youthful wisdom. "It's too hot for this, Elle. Let's go swimming already. You promised we'd get in your pool today."

"In a minute." Elle automatically dismissed her friend's demand. "They're washing Jeff's car. They don't know we're here."

Unable to tear her eyes away, embarrassment and panic grew wild when Devon turned his gaze and met hers. His dazzling smile made her blush just before he raised his hand beside his face and gave her a small, knowing wave of his fingers. Her jaw dropped, her eyes flew open wide, and her muscles froze in place.

She was so busted.

Jeff was leaned over, washing the side of his Mustang GT when Devon's movement caught his eye. Jeff followed Devon's line of sight, and anger hit him as soon as he spotted the girls hiding behind the tree.

"Elle Marie Moore, get over here right now!" Jeff yelled across the front yard and threw his soapy mitt in the bucket.

"He used your whole name," Beth whispered, her tone rife with fear. "That's not good."

Elle considered her options. She could pretend she didn't hear him and run like the wind to the backyard, or accept the consequences and get it all over with at once by doing what he said. Resigned to the fact that there was no other choice but to live in the same house with her brother for the next few years, Elle decided to go with the latter rather than the former. Her eyes downcast, her bottom lip quivered as she maintained a death grip on her best friend's hand. The pair of seven-year-old, towheaded girls marched across the grass toward Jeff and Devon. Each step brought more dread than the last and made Elle's feet feel like they were weighted down with cement blocks.

She chanced a glance at Jeff but quickly dropped her eyes again when she saw his arms folded over his chest and an irritated expression boring straight through her. She'd been caught spying on them in the past, but that had been many spy missions before this one. She thought she'd improved her technique since then, but apparently, she was too sloppy. Future excursions would require more stealth, more craftiness, and much better hiding places.

"Elle, what have I told you about spying on us?" Jeff demanded.

"Not to," she mumbled.

"Why do you keep doing it? It's weird. You're creeping me out."

"Because she's in lov—" Beth almost told on Elle, but Elle jerked her arm down hard and cut her eyes at her friend.

"Shut up, Beth," she hissed. Glancing up at her brother, she continued. Her voice quivered almost as much as her legs shook. "We're playing a game. It's not a big deal, Jeff."

"Would it be a big deal if I tell Mom to ground you from the pool all summer?" Jeff taunted.

Tears filled her eyes and spilled over her lower lids then slid down her cheeks before they dropped onto the concrete below. "No, Jeff," she pleaded. "I didn't do anything to you."

Two large hands slid under her arms and hoisted her up in the air. Before she knew what was happening, she was held by protective, muscular arms against a warm, bare chest. "Leave her alone, man." Devon's tone held a strict warning. "She's just a little kid having fun playing outside. Quit being so damn mean to her all the time."

Elle looked up at Devon, devotion shining in her big, gorgeous, hazel eyes. He wiped the lingering tears from her cheeks and talked to her with the kindest timbre in his voice. "Hey, it's okay, Elle. Don't cry, sweetheart. You're my girl, aren't you?"

Unable to speak, she nodded her head enthusiastically.

"Then you should know I'll take care of you. I'll kick Jeff's ass if he's mean to you again. No more crying. Okay?"

That elicited a small smile from her, and shyness took over, forcing her to avert her eyes. "Okay."

"Whatever game y'all are playing isn't bothering us. Go have fun, darlin'."

"Okay, we will."

Devon put her down, and Elle stood rooted to her spot for a few seconds before she tilted her head back to look up at him again. Even at sixteen years old, Devon was taller and thicker than any of Jeff's other friends, but he never once made her feel like she was a nuisance to him. A small smile played on his lips while he waited for her to say what was on her mind.

"You're my hero, Devon."

"And you'll always be my girl, Elle. You remember that when you get to be my age and all those boys are hitting on you." Devon winked at her, causing the butterflies in her stomach to flutter and turn somersaults in her belly.

"Let's go swim already," Beth complained.

With her heart full and a smile permanently affixed to her face, Elle wordlessly grabbed Beth's hand. The two rushed to the backyard to join Elle's mom in the pool.

The scorching Georgia sun didn't faze Elle at all that day as she and Beth jumped into the lukewarm pool water. Devon's words kept ringing in her ears. *"You're my girl, aren't you?"*

"What the hell was that about?" Jeff's tone was accusatory when he turned to Devon.

"She wasn't doing anything but watching us, man. You're way too mean to her. We did a lot worse when we were her age. In case you haven't noticed, your little sister is already pretty for her age. She's going to be a knockout when she gets older. And she's smart as a whip.

"If you don't quit being such a dick to her, she won't come to you later when she needs your help. And believe me, she'll have guys all over her when she hits our age. She'll need you, and you'd better be there for her, or I'll kick your ass then, too. You should be glad you have a little sister who even wants to be around you."

"I fucking hate it when you're right," Jeff huffed.

"Then I guess you're always hating on me, huh?" Devon laughed, lightening the mood.

"Hey, you weren't right about that algebra test. I almost had to go to summer school over that."

"No, my answers were right. You weren't wearing your glasses and wrote down the wrong thing."

The two best friends finished washing their cars before they joined the rest of Jeff's family in the pool. Jeff's parents, Danny and Tanya, best friends and long-time neighbors of Devon's parents, were like a second mom and dad to Devon. Mark, Jeff's younger brother and the middle child, worshiped the older boys almost as much as Elle did.

Watching the interactions between the close-knit family was bittersweet for Devon. The shadows of memories from his childhood were always on the fringe of his happiness, waiting to bring him down.

"You're doing *what*?" Tracey asked. Her hands dropped to her side, and she leaned toward her son.

"I'm joining the CIA. They offered me the perfect job, so I can't very well turn it down."

"You didn't say it was just a CIA job. You said you were joining the black ops team. That means you'll be a spy, doesn't it?"

"Among other things. Yes."

"Why are you doing this, Devon? You just got out of the Army. How many tours did you do in the Middle East? I lost count! Now you'll be permanently undercover, and I'll have no way of knowing if you're dead or alive. I'm your mother—I need more of a reason than it's 'the perfect job.' You have to help me out here."

He pulled a chair out and sat, joining his father Phil at the table. His fingers traced invisible patterns on the table while he avoided their heavy stares. His voice was uncharacteristically low when he spoke. "When Ava disappeared, I was supposed to be watching her. But I got distracted—I don't even know for how long. When I looked up, she was gone. The whole time we searched for her, I wanted to tell you it was all my fault but I couldn't bring myself to say it. I figured when we found her, you'd be too happy to punish me for not watching her. But we never found her. And I've never forgiven myself. This is my way of helping other people, even if they never know I've helped them."

Phil cleared his throat nervously, fighting the emotions welling up in his throat and constricting his ability to breathe. Tears flowed across Tracey's cheeks as she rushed to her son's side. She stroked his hair before holding his face in her hands, forcing him to look at her when she spoke.

"Devon, you were only nine years old. You were not responsible for watching your little sister. You were not responsible for Ava's abduction, and you couldn't have stopped it even if you tried. A grown man took her, and he could've taken you too. There isn't a day that goes by your father and I don't thank God to have you. You don't have to do this to make amends for Ava. We love you. Ava worshiped you. We've never blamed you for what happened, and we never will."

"I need to do this, Mom. It's important to me. I'll be okay—I'm a big boy, and I can take care of myself now." He gave her a small, reassuring smile before standing and pulling her into his arms. "I love you both. Don't worry."

"Devon, I'm your mother. It's my job to worry about you."

"If I find the man who took Ava, we'll never have to worry about him taking another child again."

Tracey sank into his arms a little farther, half in hope and half in fear he'd do just that.

There's a lot more of Shadow waiting for you in Wicked Shadows!

A MESSAGE TO YOU

Dear Reader,

From the bottom of my heart, I want to thank you for spending your time reading this book. Whether you loved, liked, or hated it, your time is precious and I appreciate you spending it with the characters I love so much.

If you will take just a few more minutes to leave a review, I would greatly appreciate it. Even just a few words helps more than you know. Your review doesn't have to be a long book report. :) A simple, "Everyone needs to read this book," or even, "This book wasn't really for me," is more than enough.

Again, thank you for your time and support.

Lots of Love,
Angel

BOOKS BY A.D. JUSTICE

Steele Security Series

Wicked Games (Book 1)

Wicked Ties (Book 2)

Wicked Nights (Book 3)

Wicked Intentions (Book 4)

Wicked Shadows (Book 5)

Crossing Lines Series

Fine Line

Blurred Line

Hard Line

The Vault Series

Precarious: Warning, Part One

Insidious: Warning, Part Two

Treacherous: Warning, Part Three

A HOMETOWN NOVEL

Intent

All I Want

All I Need

Entice (coming soon!)

The Crazy Series

Crazy Maybe (Book 1)

Crazy Baby (Book 2)

Crazy Love (Book 3, Free Short Story)

Dominic Powers Series

Her Dom (Book 1)

Her Dom's Lesson (Book 2)

Covis Realm, Easthaven Crest Series

Cloaked

Deceived

Unveiled

Stand—alone Books

Saving Grace

Completely Captivated

Immortal Envy

Mistletoe Not Required

Just One Summer

ABOUT THE AUTHOR

A.D. Justice is the award-winning, *USA Today* bestselling author of several series and stand-alone romance novels in various romance genres, including romantic suspense, contemporary, and paranormal.

When she's not writing, she loves spending time with her alpha male husband in the Northwest Georgia mountains. They're living out their own HEA, frequently on horseback with a dog in tow.

She is also an avid reader of romance novels, a master of procrastination, a chocolate sommelier, a twister of words, and speaks fluent sarcasm. An avid animal lover, she has two horses, two cats, and two very spoiled dogs.

She loves chatting with her readers. You're welcome to stalk her across all social media!

Connect with her online!

Newsletter
Facebook Reader Group
Website

facebook.com/adjusticeauthor
instagram.com/authoradjustice
bookbub.com/authors/a-d-justice
amazon.com/author/adjustice
pinterest.com/adjusticeauthor

ACKNOWLEDGMENTS

Special thanks goes to –

Tabitha – my PA, you help keep me on track and encourage me to "hurry and finish," even if it's for no other reason than you can't wait to read it. And I love you for that!

Lisa Hollett, with Silently Correcting Your Grammar – my editor and my friend, you help me polish and spit-shine my words while providing your honest feedback as you read. I'm so glad I found you!

My beta team – I want to thank each and every one of you for taking the time to read, answering my incessant questions, and not letting me get away with not doing an epilogue. ;) You're all the best!

Bloggers – I know how much work goes into what you do for free, to support others, to share the word of new releases and books you love. I just want you to know I appreciate you so much! Much love for you!!!

Readers – I am so grateful for each and every single one of you! Without your constant support and willingness to shout from the rooftops about your favorite books, none of these characters would have a chance to live, even for a moment, in this fictional world we love so much. From the bottom of my heart, thank you for everything!

www.ingramcontent.com/pod-product-compliance
Lightning Source LLC
Chambersburg PA
CBHW021005120726
47905CB00009B/2870